Praise and awards for

The Healer's Apprentice

"Alternating between the two protagonists' viewpoints, the plot unfolds at a satisfying clip with zesty supporting characters (the healer, the duke's younger son), which add intrigue."

— *Publisher's Weekly*

"In her debut, Dickerson spins a magical tale ... Laced with plenty of romance, action, faith and fantasy, it's a perfectly romantic and well-told tale."

— *Romantic Times*

The Merchant's Daughter

"A virtuous romance with characters who fall in love with each other's inner beauty in spite of outward appearance."

— *Kirkus Reviews*

"True, readers will peg the happy ending at the start, but the progression of Annabel's honorable love affair will have the rapt attention of Christian-fiction fans."

— *Booklist*

The Fairest Beauty

"This well-crafted retelling of the Snow White story leaves out magic and potions, substituting instead human emotions, faults and strengths, and romance in the post-medieval setting."

— *Booklist*

"Solid storytelling, cleverly woven references to the folktale, and historical detail combine in a novel that is a likely popular choice for girls in search of gentle romance."

— *Booklist*

The Captive Maiden

"Without magic dust or musical interludes, Dickerson delivers a wonderful spin on 'Cinderella' that is full of engaging, thoughtful characters amid lively medieval pageantry."

— *School Library Journal*

"Expect high romance, melodrama, and Christian inspiration in a vivid medieval setting."

— *Booklist*

Awards

2014 Christian Retailing's Best Award YA Fiction: *The Fairest Beauty*

2013 National Reader's Choice Awards (Romance Writers of America) YA Finalist: *The Captive Maiden*

2012 Carol Award Winner: *The Merchant's Daughter*

2012 Christy Award Finalist: *The Merchant's Daughter*

2011 National Reader's Choice Award (Romance Writers of America) Best First Book Winner: *The Healer's Apprentice*

HOLT Medallion Award of Excellence winner: *The Healer's Apprentice*

Other books by
Melanie Dickerson

The Healer's Apprentice
The Merchant's Daughter
The Fairest Beauty
The Captive Maiden

THE Princess SPY

MELANIE DICKERSON

ZONDERVAN®

ZONDERVAN

The Princess Spy
Copyright © 2014 by Melanie Dickerson

This title is also available as a Zondervan ebook.
Visit www.zondervan.com/ebooks.

Requests for information should be addressed to:
Zondervan, 3900 *Sparks Dr. SE, Grand Rapids, Michigan* 49546

ISBN 978-0-310-73098-9

Published in association with the Books & Such Literary Management,
52 Mission Circle, Suite 122, PMB 170, Santa Rosa, California 95409 - 5370.
www.booksandsuch.com.

Cover design and photography: *Mike Heath/Magnus Creative*
Interior design and composition: *Greg Johnson/Textbook Perfect*

Printed in the United States of America

14 15 16 17 18 19 20 /QG/ 19 18 17 16 15 14 13 12 11 10 9 8 7 6 5 4 3 2 1

Prologue

April 1413, forty miles southwest of Hagenheim

Colin touched John's forehead with the back of his hand. "Burning hot."

John groaned and looked at him with unfocused, heavy-lidded eyes.

The sun was low in the sky and the air was getting colder. Colin swept off his red cape and placed it around John's shoulders while they waited for the horses to finish drinking.

If only he could find someone who knew about healing herbs, a healer who could help bring down John's fever.

After their short rest, John managed to mount his horse and they set out. They had passed Arnsberg almost a day ago, which meant they were yet at least two days from Hagenheim.

"If we come to a village," Colin said, "we will find lodging and a healer to tend you."

"No, no. I can ride. We should go on."

"John, you cannot. You are too ill. We shall catch up to that murderer sooner or later, but you must get well first."

John gave him a look but said nothing, his shoulders slumping even lower.

Colin's heart twisted painfully inside his chest. John would be back home in England, comfortable and enjoying a warm fire. John had tried to talk him out of his wild scheme, reasoning that it was foolish for Colin to leave his family and his country to go running after the man who had murdered Philippa. But the heinous deed had filled Colin with outraged justice. Philippa had been Colin's sister's closest friend and had not deserved such a fate. Nor did his sister deserve to have her own sense of safety shattered in such a way.

John had pointed out the obvious: What could Colin do—only one man against an earl and all his knights and fighting men? Colin refused to be deterred, and loyal John had come with him. Perhaps he should have listened to John's wise counsel.

"I'm sorry I dragged you here." Colin looked askance at his friend.

"I came of my own accord." John's voice was weak and hoarse as he held the reins in his limp hands. "I'd hardly let you go on such a quest without me."

Just then, they heard horses' hooves pounding behind them, coming closer. Colin grabbed John's reins and guided both horses toward the side of the road. He glanced over his shoulder. Perhaps ten men were driving hard toward them. They were quite close before Colin realized—

"Go!"

They both spurred their horses, but it was too late. The horsemen caught up with them in a matter of seconds. One of them knocked John off his horse, then another jumped from his saddle and caught Colin around the neck. They hit the ground with a bone-jarring crash.

John. He wouldn't stand a chance, as sick as he was.

"Kill the one in the red cloak!" one of the men shouted. "He's the one we want."

No. Colin rolled over onto his attacker and slammed his fist into his assailant's nose. Then he grabbed him around the neck. Colin squeezed, pressing his thumbs into the man's throat until he went limp.

Colin jumped up and ran, a roar vibrating his chest as it made its way through his clenched teeth.

Their attackers stood clustered around John, who was lying on the ground.

John's eyes stared straight up, glassy and unmoving. He was already dead.

Colin cried out, drawing their attention to him. He rushed over to his horse, which had miraculously not run away, and yanked his sword from the sheath attached to his saddle bag. As he spun around, a blow connected with his head. He swung the blade in a wide arc, but he was suddenly pummeled from every side. He fought the darkness that was closing in. Then another wall of pain slammed his head and everything went black.

Colin awoke to his own groaning. He turned to avoid the sunlight as the pain above his right eye raced to the back of his head. He remembered John's lifeless body lying on the ground, and he fought the urge to retch.

How many days had it been since John was murdered? Since he himself was beaten and left for dead? Two? Four? Ten? The passage of time blurred, hazy in his confused brain.

He had to get up. Had to start walking or he would surely die. And he couldn't die. Justice must be exacted, and if he didn't do it, Philippa's killer—and now John's—would go unpunished.

Struggling onto his hands and knees in the middle of the leaves by the roadside, he paused a moment to catch his breath. He sat back on his heels, waited for the throbbing to lessen, then managed to rise to his feet.

His head was spinning like a bug on its back. His stomach gnawed at him in a way that signified he had not eaten for days, and the pain in his throat was nearly unbearable. When was the last time he had drunk any water? He'd started following this

7

road, trying to reach Hagenheim to find someone who could understand him and help him. How long had he been unconscious on the side of the road? He might have been lying there a few minutes, hours, or days; he didn't know.

"God, how low can I sink?"

He knew the answer to that question. Death. And it was imminent. He could feel it hounding him, pushing him to keep moving.

"Forgive me, John." No one was around to hear. His mouth was as dry as the dusty road, and his voice was so weak it angered him. John, dying in a foreign country where he didn't even speak the language, while that fiend, that son of hell, was free to wreak more havoc.

God, let it not be so.

Colin never should have let John come with him. It was his fault John was dead.

Forgive me, God, for not keeping him safe.

His legs were as heavy as boulders, but he forced his feet to move forward. His temples pounded with every beat of his heart. He kept his eyes open a slit to try not to trip or veer off the road.

He was lying facedown on the ground. He didn't remember falling. How long had he been unconscious? He didn't have the strength to lift his head. He wasn't even sure he wanted to. How easy it would be to simply lie here and never wake up.

God, if you want me to live, I will live. If not ... so be it. I surrender to you.

Peace washed over him. He closed his eyes. Just as he was drifting into unconsciousness, he heard the creaking of a cart drawing closer, and men's voices. But he saw nothing but darkness.

Chapter 1

Margaretha sat in the Great Hall listening to her newest suitor, Rowland Fortescue, Earl of Claybrook, who had cornered her after the midday meal.

Perhaps it was unkind of her to use the word "cornered." He was her suitor, after all, and she should be pleased that he wanted to talk to her. Some of her other suitors had barely said two words to her, but this man seemed to enjoy talking to her—in very fluent German for an Englishman, but his mother *was* from the German regions of the Holy Roman Empire.

Everyone, especially her brothers, accused Margaretha of talking too much, but Lord Claybrook often left her speechless. Could that be a good thing?

This morning, Lord Claybrook had been telling her of his prowess as a hunter, both with his falcons and his oh-so-remarkable hounds, a subject so boring that it wasn't her fault if she was distracted by his hat.

Truly, it was an astonishing hat. But then, all of his hats were astonishing. Every day since he had come to Hagenheim Castle, Margaretha had found herself staring at the man's hat.

Today's hat consisted of a gray fur band as wide as her hand and padded to make it twice as fat as his head, with a large jewel inset in the front, and folds of red cloth protruding from inside, draped over his right temple like the coxcomb of a rooster. A piece of matching cloth hung from the other side of the hat, reaching to his left knee.

While his hat's liripipe was ridiculously long, his tunic was scandalously short. He wore only tight hose underneath, so she was careful not to let her eyes stray too low.

But she must make allowances for him. He was a foreigner, after all. Perhaps everyone in England dressed that way.

Lord Claybrook described his favorite hunting dog, explaining how the animal had tracked a deer for three days while he and his guests had followed close behind. As he paced the room, his tunic, trimmed in fur at the cuffs of his sleeves, shimmered, as it was embroidered all over with an elaborate design of curly leaves done in shiny gold thread. She hated to admit it, but she was beginning to agree with her brothers—the man was overdressed even for an earl. Her oldest brother, Valten, was an earl, and he never dressed so elaborately. For that matter, her father was a duke and rarely wore velvet and silk except on special occasions.

But perhaps Lord Claybrook was only trying to make a good impression on her. After all, he had been very courteous to her, never complaining that she talked too much. Was he her perfect match?

Margaretha was good at choosing other people's perfect match. A few weeks ago she had noticed her maidservant, Britta, and one of the guards, Gustaf, eyeing each other. Margaretha inquired about the guard, discovering that Gustaf used his wages to help his sickly mother and two sisters. So Margaretha managed to arrange for the guard to accompany her, her sisters, and Britta on a picnic. Margaretha and her sisters went to pick flowers, leaving Britta and Gustaf alone together to guard the food. Later, she sent the two of them to pick apples. Soon her matchmaking was rewarded with seeing them smiling at each other and talking quietly.

Lord Claybrook seemed kind, and he wouldn't force her to go back to England with him. He had said he wanted to stay within the Holy Roman Empire, as he would inherit the nearby estate of his uncle, the Earl of Keiterhafen. If she married Lord Claybrook, she could stay close to her family.

As a duke's daughter, it was her duty to marry as advantageously as possible. How spoiled she would seem if she ignored her parents' wishes by refusing to accept a suitor who would advance their family's holdings and bring about peace and harmony to the people whose lives depended upon it.

She had already delayed the process so long, her younger sister was now of age to marry. It didn't seem too much to ask, however, that she be allowed enough time to get to know him. She must first believe she could love him and that he loved her. But if she could not find a good reason *not* to accept Lord Claybrook, he seemed her best choice.

Lord Claybrook, she realized with a guilty feeling, had stopped talking and was staring at her with a look of frustration on his face. Oh dear. She had insulted him by not listening to his long diatribe on hunting.

"Forgive me, Lord Claybrook. My mind wandered. What were you saying?"

"I was telling you about my hunting dogs. I thought you were interested in learning about me, Lady Margaretha. But I shall not bore you any longer."

"Oh no! You mustn't think—" That she wasn't interested in his hunting exploits? She couldn't lie. "I was rude, and I hope you will forgive me. I do want to learn more about you. Most people complain that I talk too much, and I didn't want to annoy you with too much chatter." She smiled, hoping to return him to a good humor.

Lord Claybrook smiled back and reached out a hand to her. Straight white teeth shone among his good-looking features—hard-planed chin and cheekbones, a prominent brow, and dark brown eyes that were perfectly spaced. Her maids all told her he was her most handsome suitor yet.

Margaretha allowed him to take her hand, and he raised it to his lips and kissed her knuckles. "You are much too beautiful to offend, Lady Margaretha. Of course, I must not expect a gentle lady to be interested in hunting. Although many ladies do go out hunting with their men. But your delicate nature becomes you." Still holding her hand, he bent to kiss it again.

Perhaps she should be moved, at least a little, by his gesture, but it didn't make her heart flutter in the least, the way Britta said hers did when Gustaf smiled at her. But perhaps it wasn't Margaretha's way to be moved to flutterings of the heart by a man's smile or kiss. Her mother said love grew out of mutual respect and friendship. So far, Lord Claybrook hadn't given her any reason to not respect him. Unless she considered his irrational choices in clothing.

Just then her father, Duke Wilhelm, and her eldest brother, Lord Valten, came into the Great Hall wearing leather tunics, leather breeches, and shoulder capes—their usual riding attire.

"Shall we hunt?" Lord Claybrook asked them, an eager glint in his eyes.

"Perhaps tomorrow," her father answered him. "I shall ask my falconer and the dogs' handler to be ready in the morning. For now, I thought we could take a ride around the town."

"It would be my pleasure, your Grace. Do I have time to change my hat?"

"Of course," her father said, as a flicker of amusement

crossed his face. Her brother Valten's expression, on the other hand, was openly scornful.

Lord Claybrook made an elegant bow to his host and then turned to Margaretha. "Will you join us, my lady?"

"No, I thank you." She knew her father was still trying to make out the man's character, and he could do it better without her along. "Enjoy your ride. I will be here when you get back." She smiled, trying to seem amenable and friendly.

Lord Claybrook's gaze lingered on her before he bowed and strode away.

Her father smiled at her, looking pleased. Valten just scowled.

"How is my beautiful daughter this morning?"

"Very well, Father." Margaretha went forward and embraced him. If only she could find someone as perfect as her father. He made every other man she'd ever met seem unworthy.

Perhaps this was the reason she'd never found a suitor very appealing; she always compared him to her father.

She pressed her cheek against his shoulder. He would never force her to marry, but she also felt he had been a little disappointed that she had rejected the Duke of Beimerberg last fall, and the Earl of Rimmel last summer, both within the first week of meeting them.

Some others hadn't even lasted that long. Would he ask her how things were progressing with Lord Claybrook?

When she pulled away, he looked into her eyes. His knuckles grazed her chin and jawline, and he winked. Then he and Valten left.

Margaretha wandered through the castle, trying to imagine herself married with two children, like her brother Gabe's wife, Sophie. Or pregnant with her first child, like Valten's wife, Gisela. Her sisters-in-law both seemed content. Gabe and Sophie were perfect for each other, and Valten and Gisela were also well-matched and in love. But Margaretha didn't think she would be pleased with a man like either of her brothers. She wanted someone extraordinary, a man who was bold, fearless, and impulsive, yet humble, kind, and gentle. He should be intelligent and confident in his ability to love her and make her happy. He had to be passionate about right and wrong, and passionately in love with *her*, not her father's title and wealth.

All Lord Claybrook seemed passionate about was hunting . . . and hats.

But after all, she barely knew him. Did she want him to behave unseemly, attacking her in his ardor?

She didn't know what she wanted.

She wandered through the outside door and into the courtyard, which was surrounded on three sides by the castle walls. To her right was the blacksmith's stall, which was always busy with people bringing work or retrieving mended tools and horseshoes. Straight ahead, three maids stood at the well, talking as they waited their turn to draw water.

To her left was the open door to the healer's chambers. Frau Lena left the door open in good weather to let out the bad humors. Margaretha could hear her singing, her clear voice carrying into the courtyard.

The early spring sun was more than halfway up the sky, but it was pleasantly cool, as the weather had turned mild. Only a few white clouds dotted the blue sky, but three vultures, circling lazily overhead, marred the perfection of her view. What were they doing here? Vultures only came around when something was dead—or dying.

A cart, pulled by a gray mule, rolled through the castle gate from the *Marktplatz* and headed toward Frau Lena's tower chambers. A long bundle lay on the otherwise empty cart. She stared absentmindedly at it, until she began to notice the angles and bulges of the cloth. Then, as it drew near the healer's open door, Margaretha realized—those were feet dangling off the end of the cart.

The motionless heap was a person.

Chapter
2

Margaretha crept closer to the cart, trying to look inconspicuous. At any moment Frau Lena might notice her and warn her away.

The boy who had been leading the mule and potter's cart must be the potter's apprentice. He peeked into the open doorway of the healer's chambers in the southwest tower, then called, "Frau Lena? Are you here?"

Margaretha peered over the side at the unconscious body.

A young man, perhaps a little older than her own age of eighteen, lay motionless, his eyes closed. His black hair was plastered to his head above his right eye with what looked like dried blood, and dead leaves were tangled up in his thick, wavy locks. He had been beaten, as there were bruises over his face and on his collarbone, which she could see because his shirt was ripped and lay open, exposing his chest. In spite of the smudges of dust and grime on his face, his bleeding, swollen lips, and the dark circles under his eyes, he had noble features and might be considered handsome if he were cleaned up. His fine linen clothes were dirty and torn, his feet bare. Although he was thin, his chest and shoulders were broad. He must be cold, lying there with nothing warm to cover him.

She stared, trying to tell if he was breathing. Was he dead? Her heart squeezed painfully, as if trying to beat for him.

Frau Lena came out of the tower door and walked to the other side of the cart. She bent her face close to the unconscious man's.

"My master and I found him on the south road to Hagenheim." The lad who had brought him followed Frau Lena and stood beside her, staring down at the dark-haired man.

Frau Lena pressed two fingers to the side of his neck. She glanced up and her eyes locked on Margaretha, then widened, as though she was startled to see her.

"Is he alive?"

Frau Lena nodded. "He is breathing. I'll need help carrying him inside."

Margaretha turned and hailed one of her father's knights, who was strolling through the courtyard. "Sir Bezilo! *Kommen Sie hier, bitte!* Over here, please."

Sir Bezilo strode forward and slipped his massive arms underneath the body and picked him up.

The unconscious man opened his eyes — they were a stunning dark blue — and began trying to speak, but his voice was so hoarse and cracked that he sounded more as if he was croaking than speaking words. But even in his weak state, he struggled against the larger knight.

"*Sei still,*" Sir Bezilo told him. "You are safe now."

But the poor man continued to struggle and try to speak as the knight carried him inside.

She asked the boy who had brought the stranger, "Did he tell you anything?"

"He never awakened until now. Did you understand what he was saying?"

"No. But now that I think about it, perhaps he was speaking another language."

The boy raised his brows. "No one around here knows how

to speak other languages, only a few words of Latin or French. No one except some of the duke's family." His eyes fixed on her for the first time and his mouth fell open. "Oh. Begging your pardon, Lady Margaretha." He bowed to her, his ears turning bright red.

"Nothing to pardon," Margaretha said gently. "And thank you for being so kind as to bring the poor man to our healer. You saved his life, I am sure. Please inform the potter of my family's gratitude."

"Of course, my lady." He bowed again, then took his mule and led him away, the cart wheels rattling over the cobblestones.

Margaretha turned back to the open doorway. Frau Lena was rummaging through a basket by the sick bed, while her patient lay motionless and quiet once again, his eyes closed.

Margaretha stepped inside, not sure what she intended to do. She'd never entered the healer's chambers before, as Frau Lena always came to Margaretha's own chamber when she was ill. She was certain her mother and father wouldn't like her being here—she might see things a duke's daughter ought not to see. But curiosity compelled her.

Frau Lena pulled a cloth from the basket and glanced up. "Lady Margaretha." She seemed about to say something, then turned and dipped some water from the kettle over the fire in the fireplace into a bowl.

Margaretha took a deep breath, then said, "Please, Frau Lena, may I stay, only until I can see if the young man will recover?"

"Yes, you may stay and help me, if you wish. My apprentice has gone to the market and may not be back for a while."

Margaretha stepped closer. "Oh, thank you, Frau Lena. I would like to help. The poor man looks as if he was beset by robbers and left for dead. What should I do? Do you think he will live?"

She was asking questions faster than Frau Lena could answer them. She literally bit her tongue to stop herself.

"I think he will live." Frau Lena smiled as she handed Margaretha a wet cloth and the bowl of warm water. "Bathe his face with this while I make him a special herbal drink."

Margaretha sat on a stool by the narrow bed and began gently washing his face, which was so dirty she had to continually rinse out her cloth. "What do you think is wrong with him?" she whispered.

"He has gone too long without water and food. He also has had a nasty blow to the head, which is probably affecting his mind."

Frau Lena went inside the storage room and came back out with some flasks of herbs. She placed some of the dried leaves in a small, porous piece of cloth, brought the corners up and twisted it closed, tying it with thread. She then dropped the herb ball into a cup and poured hot water over it. Frau Lena had often made tea for Margaretha's sicknesses and minor ailments in the same way.

The longer Margaretha leaned over the young man, cleaning the blood and dirt from his face, the more she noticed his features, his long, sooty-black eyelashes, and his thick black brows. She cleaned his square chin and stubbly jaw. His cheeks were hollow, but he had strong cheekbones.

After cleaning most of the dust and dirt from his face, she found the dried blood that was matted in his hair a bit harder to remove. She dabbed at it over and over with the wet cloth, but gently, trying not to cause him pain or wake him.

When Frau Lena turned away and went back into the storage room, Margaretha worked up enough courage to wipe the dust from the man's poor, cracked lips.

She dipped the cloth into the pan of water and went back to work on his bloody hair. Slowly, the blood disappeared and she could see the deep gash extending from his hairline to about three inches into his hair.

He moaned and turned his head slightly, as if trying to get away from her ministrations. Margaretha drew back and looked to Frau Lena, who had reentered the room.

"Let me see if I can get him to drink a bit."

Margaretha stood, and Frau Lena took her place on the stool at the young man's shoulder. Frau Lena leaned over him and spoke gently. "Can you hear me?"

He didn't move or speak, his eyes still closed.

Frau Lena slipped a hand under his head and lifted him while putting the cup to his lips.

Margaretha watched the steam rising from the cup. She hoped Frau Lena's drink would rouse him. She was curious to know where he came from and who he was.

As Frau Lena let a bit of the drink dribble out onto his lips, his eyes flew open and he began to speak. At least, it seemed as though he was speaking, but his voice was hoarse and the sounds he was emitting seemed fragmented, as his voice was cracking. His eyes were wide and wild as he seemed to rant at Frau Lena. His manner matched the intensity in his bright blue eyes.

"Do you think he's lost his mind because of his injuries?" Margaretha whispered, keeping out of the young man's line of vision.

"It seems likely," Frau Lena whispered back.

Margaretha glanced toward the open door. If she needed to, she could run fetch help and be back within a few moments. She didn't want the young madman hurting Frau Lena.

Colin felt something hot burning the cracked places on his lips, and opened his eyes, ready to fight. But it was only a woman before him, holding a cup.

"What is this place? Where am I?" He stopped speaking, realizing from the look on the woman's face that she didn't mean him any harm—and that she didn't understand a word he was saying.

His head throbbed and his thoughts were hazy, like clouds he couldn't grab hold of. His face felt hot ... so hot ... but his feet were cold. The pain in his head made him want to go back to sleep. He heard himself moan.

The red-haired woman turned and began whispering to someone behind her. By the voice that whispered back, it became evident there was another woman in the room.

The redhead turned back to him and held the cup of hot liquid to his lips again. Her words were foreign. He concentrated, trying to make them out.

"*Trink.*"

He hoped she wasn't trying to scald him. She looked kind, so he let her pour a bit of the hot liquid into his mouth. It burned not only his lips, but his parched throat as well, yet he drank another gulp, then another. Suddenly, the liquid seemed to go down the wrong way and he started coughing, which made his head throb even more.

He finally stopped coughing and sank back onto the bed.

The red-haired woman spoke again. The first word sounded like "*Trink,*" but the rest was gibberish to him. She held the cup to his lips and he drank some more. The liquid—whatever it was—was starting to feel good going down his throat. He reached up and took the cup in his own hand.

"*Trink langsamer,*" she said, wrinkling her freckled forehead, concern in her voice.

Colin drank the rest of what was in the cup in two big swallows. He handed the cup back to the woman. He didn't understand a word she was saying, but if she didn't just poison him, she probably saved his life.

He lay back against the pillow and closed his eyes. The woman began to whisper again to her friend.

God, why didn't I listen to my mother and learn to speak German? He hoped someone here spoke English, the only language he was fluent in. He knew a bit of Latin, but not enough to communicate what he needed to say.

He opened his eyes again. The redhead who had given him the drink was staring at him. At her left shoulder stood a beautiful young lady dressed in a gown of purple silk. Her eyes were also fastened on him.

The beautiful girl moved toward him. "Do you speak English?"

Praise God! "Yes! Do you?"

"Where do you come from? Are you from England?" she asked in English. Her brown eyes sparked with intelligence, and her full, perfect lips turned up at the corners. She spoke with a heavy accent, but she enunciated clearly. As she moved in front of the window, the light streaming in created a warm glow around her fair face, setting the rich brown of her hair on fire.

"Thank God." Truly, God was watching out for him after all.

Chapter
3

Margaretha concentrated on bringing forth the correct words. "What is your name and how came you here?" It had been several months since she'd practiced her English, as that was when her tutor had left.

The stranger's face was pale and he seemed barely able to focus his eyes—those dark blue eyes with their wild intensity.

"I do not believe I should tell you." His voice was still weak and hoarse. "I do not want to endanger you, and my name must remain a secret until . . . but I must not reveal that either."

His head lolled to one side and his eyes fell closed, as if he'd lost consciousness again. He seemed almost to be talking to himself as he ended his mumbled speech. She still feared his mind was seriously addled.

"What does he say, my lady?" Frau Lena asked.

"He says he doesn't want to tell me his name, that he is in danger, and I believe he said that I would be too if he told me." Margaretha shook her head and frowned. "He was mumbling a lot, almost as if he was not conscious of what he was saying."

"He is certainly agitated. Ask him to tell us where his injuries are. And if he's able to talk, ask him who beat him."

Margaretha touched his shoulder and he opened his eyes again. She wasn't sure of the English word for *injury*, so she asked, "Where do you hurt?"

He turned his head slightly and winced. "I am not seriously hurt. I need only justice ..." His voice trailed off, but then he finished by saying, "And I shall be perfectly well."

Margaretha translated for Frau Lena, who frowned. "What he needs is food and rest. I shall get him something to eat. Ask him about his head."

"Your head," Margaretha began, pointing to her own head. "How did you hurt it?"

"I did not hurt my head," he grumbled irritably. "Someone hit me. *He* did it!" He gestured with his hand. "His men tried to kill me. They killed John ... they killed him ... then beat me and left me for dead."

"Who?"

"I mustn't tell you."

"Very well. But you must not become so ..." Again, Margaretha couldn't remember the correct English word. "You are too excited, and it is not good for you. You must rest, and eat and drink something. Rest."

The man closed his eyes, but not as though he was trying to rest. More out of frustration. How could she convince him to be calm and rest?

He suddenly sat up and put his feet to the floor. His breath was labored, and he pressed his arm against his middle.

"No, no, he mustn't get up!" Frau Lena put her hands on his shoulders to stop him, and he collapsed again onto the bed, his eyes closed. Frau Lena pulled his legs back up on the bed.

He lay, pale and limp. After a moment, Margaretha realized he'd passed out.

"How unfortunate that his injuries have him so addled," Margaretha whispered.

"Perhaps he will recover his senses in a few days," Frau Lena answered.

Margaretha set back to work, dabbing at his bloody head

wound. Lena leaned over to examine it and said he needed stitches. "But I'm afraid to try to stitch him up. He might wake up and injure himself further."

Might he not also injure Frau Lena?

A few minutes later, he awakened again, groaning.

"Now will you tell me where you hurt?" Margaretha frowned down at him, wondering if he would try to get up again. What made him so frantic?

He only blinked at her. "Where am I?"

"You are at *Hagenheim Burg*, Hagenheim Castle."

"Thank God." He blinked, then licked his swollen lips. "Who are you?"

"I am Margaretha, the oldest daughter of Duke Wilhelm, and this is Frau Lena, our healer." Margaretha indicated the thin, red-haired woman behind her. "You must listen to her and do as she says, for she is trying to help you."

"When might I be able to speak to Duke Wilhelm?"

Margaretha shook her head at his boldness. "You have not told me who you are."

"I do not want to endanger you. I need to speak to your father first."

"You are in no condition to have a meeting with the duke." Margaretha smiled indulgently as she tucked the blanket around him. "If you lie still and answer Frau Lena's questions, I will try to arrange for you to meet with my father when you are feeling better." *And looking and smelling better.* "You did not answer my question about where you hurt."

His jaw clenched. He seemed to try to take a deep breath, but he winced, then took several shallow breaths. "I am grateful for your help to me, Lady . . . What did you say your name was?"

"Though you refuse to tell me yours, I shall tell you mine again. It is Margaretha."

"Lady Margaretha. Forgive my lack of manners." He spoke

slowly, as he was obviously in pain. "And please tell your healer I am grateful to her as well. But the man who tried to kill me would come after me again if he knew I was still alive. I must bring him to justice, and I will need Duke Wilhelm's help."

"So you know who tried to kill you?"

"Yes. But I cannot tell you his name. It is too dangerous."

"Very well, very well. We can talk about all that when you are better." Best to placate him for now, but the idea that she, Duke Wilhelm's daughter, could be in danger seemed preposterous. "Now you must tell me where you feel pain so Frau Lena can help you."

He looked rather sullen, but finally said, "My head throbs, it hurts to breathe, and I feel like I've been trampled by a horse. Other than that, I feel very well."

Margaretha smiled. "How humorous you are." She turned to translate to Frau Lena.

Humorous? There was nothing humorous in his situation. He probably did seem lacking in sense, as he was murmuring to himself and telling a duke's daughter that he couldn't tell her his name or she would be in danger. But his head hurt so much, it was hard to think straight. Another moan slipped, unbidden, from his throat.

After speaking in her language to the healer, she turned back to him with a cup and a small loaf of bread. "You must eat and drink something."

He took the cup from her and drank more of the bitter herbal concoction. Then he took the bread and ate a bite. It was the best bread he had ever tasted. He began to feel better instantly. Even his pain seemed dulled.

He watched the beautiful Lady Margaretha as she took a clean cloth and new bowl of water from the healer. He continued to eat and watch her as she wet the cloth and started dabbing at the cut on his head. He liked the way she smelled as she leaned over him—like flowers and fresh air and feminine warmth.

"Frau Lena needs to"—she motioned with her hands, mimicking sewing with a needle and thread—"your head closed so it will heal more quickly."

He should have known the sweet moment wouldn't last.

"Will you promise to stay still and let her close your wound?"

She spoke to him as if he was slow-witted. "Of course. I'm not a child."

"No, of course you aren't." She smiled in the exact same way she might smile at a child—a very small child.

She was hurting his head with the way she was dabbing at it, and he certainly didn't want her around when Frau Lena sewed up his head. But he felt drowsy ... so drowsy he almost stopped chewing the bread that was in his mouth. He wasn't entirely sure he hadn't been poisoned, but he was too sleepy and warm and full to care.

Colin awoke to a sharp pain in his head and remembered that Frau Lena had stitched the wound there. She'd sent Lady Margaretha away, for which he was grateful. He didn't want the beautiful duke's daughter to witness him in pain. Had he cried out? His memory of it was blurry.

He seemed to be alone in the room. The light was gray through the window, but he couldn't tell if it was morning or twilight. The walls around him were of gray stone and curved, as if he were in a round tower. His stomach growled over the faint noises coming from outside. The lady had told him he was at Hagenheim Castle.

He'd demanded to see Duke Wilhelm, but she'd refused. Lifting his head, he could see why. He surveyed his condition—

horribly skinny and in need of a bath. His clothes were dirty, stained, and torn beyond repair.

Just lifting his head off the pillow made him dizzy, so he sank back.

It would take him a day or two to get at least a modicum of his strength back before he could confront Duke Wilhelm, not to mention his enemy—that deceitful lump of pond scum whose men had killed John. But he was alive, and he would not give up until he found Claybrook.

Chapter
4

Margaretha couldn't stop thinking about the poor young Englishman who had been brought to Frau Lena's chamber. He seemed desperate to talk to Father about whoever had tried to kill him. But why couldn't he simply tell her? Why did he think it would endanger her to know who his attacker was?

She was sitting in the Great Hall when Lord Claybrook entered carrying a whole armful of flowers after his ride with her father and brother. Lord Claybrook presented them to her with a charming smile.

"They're lovely!"

A kitchen maid scurried to find a vessel to put them in while Margaretha took them from him. The profusion of color from the different types of flowers made her nearly giddy.

"They are so bright! Are they selling these in the market? I didn't know the geraniums were blooming already." Instead of prattling on about the flowers, Margaretha brought herself up short and remembered to ask Lord Claybrook how his ride had been and what he had thought of Hagenheim.

"It is such a charming place." Lord Claybrook went on to compliment her father's leadership skills, as well as the peace and lawful atmosphere of the town. He praised the strength of the walls and the gates and gatehouses around the town. He spoke of the friendliness and cheer of the people, as well as their cleanliness and the beauty and upkeep of the buildings.

While he talked, Margaretha arranged and rearranged her flowers in the large pottery jar. The pink flowers looked pretty next to the lavender, and the daisies set off the geraniums perfectly. Perhaps she could take a small bunch of them to the healer's chamber. They would brighten up the room so nicely, and the English boy, whatever his name was, could enjoy them while he was getting well. The poor thing had looked so pale when Frau Lena was about to stitch him up. Her presence in the room seemed to be disturbing him, and Frau Lena asked her to leave, but she wondered if he was feeling better. Maybe she could sneak away later and see if he—

"Lady Margaretha."

"Oh, yes, Lord Claybrook."

He smiled at her with narrowed eyes, then he made a "tsk-tsk-tsk" sound with his tongue against his teeth. "You were not listening again." He shook his finger at her.

"I was listening. You were telling me all about the town and how much you liked it and the security of the gates and—"

"And then I asked you what you would do tomorrow while I am out hunting with Duke Wilhelm."

"Oh, well, I shall find something to do, I am sure. I never have trouble keeping myself busy." Margaretha smiled at him.

"I have another gift for you." Lord Claybrook pulled something from a pocket inside his surcoat, and while holding it behind his back with one hand, he held out his other hand to her.

Margaretha reached out, palm up, to receive it. "I am not at all sure you should be giving me so many gifts." She almost said, *since I have not accepted you*, but she was sure he understood she hadn't agreed to marry him yet. At least he was making the effort to woo her. And what girl could resist gifts?

Lord Claybrook took her hand in his, then pulled his other hand from behind his back and deposited a small purple velvet pouch in her palm.

"What is it?"

"Open it and see."

Margaretha pulled open the mouth of the tiny drawstring bag and upended it into her hand. A ring tumbled out. It held a large ruby in the center, encircled by sapphires and diamonds.

"Oh my! It is much too extravagant a gift. I mustn't accept it." But Margaretha held it up and let it catch the rays of the late afternoon sun that were streaming in the windows. The precious stones seemed to wink at her and spark with inward flames. "It is beautiful."

The ring would perfectly match the beautiful ruby, diamond, and sapphire bracelet her grandmother, the Duchess of Marienberg, had given her as the oldest girl in the family. Perhaps it was a sign from God; Claybrook had given her a ring that matched the bracelet that was a family heirloom.

Before she knew what he planned to do, Lord Claybrook took the ring from her and slipped it on her finger. It fit perfectly.

"It is yours, my dear," he said in a deep, low voice. "You have only to accept my suit for you as my wife." He stared into her eyes, leaning close.

"Oh. I don't know if I am ready yet." Margaretha laughed nervously, pulling her hand out of his grasp and taking a step back. She slipped the ring off her finger.

He grabbed her hand to stop her. "Please. It is a gift and I do not want it back, even if you choose not to marry me." He looked into her eyes again.

"I should not accept the ring."

"But I insist. For putting up with my clumsy attempts to woo you." He smiled, as if he didn't believe his wooing was actually clumsy at all. There was something almost feline in the curve of his lips. She began to feel uncomfortable, and looked over his shoulder in hopes that someone else might be entering the room.

"Very well. I will keep it for now."

"And wear it?"

"I suppose. For now."

He kissed her hand again. Apparently, he thought it was attractive to stare into her eyes as if he couldn't look away, for he was doing it again. Margaretha had a nearly uncontrollable urge to giggle.

"Excuse me, but I must go and see what my sister needs."

"Is she calling for you? I didn't hear anything."

"Oh, no, but if I don't go to her, she may start." Margaretha's excuse was awkward, but it was enough to break away from him.

"Don't you want to take your flowers with you?"

"I like them here, in the Great Hall," she called over her shoulder. Once in the corridor, she ran all the way to her sister's chamber.

Margaretha awoke at dawn the next morning, hearing faint sounds outside her window of the hunting dogs and their trainer, as well as the voices of her father, brother, and Lord Claybrook, all assembling and getting ready for the hunt.

She threw the covers back and leapt out of bed. By the time she was able to dress, the men would be long gone and on the trail of some wild animal. No one would be around to see her enter the healer's tower to check on the English stranger.

Why was she so interested? Perhaps she hoped he would be more lucid today, that he would tell her his name and more about himself and where he came from. He was so passionate about wanting to speak with her father, and about the necessity of secrecy. Would he have calmed down, his senses restored now that he was safe and well fed? Perhaps he would tell her how he'd left his native England and come to be in Hagenheim and the Holy Roman Empire.

Margaretha dressed quickly and hurried down the stairs to the Great Hall, where she exited into the courtyard. Several maids were gathered around the well, taking their time as they filled their buckets and gossiped. They stood straighter when they noticed Margaretha, but she only smiled and waved as she sped past them on her way to Frau Lena's southwest tower.

She peeked inside the door, which was ajar on this warm, late spring morning. The bed appeared empty. She pushed the door farther open and stepped inside.

A movement to her left caught her eye. The stranger was standing up, combing his hair. He stared back at her with intense, suspicious, startling blue eyes.

"How well you are looking!" Margaretha burst out, then realized she'd said it in her native German, so she restated it in English.

Truly, he was still gaunt, and his cheeks were pale, but at least he was able to stand.

His hand shook as he stopped combing. He opened his mouth as though to speak, then closed it again. He put out his hand, leaned against the wall, and swayed. "Don't try to stop me."

"Stop you from what?"

"I'm going to see Duke Wilhelm." He pushed himself off the wall, then wobbled again.

"You will never make it across the courtyard. You should rest a bit longer. You are not well yet." She stepped forward and caught him by the arm, hoping to keep him from falling.

"I said, don't try to stop me." His tone and his eyes were fierce, but the rest of him looked as weak as a newborn kitten.

"I am not trying to stop you." Margaretha hoped her voice sounded soothing. "*Stille, ruhig bleiben.* Everything is all right."

"I am well enough to see him. I shall see him. You will not stop me."

"*Stille, ruhig bleiben.*" It was hard to think in English. She tried to think of some comforting phrase, something appropriate for the situation, and remembered her English tutor teaching her a lullaby with the words, *Hush, now.* So she said, "Hush, now. All shall be well. No one is trying to stop you."

"Then why do you have hold of my arm?" He swayed again and blinked hard. His voice was getting weaker.

"I didn't want you to fall. I would take you to Duke Wilhelm myself—he is my father, as you know—but I'm afraid he has gone hunting." Her memory of the language seemed to be coming back to her, the more she spoke it. "He'll be away most of the day. So you see, you couldn't go and see him, even if you were able."

"A-ha!" he yelled, then sagged forward.

Margaretha grabbed his shoulders and pushed, to keep him from falling to the floor on his face. Once she had him more upright and balanced than not, she asked, "What is 'a-ha'?"

"You think I am not able to go to him ... to speak to him." He was huffing, as if it was taking all his strength simply to talk and breathe. "But I am ... full able."

"*Ja, klar.* Of course, of course." She pulled his arm over her shoulder, taking much of his weight upon herself, and slowly turned him back toward the bed. He seemed beyond protestations now.

"What is happening here?" Frau Lena strode toward them. "He shouldn't be out of bed." The healer put her arm around him on the other side, and they helped him down onto the bed. Margaretha supported his shoulders as she laid his head on the pillow. Almost instantly, he was unconscious.

His face was as pale as death. Even his lips were colorless. His eyes were closed, and his unusually long black eyelashes did not even flutter. "Is he very ill? Will he die?"

"I don't think so." Frau Lena was smiling. "He is only weak from blood loss and going so long without food or water. Besides that, he took quite a beating and has a fever."

Together they stared down at him, his chest barely rising and falling. Then Margaretha noticed his clothing. "Wherever did he get such clothes?" Over a coarse woolen shirt, he wore a leather jerkin and leather breeches. That wasn't so unusual, but the color *was*—bright green and mottled with greenish yellow spots.

Frau Lena shook her head. "It was the only thing I could find that would fit him. I had to go to the laundress and beg for something, and she gave them to me. Apparently the tanner's wife was experimenting with new dyes."

"The experiment was a failure." Margaretha frowned at the strikingly ugly garments.

"These clothes fit the laundress's son, but he refused to wear them." She pursed her lips, as though trying not to laugh.

"Well, it's cruel to force this poor foreigner to wear them."

"I didn't force him to wear them." They were whispering, watching him breathe. "He must have awakened this morning and found them by his bed and put them on. His other clothes were beyond mending, I'm afraid."

"I shall try to find him something better. He is determined to speak to the duke no matter if he does look like a ... a giant frog." Margaretha shook her head.

"I imagine he will fill out his clothes better when he is able to eat more. For now, these will do. I don't want him escaping here before he is completely well, and we can better track him while he's wearing these ... green clothes."

Margaretha could see the sense in that. Still, it was a shame anyone should have to wear such an outfit. It was almost as bad as Lord Claybrook's ensembles.

"Cook is preparing some special soup for him," Frau Lena

went on, "and I plan to feed him more today. Yesterday, he wasn't able to eat much."

"I wish I could do something to help."

Frau Lena smiled, her freckles stretching across her cheeks. "Pray for him. He needs to get his strength back and stop being so frantic. I'm afraid his mind is still affected."

Margaretha embraced the healer. "That is what I shall do. Thank you for caring for him. Do you think you will need one of the maids to come and help?"

"If I do, I shall ask them. Don't worry."

Margaretha left her, feeling a strange urgency to pray for the poor young man who seemed so lost.

Chapter 5

Margaretha managed to sneak away again the next day and go to Frau Lena's chamber.

She translated Frau Lena's instructions to the stranger as he lay still on the bed. He may have looked tranquil, lying still and unmoving, but it was plain by the intense, rebellious gleam in his eyes that he was anything but.

"You must rest, because that is the only way you can fully recover and get your strength back. You must eat what Frau Lena gives you, because it will keep you from getting sick, and you must not be pacing around the room, raving like a madman." She surprised herself by remembering the English word "raving."

"If I do rave like a madman," he said, sitting up and balling his hands into fists, "it is because there is a murderer out there, probably in this very castle, who is free to kill again. He is evil, and if I do not—"

"Please. Frau Lena says you must lie still and not excite yourself. You will bring on another fever." Margaretha pushed gently on his shoulder, trying to get him to lie back down. "This is not good for you."

A muscle in his jaw flexed, as though he was clenching his teeth. But he lay back and closed his eyes. "I am not so weak I can't speak. Won't anyone listen to me?" He lifted his hands to his face, rubbing his eyes, scraping his hands down his stubbly cheeks and chin.

"*Sei still.*" What was that English phrase she'd used before to try to comfort him? "Hush now. Everything will be well. Why don't you tell me what you want to tell Duke Wilhelm? I can write it down for you and give it to him myself."

"No, it is too dangerous to write it down." A growling sound came from his throat.

"Then just tell me. Why don't you start with your name?"

"You don't understand." He covered his face with his hands again. His voice was muffled as he said, "I probably shouldn't tell even Duke Wilhelm, but I have no choice. We should find out what he plans to do, why he's here. You could all be in danger."

"Who? Why who is here?"

He lay still and quiet, and she thought perhaps he had fallen asleep. He finally let his hands fall away and looked at her. "I want you to teach me to speak some German."

So he wanted to change the subject. He was so adamant. "I shall try. But it would be helpful if you would tell me your name."

"Very well. I will tell you my given name if you will promise not to tell it to anyone."

"Oh." She hesitated before saying, "I do tend to talk a lot, but when it is important to keep something a secret, I certainly will not babble on about it. My brothers tease me about talking too much, and I do sometimes say things before I think."

"Is there anyone else in Hagenheim who speaks English?" He fixed her with those dark blue eyes.

"Oh. Well, no, no one who speaks it as well as I. My younger sisters studied it, but they do not like languages as much as I do. My brothers say it is because I like to talk so much, but little brothers always tease their sisters, my father says. It's the way of siblings, and they were jealous when they often heard me speaking English with my tutor. Even my tutor said my English was very good for someone who had never been to England. But languages are so interesting, and I like to know the origins of words."

He was staring at her with narrowed eyes. She was annoying him.

She cleared her throat. "I promise not to say anything you don't want me to say, and if you only tell me your given name, I don't see how that could put anyone in danger, especially if it is a common name."

"That is the problem. It is not a common name here. Perhaps you could call me ... Otto."

"Oh, no. That name doesn't suit you. You don't look at all like an Otto. You are much too tall and handsome to be an Otto."

"Then you pick a name for me." His voice sounded tired, or perhaps frustrated. At least he had ceased glaring at her.

"Very well. It shall be as you wish. I shall call you ..." What an odd thing—to name an adult. "Gawain."

"Gawain?" His upper lip curled on one side while one brow went up.

"Yes. With your thick, wavy, dark hair and blue eyes, you look like a Gawain." Very handsome, like a knight. Her heart skipped a little as she pictured him in her father's armor.

He sighed. "Very well. I am Gawain."

Colin's head was spinning, partly from sitting up too abruptly a few moments before, and partly from his maddening inability to convey to Lady Margaretha the danger they were all in. He couldn't expect her to understand. She was a sheltered, wealthy duke's daughter. What could she know of intrigues and murders and people who were not as they seemed? But the fact that she was the only person who could communicate with him, and he with her, made her the most valuable person in the world to him.

And, he had to admit, he liked looking at her, even if her aimless chatter did give him a headache.

She began his first German lesson, in which she taught him to say, "My name is Gawain. *Mein Name ist Gawain.* I speak a little of your language. *Ich spreche ein bisschen von Ihrer Sprache.*"

She also told him all about her family and asked him about his. He was obliged to tell her he had a mother and father and several younger siblings, that he was the oldest child, and that he had left home abruptly a few months before, leaving word where he was going but not speaking to his family about his quest, since they would have forbidden him to go.

Frau Lena came into the room. When the healer saw Margaretha sitting close to his bed, her forehead creased. She spoke softly—chidingly, if he understood her tone—probably about spending so much time at his bedside. The healer clearly thought him merely a lost beggar with a few eggs short of a dozen, but Lady Margaretha must have talked Frau Lena into letting her stay and teach him German. He hardly understood a word they were saying in that strange, guttural language of theirs, but he read a lot in their facial expressions and tone.

Lady Margaretha turned back to him with a smile. "Now what else shall I teach you? Thank you is *danke.*"

Frau Lena left through the doorway in the back of the room, which led to what looked like a storage area.

Colin said, "Lady Margaretha, won't you take me to see your father?"

"I don't believe you are well enough yet, and I don't want you to become frantic. It is not good for you. You want to get your strength back, don't you?"

"Will you take me to see him tomorrow?"

"I don't know." She bit her lip and her brows came together, forming a wrinkle above her nose. "I would have to ask Frau Lena."

"Oh, no you wouldn't. You and I could sneak away when she was not watching us. It could easily be done."

"I wouldn't want to anger Frau Lena. She knows what is best for you."

"If you will not take me to see him, then I shall go by myself." Would she give in to him? She seemed a sweet, compliant sort of girl.

But she only smiled and shook her head. "You would not be allowed to get anywhere near him. We have many guards, and a stranger like you would be noticed and escorted out of the castle."

He looked down at his hideous green clothes. She had a point.

"Besides, my father knows very little English. You would have a difficult time communicating with him without me."

Had he really thought she was lovely? Sweet and compliant? That smug, knowing smile was making his headache worse. If only she wasn't right.

"If you will promise me that you will do everything Frau Lena says, I will try to get you a private audience with my father in a few days."

Perhaps that was the best he could hope for. "Very well, I promise—if you will promise to get me something to wear other than these hideous green clothes."

She smiled sweetly again. "I agree. You need proper clothing. I am sorry Frau Lena couldn't find anything better. One of my brothers should have something. You are closest to my brother Gabe's size, though you are thinner. I may be able to find some clothes he left here when he married Sophie and went to Hohendorf."

She didn't have to remind him how thin he had become.

He'd never been brawny, but he looked out-and-out puny since nearly getting beaten to death and left to die at the edge of nowhere. But he must be polite to her, as she was his only friend. Softly, he said, "If you can find me some clothes that don't make me look ridiculous, I would be obliged to you."

"I shall. And when I bring them to you, you must say, *"Danke für die Kleidung."*

"What does that mean?"

"Thank you for the clothes."

"Danke für . . . what was it?"

She repeated the phrase, and he said it after her.

Frau Lena came back, bringing him a bowl of soup and a small loaf of bread. *"Danke,"* he told her, which made the fair, red-haired healer smile and say, *"Sehr gut."*

"That means, 'very good.'" Margaretha reached out as though to take his bowl of soup.

"Nein!" He already knew how to say no. "Why are you taking my soup?"

"I only wanted to help you."

"To feed me? No, thank you. I'm not that helpless." He held the bowl in his lap and picked up the spoon. Putting the first spoonful of soup in his mouth, he glanced up at her to make sure she wasn't offended by his rebuff. He was not exactly behaving properly toward the daughter of a duke, but in his defense, she wasn't behaving like any daughter of any duke he knew.

She was smiling the way one might smile at a small child. Irritating.

The soup was good, and he ate and listened to her talk about her family. They sounded like a jolly group, the many brothers and sisters, and she obviously loved her mother and father. He tried to think how he might get her to mention that fiend, if indeed he was in Hagenheim.

Between bites, he interrupted her to ask, "What do you do

every day?" He was just finishing the soup—he didn't want to waste a drop—and started on his bread.

"Oh, I like to ride my horse, Blüte, which is 'Bloom' in English. She is a sweet, gentle mare, but I would dearly love to ride my father's new stallion. My father says no, that the horse is too wild for me, but I know he likes me. I always bring him a carrot or an apple, and he lets me pet him and never bites me. He bit my brother so hard he drew blood. But he likes me, so I'm sure there is no danger.

"I also like to read and study languages. I like music too—we are a musical family. My father plays the lute and we all sing. Although some of my brothers sing badly. And for the last year, my father has been trying to find me a suitable husband." She paused long enough to let out a sigh. "Until now, I haven't liked any of my suitors. But I must marry, so that my younger sisters can get their chance to make a good match."

That she had not married yet was surprising. Her beauty should have attracted an abundance of eligible suitors, and she was the oldest daughter of one of the most powerful dukes in the German regions. Although the fact that she prattled on so often might have driven off a few.

"But my current suitor seems very kind. He brings me gifts, and I could learn to like that. Also, he talks so much that I am learning to listen and not speak so much myself." She sighed again. "My father says he would be a suitable husband, as he is an English earl, and he stands to inherit a second earldom not far away, a region adjoining Hagenheim."

Colin began to feel ill, and it wasn't from overfilling his stomach.

"My father says if I marry Lord Claybrook, I will be able to stay near—"

"Claybrook." Colin ground his teeth. "Marry Claybrook."

He sat straight up and threw his legs over the side of the bed. His empty soup bowl and spoon clattered to the floor.

Lady Margaretha jumped up from her stool and backed away.

All he could see was red, like a film of blood over his eyes. That devil was here! He was here wooing Lady Margaretha. And she was considering marrying him! She had no idea what a cruel, heartless murderer he was, what danger she was in!

He stood up and his head seemed to drift right off his shoulders. His vision started to go dark. He grabbed for the wall but missed and fell back onto the bed.

"Frau Lena!" Margaretha came toward him and helped pull his feet onto the bed.

He could barely see her for the darkness coming over him.

"Curse this weakness!" he muttered. He put his hands on his head, trying to make it stop spinning. If he were fully recovered, he'd go find Claybrook and fight it out with him once and for all. And probably get himself killed. For if he knew Claybrook, the man would have plenty of men around him to protect his worthless skin.

But at least Colin knew Claybrook was here. And as soon as he was able, he would bring his enemy to justice. He couldn't let him get away a second time. And he couldn't let him hurt Margaretha or her family. If only he wasn't so weak.

Chapter
6

Margaretha called for Frau Lena, and she came hurrying down the stairs.

"What is it?"

"He became extremely agitated, jumped up, and nearly fainted."

Frau Lena approached the bed where Gawain lay mumbling and moaning, his hands on his head. Frau Lena felt his cheek. "He doesn't seem to have a fever any longer. What was he so agitated about?" She bent down and picked up the bowl and spoon from the floor.

Margaretha thought back to what he had said. "I was telling him about my new suitor, and when I said his name" — Margaretha mouthed the words "Lord Claybrook" so as not to send the young stranger into another frenzy — "he became extremely agitated and kept repeating it. His face turned red and he was clearly disturbed. What could have caused him to behave in such a way?"

Frau Lena looked thoughtful, touching her finger to her chin. "Did he say anything else? Did he say only the name," and Frau Lena whispered, "Lord Claybrook?"

The stranger moaned again and Margaretha placed her finger to her lips. "He did say one other thing. He said, 'Curse this weakness.' What do you think it means?"

Frau Lena shook her head slowly. "I can only think of one thing: He must be in love with you, and the mere thought of another suitor sends him into hysterics. He must regret he is too weak to challenge your suitor."

"Oh no." Margaretha sighed. "I wish it were not so, but I'm afraid that is the only explanation for such a wild reaction. He was calm before I began talking of my new suitor." Margaretha clicked her tongue against her teeth. "His mind seemed to be improving. He ate his soup and bread and seemed perfectly sane when he asked me to get him some clothes that didn't make him look ridiculous."

At the moment, he was lying perfectly still on the sick bed. One would never know he was insanely jealous of Margaretha's suitor.

"Perhaps you should go, so as not to disturb him again." Frau Lena patted Margaretha's arm.

"Let me just say good-bye to him and see if he remembers the words I taught him."

"Very well. I shall be upstairs if you need me." Frau Lena gave him one last long look and left.

Margaretha righted her stool and sat down next to him. "Gawain? Are you feeling well?"

"Who? What?"

Already he had forgotten. "Remember? You didn't want to tell me your name, so we agreed I would call you Gawain."

He frowned. His hands still covered his eyes.

When he didn't say anything, she asked, "Do you remember our German lesson? What will you say if I find you some clothes?"

"Danke für die Kleidung."

"That is very good."

"Das ist sehr gut."

"Excellent!" She hadn't taught him that sentence, although

46

he must have put the words together from other sentences she taught him. Was he only pretending not to know German?

Gawain was half sitting, propped up on one elbow. He'd moved so fast, she hadn't even noticed. He grabbed her arm.

"Listen to me," he said, returning to English. "You must not mention me to Lord Claybrook. Promise you won't say a word. If he knows I'm here, all will be lost."

What was he talking about? Should she call for Frau Lena? "Hush now, Gawain. All will be well. You are distressed at the moment, but——"

"You must promise me." He tightened his grip as his eyes bore into hers. "Your life could be in danger, especially if he thinks you know about me."

"Lord Claybrook? He would never harm me. You only need to rest——"

"No, it is you who do not understand." Gawain pulled her closer, and she almost lost her balance and fell off the stool. "The man is evil. He has killed before, and he will do it again."

The gleam in his eyes frightened her, as well as the fact that she couldn't pull loose from his grip on her arm. "Frau Lena!"

He leaned even closer and spoke in a hoarse whisper. "You must listen. Please, Lady Margaretha. All our lives depend upon it."

He was clearly delirious again. His words and the intensity in his eyes were frightening, but he obviously believed what he was saying.

"Are you sure it is the same Lord Claybrook? That he killed someone?" What if he *was* right? Could Lord Claybrook be a killer? It seemed impossible, but now that she thought about it ... there was a coldness in his eyes sometimes. And when he talked about hunting, there was a bloodthirstiness in his voice. Shouldn't she at least consider it a possibility?

"Yes, I am sure! Lady Margaretha, you must not trust him."

Frau Lena came hurrying into the room again. Her eyes went wide with horror.

Gawain glanced down at his hand gripping Margaretha's arm and let go, as if dropping a burning ember. He must have realized how it would look to Frau Lena.

Frau Lena hurried to her. "Did he hurt you? Are you all right?"

"I am not hurt." Margaretha's arm tingled where his fingers had pressed into her flesh. "He is only dismayed about Lord Claybrook, I think."

She couldn't break away from his gaze, as he stared at her with those intense blue eyes.

"Please," he begged her as if her life depended on her believing him. "Please."

Her heart tripped strangely. "How do you know Lord Claybrook?"

He stared into her eyes for a moment, then sighed. "You need to know, since he is here." He frowned, but the intensity never left his face. "We are from the same part of England. He murdered my sister's friend, a young woman, the daughter of a wealthy landowner, because she was pregnant with his child and he didn't want to marry her. He came here to escape justice, and for who knows what other evil intentions. He has been amassing an army of knights for the past several years and has brought them with him." His lips parted as he stared at her. "You don't know what he is capable of. Please believe me."

"What is he saying?" Frau Lena's voice was tense by her side.

"Don't tell her what I'm saying," Gawain said. "Don't tell her any of it. Please."

Margaretha stared at him. Then she looked at Frau Lena. "He . . . he is only ranting." She shrugged and shook her head. "I am not sure."

Frau Lena's forehead was still creased. "You should go. He may be dangerous. I don't think you should visit him anymore."

Gawain leaned toward her again, that intense look in his eyes. "Please promise me you will come back. I must talk with you again."

"Did you understand Frau Lena?" Was he only pretending not to understand the healer? Or had he simply anticipated what she would say?

"No. What did she say?" He looked as if he sincerely wanted to know.

Again she wondered if he was only pretending not to know German. But she thought she'd better play along with him—for now. "That I must leave."

"Please, Lady Margaretha. Promise me you will come back. Promise me you will remember what I said, and go and tell your father. Yes." He frowned again. "I'm afraid you must go and tell Duke Wilhelm. But you must not let Lord Claybrook hear you or know you are suspicious of him in the least. You must be extremely careful with what I have told you and not tell anyone except your father. Promise me."

Margaretha's mind was spinning. She wasn't sure what to believe. She had thought him mad, until he'd told her the story about Lord Claybrook murdering his sister's friend because she was pregnant with Claybrook's child. Had his unbalanced mind invented the story? The details, including the fact that he claimed they were both from the same part of England, made his story seem more authentic.

If his story was true, then he was indeed in danger, and so was she, simply because he had told her. Now she understood why he hadn't wanted to tell her his name.

Still, it was all so difficult to believe. Lord Claybrook a murderer? It hardly seemed possible. A man who cared as much as he did about the fashion of his garments didn't seem likely to murder anyone, did he? But it wasn't as if she knew any murderers or their clothing preferences.

His deep blue eyes pleaded with her, even as Frau Lena stood next to her, urging her to leave the room.

"Very well, I promise," she told him.

"Please be careful." The expression on his face made her feel as if they shared a secret, as if he trusted her.

No one had ever trusted her with a secret, not since she had revealed to her mother that her older brother, Gabehart, was sneaking out at night. And there was the time her sister had accidentally broken her mother's looking glass. Once pressured to tell what she knew about it, Margaretha had spilled the entire truth. Her sister didn't speak to her for two days.

Frau Lena nudged her toward the open doorway. "Go on. Let him get some rest."

Margaretha looked over her shoulder at him as she walked out of the healer's chamber. He watched her go, as sane and solemn as the priest during Holy Eucharist.

It was only too sad that he likely was not sane at all.

"My name is Colin," he said softly.

She stared back at him, then nodded. "Colin. It suits you."

"Please be careful," he said, as Frau Lena nudged her out the door.

Chapter
7

As Margaretha went to look for her father, she couldn't stop thinking about Gawain—or Colin, if that was his actual name. In a certain manner, she felt responsible for his welfare, perhaps because she had been there when he was brought in, nearly dead, by the potter's apprentice. Or perhaps it was because she was the only one who could speak his language. He couldn't even communicate with Frau Lena. Margaretha was nearly the only person in Hagenheim who spoke English.

Being needed was a good feeling.

Her father was not in the solar, and neither was anyone else. She came down the stone steps to the first floor. Hearing voices in the Great Hall, she went in.

Margaretha's mother and sisters, Adela and Kirstyn, were sitting at a trestle table with a chessboard and chess pieces.

"Come play with us," Kirstyn called. "I'm playing chess with Mother, and you can play something with Adela."

"Yes, Margaretha. Play with me!" Adela jumped up and ran toward her. "I don't like chess and there's no one to play backgammon with me." Her blue eyes sparkled and her little hands grasped Margaretha's arm.

"In a minute, Adela. Don't pull my arm off." Margaretha's mother was staring down at the chessboard. "Mother, where is Father?"

She smiled and patted Margaretha's cheek. "He and Valten have gone to the training field with the knights to show Lord Claybrook their drills."

"Do you know when he'll be back?"

"No, but I don't expect them until late in the afternoon. They took food with them. Why do you ask?"

"I wanted to talk to him ..."

Her brothers, Steffan and Wolfgang, burst into the room. They made so much noise, shouting and fighting over a sheathed sword, that her voice was drowned out.

When the two boys stopped fighting long enough to look over at their mother, she was giving them her stern look.

"Boys, why are you fighting over that sword?"

Steffan and Wolfgang looked at each other, then turned back to their mother. "It's a secret," Wolfgang said.

"Yeah," Steffan chimed in, "and we can't tell secrets in front of Margaretha, because she talks too much."

Margaretha's chest tightened. "Well, you fight too much. Why don't you go annoy someone else." She had a secret at this very moment, and she wouldn't tell anyone but her father. It was a shame she couldn't tell her brothers how wrong they were about her.

Steffan shrugged. "Everyone says you talk too much."

"That is unkind, Steffan." Mother's look had changed from stern to shocked. "Apologize to your sister."

Her mother didn't say it was untrue, only that it was unkind.

"But, Mother, *everyone* says it."

"That is enough. You will not speak of your sister that way. Besides, most secrets should not be kept. We don't keep secrets in this family."

"I am sorry, Mother." Steffan gave his mother his best contrite face. When Mother looked away, he shifted his gaze to Margaretha, and the corners of his mouth went up in a smirk.

Margaretha was tempted to give him a quick cuff to the head while Mother was looking away. She decided instead to mollify his teasing by admitting, "I do talk too much sometimes." Margaretha allowed Adela to take her by the hand and lead her to the backgammon board. She shook her head at Steffan. "But I can't help it that your mind is too slow to process all my words. It is your fault for not stretching your mind with reading and studying—"

"There you go again, talking more than a person's brain can take in. You couldn't stop talking if you tried."

"I certainly could."

Wolfgang laughed, and Steffan joined him. They laughed so hard, the two brothers grabbed each other's shoulders, holding on as if they would fall down laughing if they didn't.

"That is enough," her mother said. "Margaretha is lovely, and therefore her thoughts and her speech are lovely. Anyone with a pure heart may speak as much as they like and their words will always be welcome."

"Thank you, Mother." She smiled and pretended her brother's words didn't bother her. If only she could be quiet and demure, like her sister Kirstyn, or wise in everything she said, like Mother. Even her sister-in-law, Gisela, seemed to command attention, and what she said always seemed pertinent to the conversation. They did not change the subject abruptly, as Margaretha often did, or forget to ask the other person about themselves.

Margaretha sat down opposite Adela, who was readying the game board. Her brothers moved closer to her, glancing several times at their mother, who was staring down at the chess game between her and Kirstyn.

Steffan made his way to Margaretha's side, bent down close to her ear, and whispered, "Aren't you planning to tell Mother about the mad fellow in the Frau Lena's chamber? I'll wager you can't keep it a secret, even though Mother would disapprove of you visiting him."

"What do you know of it?" Margaretha caught him by the collar of his tunic.

"I was walking by the healer's chamber and saw you talking with him. The blacksmith's apprentice, Frederick, saw when they brought him to Frau Lena. He told me the man took a blow to the head and now he is mad. He raves like a lunatic, and no one can understand what he says."

"You don't know anything," Margaretha whispered, while her mother was talking to Kirstyn. "I can understand him perfectly because he speaks English. You only know German and are ignorant because you neglect your studies." Oh no. She probably shouldn't have said anything about him knowing English. Colin would be angry with her if he knew. She hoped she hadn't put him in danger.

Steffan snorted. "No one around here speaks English."

"Leave me alone, Steffan." Margaretha was determined to ignore him as she sat down to begin her game of backgammon with her little sister. Did people laugh at her behind her back? Did they hide things from her? So many times she felt she was the last person to find out what was going on.

It must be true. No one wanted to tell her anything because she would repeat it, even without meaning to.

Her face burned as she went through the motions of the game, rolling the dice and moving her game pieces.

Little brothers were a plague. But Steffan didn't know how much his words hurt her. Besides, everything he said was true. Talking too much was one of her worst faults, no matter how much her mother tried to make her not feel bad about it.

Did her suitors think she talked too much? Would any of them have wanted to marry her if she was not the daughter of

Duke Wilhelm? Could anyone overlook her faults enough to truly love her?

What if she married, but her husband thought she was annoying? What if he stopped loving her because she talked too much?

She couldn't think of anything worse.

Chapter
8

*Margaretha walked toward the stables, hop-*ing a ride on her favorite mare would take her mind off the stranger, Colin.

Six days had gone by since Colin had been brought to Frau Lena's chamber, speaking English and raving about being in danger. And still Margaretha had not been able to speak to the duke about him. The first night, her father had come home late and she hadn't wanted to bother him. The next morning, he had left early. He'd been called away to the far side of the region to settle a dispute and track down some robbers who had been terrorizing the roads.

She had not fulfilled her promises to the English foreigner. It hadn't exactly been her fault that she had not spoken to her father, but she had also not come back to visit him in the last three days, or found him some better clothes in which to meet Duke Wilhelm.

Her mother had remarked about her being so quiet. How could she tell her mother that she felt bad for not fulfilling a promise? Her mother might scold her, and she couldn't break another promise—the promise not to tell anyone about Colin.

But was it her fault that Frau Lena thought it best she not visit the Englishman anymore? If Lord Claybrook had been there, she might have watched him to try to find out if what

Colin said about him was true. But Claybrook had taken some of his men and gone with her father.

Margaretha kicked a weed. She stopped to pull it out of the ground, absently shredding the leaves one by one and continuing on to the stable. She would go and visit him again even if Frau Lena didn't approve. She would also brave his displeasure at her not having been able to talk to her father yet, just as soon as she'd taken her ride.

A stable boy walked past her carrying water and dumped it into the trough for the horses. He must be new, since she didn't recognize him. His hair was thick and dark and curled at his ears and neck, and he was tall.

If he was new … A smile spread over her face. He wouldn't know that she was not allowed to ride the black stallion Lord Claybrook had given her father.

The new stable boy seemed to be muttering to himself as he emptied the bucket in the trough, then went to the well to refill it. Margaretha went into the stable, undetected, and found the black stallion in his stall. He allowed her to stroke his neck, and when she offered him a carrot, he took it carefully from her palm.

The new stable boy returned to empty another bucket into the trough. There was something appealing about the confident way he held his head and shoulders. He was almost regal. Perhaps she could find a sweet kitchen maid who would be a good match for him. If only he would look up and let her see his face. But he dumped his water and went back to the well for more.

The stable master, Dieter, was coming toward her, talking with another of the servants. Margaretha slipped quietly into her own mare Blüte's stall, rubbing the gray horse's cheek and giving her the last carrot in her pocket to keep her quiet until Dieter and the other stable boy had passed through to the other side of the stable.

Through the open doorway she heard the new stable boy coming back, so she slipped out again, closing Blüte's stall door quietly, and hurried out to stop him. He poured out the last of the water and set his bucket on the ground.

"Stable boy, I need you to saddle a horse for me."

The boy froze, then turned on his heel to face her. His flashing blue eyes were unmistakable as they pierced her through.

"Colin! *Es ist-du!*"

Spirits above, but he did look good. He was shaved, his cuts and bruises were almost healed, and she could see by the way he filled out his brown woolen tunic that he had already gained some weight. She switched to speaking in English, which she had recently refreshed by looking at the texts her English tutor had left her.

"You don't look at all pitiable anymore."

He raised one black eyebrow, the side of his mouth twisting downward. "Thank you. A man always prefers not to look pitiable, if possible."

"Oh, I'm sorry. I didn't mean to be insulting. I only meant that you look … good." It would require a special kitchen maid indeed to be a match for him now.

"Are you healed? And what are you doing working in the stables? Did Frau Lena say you were well enough?" She felt her face turn red. What must he think of her? After she had completely ignored his pleas to come back and visit him, after she had deserted him for three days, he must hate her. And worst of all, he must realize that she had not fulfilled her promise to speak to her father on his behalf.

She fidgeted with her sleeves, shifting from one foot to the other, waiting for him to reproach her.

He started toward her, then walked past, entering the stable and heading for the room where the horses' saddles and tack were kept. "I was assigned to work in the stables only yesterday because I refused to leave Hagenheim until I had spoken to Duke Wilhelm."

Was his mind healed? It seemed to be so at the moment.

"I know you must be angry with me for not speaking to the duke as you asked me to. Truly, after the first couple of days, when you were too weak to talk to him yourself, I had no chance to speak to him. He was called away on urgent business. Lord Claybrook has been away as well." She cringed as she said the name that had elicited such an extreme reaction from him before. But he didn't even flinch. Instead, he leaned down and lifted a sidesaddle from its place near the wall.

"I am not angry about that."

His voice sounded deep and strong, not at all weak anymore. Staring at his back, she felt a little shiver race across her shoulders.

He faced her, the heavy saddle in his grip. "Which horse would you like me to saddle?"

"Oh. Yes." She turned and pointed to the new black stallion's stall. "That one."

He looked at the horse, then fastened his dark blue eyes back on her. "Are you sure?"

"Of course I'm sure. I want to ride that horse, the black one with the white patch on his forehead."

He didn't move. "I do not believe you should be riding that horse. Is he the one your father told you not to ride because he was dangerous?"

"Oh, he isn't dangerous with me." Margaretha motioned carelessly with her hand. "He likes me and is always gentle with me. It is nothing to you which horse I ride, although I do appreciate your concern for my safety." She smiled to soften her words, but she was the duke's daughter and was not used to the servants speaking to her in such a manner. Perhaps her sitting by his bed when he was so ill and ministering to his wounds had caused this young man to assume a familiarity with her that was not proper.

He snorted, then rolled his eyes toward the ceiling of the stable—actually rolled his eyes at her!—and started toward the stallion. She, Margaretha, was speechless.

He stopped when he got to the stall door. She might have hurried forward to open the door if it had been one of the other stable boys, the ones who treated her with respect and deference, but not this churlish man, who dared to snort and roll his eyes! She let him struggle with the heavy saddle, holding it with one hand and half propping it on his knee while opening the stall door with his other hand.

He lifted the saddle onto the horse's back. The stallion snuffled angrily and turned his bared teeth toward Colin and tried to nip his shoulder. Colin muttered under his breath, then led the huge black horse out into the sun to finish strapping on the saddle.

Putting on a saddle usually only took a few minutes, but the way he was fumbling around, it might take him all morning. Just when she thought he was getting along better, the saddle slid all the way off and onto the ground.

"Have you ever worked in a stable before?" She might as well talk to him. Perhaps it would cover up his embarrassment at being so unskilled at his job.

He turned to face her with raised brows and a frown. "I am the son of a wealthy landed lord in England." He picked up the saddle and put it back on again. "Saddling horses and shoveling manure were not among my activities. But I might as well be a penniless beggar here. I have no choice if I want to stay here and stop a murderer from accomplishing whatever plan he is scheming."

The son of a wealthy landed lord? Was he telling the truth? His mind certainly seemed healed, and he looked well physically. She must at least believe in the possibility.

"You still don't believe me, do you?"

"I must admit, it does appear someone tried to kill you, or at least attacked you. Also, you must be telling the truth about being from England. You could not speak English so well if you were not. But you are hardly older than I am—"

"I am twenty years old."

"Precisely, and it seems a bit unlikely to think that a wealthy lord's son would come all the way here after uncovering some sort of plot by Lord Claybrook, of all people. Lord Claybrook simply seems too timid to plot murder. The man hardly—"

"Which is the exact kind of man who plots murders—a cowardly, seemingly timid person who is so deceptive, no one suspects him." Colin's eyes flashed, his whole body tense as he gripped the horse's reins and slapped his own leg with the horse's riding crop.

Just then, the black stallion turned his head and nipped Colin's arm. Too late, Colin jumped out of reach.

"Did he draw blood?" Margaretha stepped forward to look at his arm, but he pulled away from her.

"It's nothing." He rubbed his arm, the lids hanging heavy over his eyes.

"I must say, Colin, that look on your face seems far more dangerous than any I've ever seen on Lord Claybrook's."

Colin turned back to test the horse's saddle, making sure it was secure. "Time will reveal who is telling the truth, who is dangerous, and who is trying to protect you."

"The anger and resentment in your voice makes me sad. But I daresay you are right." Margaretha rubbed the side of the stallion's head to distract and calm him.

He kept his back to her as he dodged another attempt by the stallion to bite him.

"I like the name Colin. It suits you."

"I would prefer you not allow anyone to hear you call me

that. My life, and yours as well, would be in danger if Claybrook knew I was here."

"Lord Claybrook is away with my father."

"But he will return." He spun around to face her. "Do you know when they will return?"

"No, but Mother said she thought Lord Claybrook might return before Father. He could come back tomorrow."

Colin straightened and his eyes widened. "Does he have a guard named Reginald?"

"Yes, Reginald is the captain of Lord Claybrook's guard." The fact that he knew Claybrook's captain's name sent a chill through her.

"I need you, once Claybrook returns, to spy on him and Reginald."

"Spy? Me?"

"Yes."

"Oh, I don't think I would be good at spying on anyone."

He gave her a hard look.

"I don't know if I could spy on Lord Claybrook and the captain of his guard. How would I even do that? I've never deceived anyone." She stopped and drew in a quick breath. "No, that isn't entirely true. I am very good at matchmaking between our servants, and when I am matchmaking, I do temporarily neglect to tell them something, sometimes, in order to —"

"All I ask is that you listen to his conversations with his captain without him knowing it, and to tell no one except me what he says."

"You want me to purposely and secretly listen to a conversation and then tell you—and no one else—what they said."

"Exactly."

"What if I make a mess of it? What if I'm found out?"

He gazed across the distant meadow, beyond the town wall.

"Yes. Perhaps you are right. It would be too dangerous for you." He turned away so she couldn't read his expression.

"I didn't say it was too dangerous." She suspected he was only baiting her, but she suddenly didn't want him to think she couldn't do it. "I'm sure I could spy for you. But I still think you must be wrong about Lord Claybrook. He would never hurt me."

He turned to stare at her again with those intense blue eyes of his. "He killed my sister's friend, and she was every bit as young and innocent-looking as you. Although in her case, looks were deceiving." A grimace of pain flitted over his face. He cleared his throat. "No, I don't want you to do it. I would never forgive myself if he hurt you. I am sorry I mentioned it. Let us not speak of it." His voice was quiet and resigned.

He seemed sincerely concerned for her. But before she could respond, he went inside the black stallion's stall.

Colin took the horse's reins and began to lead him out of the stable. "Are you sure you want to ride this horse?"

She still wanted to pursue the matter of spying on Claybrook and his captain, but she didn't want to waste the opportunity to ride the new stallion. "Of course. He is completely gentle with me."

Colin looked doubtful. "I hope I don't get into trouble for saddling this horse for you."

"Oh, you won't get into trouble. I will tell them I forced you to do it."

He pointed his finger at her. "So I was right. You aren't supposed to ride this horse."

"I never said that. I only said you won't get in trouble. And earlier you said you weren't angry about me not speaking to my father about you. But you are angry with me." Her guilty conscience seemed to demand that she extort some sort of rebuke from him. Besides, she was desperate to distract him from the subject of the horse, since she was horribly close to admitting she wasn't supposed to ride him.

He took the horse's reins, ducking out of the way of his nipping teeth, and led the animal into the stable yard. "I was angry that you didn't believe me." After a pause, he added, "And that you didn't come back."

The hurt look on his face, which she only caught a glimpse of as he turned away, sent a stabbing pain through her chest. An angry rebuke would have been preferable.

"I am sorry. I should not have left you alone when you were a foreigner and without a friend to help you."

"I did have someone," he said quietly, not looking at her. "The priest speaks English. He came and translated for me and convinced the stable master to allow me to work in the stable in exchange for food and a place to sleep."

"I am glad." Margaretha drew closer to him. "I truly am sorry I did not follow through on my promises to you. Will you forgive me?"

He looked down at her, a softer expression on his face. "I forgive you. But I was not only angry with you. I was worried about what Claybrook might do to you. He is a craven weasel, but also cruel and dangerous."

Examining the serious look on his face, she was convinced again that he at least believed what he was saying. However, she still wasn't sure if she believed it herself.

He stared at her, a muscle twitching in his jaw. "But he is not here, so we need not be afraid of him now. Are you ready for your ride?"

"Yes."

He bent and held his hands at knee level to help her mount the horse. She quickly placed her foot in his hands, before he should change his mind about letting her ride the stallion. In a moment she was sitting high in the sidesaddle, higher than she had ever been, since the stallion was so much larger than her mare. Her heart galloped, but she smiled, hoping she looked at ease on the powerful beast. She sat still a moment to let the horse get used to her—and said a little prayer that he wouldn't throw her. Then she nudged him forward with her knee.

Out of the corner of her eye, she saw the stable master rushing toward them from the other side of the stable yard, his mouth hanging open.

The horse started forward, then reared. Margaretha clutched the reins, grabbing a fistful of mane along with them. The horse reared again as Colin tried to grab the horse's neck—and the horse's pawing hoof came within a finger-width of striking him in the head.

Somehow Margaretha managed to hang on and stay in the saddle. When he pounded his hooves to the ground, Margaretha's teeth slammed together so hard she hoped they didn't break.

The horse immediately bolted. Again, she was hard-pressed to keep from falling off as her bones seemed to rattle at the violence of his gait. The stallion's hooves pounded faster and faster, heading straight for the stone well where the horses' water was drawn.

The roaring in her ears nearly drowned out all other sound. Her heart pounded in rhythm to the horse's hooves.

Was this the end of her life? Why hadn't she listened to her father? Even Colin had warned her that the horse was dangerous. *O God, I don't want to die.* How dishonorable it would be to die this way. Her father would be so disappointed in her, and poor Colin would be blamed for it. *O God, help me!*

The horse thundered at an amazing speed, never wavering from his path toward the stone wall around the well. She held on to the horse's mane with all her strength. Somehow she'd lost her grip on the reins. If they became tangled around the stallion's legs, he would surely tumble head first and kill them both.

Still, he continued toward the well. Just when she was certain he would crash into the four-foot-high wall around it, he turned and headed back the way they had come, toward the stable, at the same breakneck speed. The stable master jumped out of the way, but Colin came toward them, raising his arms and yelling at her, "Jump! I'll catch you!"

He must be insane to offer to rescue her this way. Still, it was her only hope to be saved from this horse that seemed bent on killing her. As soon as he was almost close enough for her to jump, the stallion changed his direction so that Colin was on the opposite side, making it impossible for her to leap from the sidesaddle into Colin's arms without landing upside down.

The horse headed back toward the well again, galloping faster than ever, ignoring her shouts for him to stop. He drew closer and closer to the four-foot wall — it seemed inevitable that he would break his forelegs against the well. At the last moment, he halted.

Only Margaretha kept going. She braced herself as she landed on her back on the ground a hand-breadth from the well.

Chapter
9

She couldn't breathe. She rolled over onto one side, and after a long, horrible moment, the breath came back into her lungs.

As she clutched at her chest and gulped the air, sharp pain shot through her left arm and shoulder. Someone ran toward her, then fell to his knees at her side.

She blinked hard.

Colin leaned over her. "Are you hurt? Lady Margaretha, can you hear me?"

She blinked again. The black stallion grazed placidly several feet away, beside the well where he had stopped. She shuddered. The horse's wild plunge toward the well had jarred every bone and tooth in her body. A few more inches and she would have cracked her head open on the wall.

She moaned.

"Where are you hurt?" Colin leaned even closer, bringing his face more into focus.

"I must have landed on the back of my shoulder." Her shoulder hurt, but it would hurt more if any bones were broken. She hoped.

"I'll go get Frau Lena."

"No! Please don't. I think I am well. Only help me sit up."

Colin leaned even closer as he slipped his arm underneath

her back and lifted her into a sitting position. She gasped at how easily and swiftly he lifted her, then at the pain in her left shoulder. She cradled her left arm close to her stomach.

"Is it broken? Are you in much pain?"

"No, no, I am well. I've fallen off horses before, and I don't think any bones are broken."

"Are you certain?" Colin still knelt in front of her. "I think you should see Frau Lena and let her look at you. I will carry you."

"That won't be necessary. Perhaps if I could just stand, maybe have a drink of water ..." She kept her left arm close to her side and let him lift her by her right elbow. Her left hip was sore, but her legs held her up, and her left arm hurt, but at least she could move it. She leaned on the well and drew a ladle-full of water out of the bucket.

He hovered over her, making sure she was steady. She moaned again. What a disgrace she was. "Please promise you won't tell anyone about this." The bones in her legs seemed to have turned to water, but it was only from fear. "If I rest here a moment, I'll be well. But I don't want my father to know how foolish I was. Please don't tell anyone about this."

"I won't. But what about the stable master?"

"He won't tell. He is a man of few words and not a person to make trouble. But if my younger brothers found out ..." She glanced around to make sure no one else had seen. "They would never let me forget it, and then my father and my mother might hear of it and be angry with me."

"I should think you would be more worried about whether or not you are injured."

Staring down at her wrist, she realized it was bare. "Oh no. I've lost my bracelet." Her heart sank. She looked at the ground around her feet but didn't see it. "How will I ever explain losing that bracelet? It was my great-grandmother's. My mother will be so disappointed in me." Tears filled her eyes. She blinked them back so she could better see as she searched the ground.

"I'll help you look for it," Colin said. "If it fell off between here and the stable, we should be able to find it." He began searching the ground just as she was doing.

"*Du!*" someone yelled. It was the stable master, pointing at Colin. "You! Frog boy!" he said in German. "What do you think you're doing, putting the Lady Margaretha on that devil of a horse?"

Colin merely looked at him, shook his head, and kept searching the ground for the bracelet.

The stable master stomped toward Colin and shoved his shoulder. "Answer me, frog boy."

Colin ceased his search and stared back at the stable master.

"He doesn't understand you," Margaretha offered.

"Oh, he understands." The stable master, Dieter, shoved Colin's shoulder again. "He understands he put you in danger by letting you ride that horse."

Margaretha stepped forward. "Please. I beg you not to punish him. It was not his fault. I forced him to saddle the stallion for me. He tried to tell me not to ride him, that he was dangerous, but I refused to listen."

Margaretha translated for Colin into English. "He is blaming you for me riding the stallion, but I am telling him it was my fault." Then she turned back to Dieter. "I'm sorry. I realize I put myself in danger by trying to ride him. It won't happen again, you have my word, but please don't blame this man. He tried to save me and would have risked his life."

"As well he should." He made a gruff sound in his throat as he shot a scornful look at Colin.

Margaretha watched Dieter grab the black stallion's reins. Surprisingly, the animal didn't resist him, and he took the horse with him as he stomped toward the stable.

"Thank you," Colin said quietly. "I'm sure you must have

talked him out of sending me to feed pigs or empty chamber pots."

"It was my fault I was nearly killed, not yours." But why had Dieter called him 'frog boy'?

Margaretha's cheeks burned as she realized his nickname was her fault too. No doubt, the first time Dieter had seen Colin, he had been wearing the ugly green-speckled clothing Frau Lena had given him. She had promised to bring Colin some better clothes, something of her brother's, and she had failed to keep her word. The fact that he had gone back to looking for her bracelet made her feel even worse.

Margaretha started searching again too, imagining the look on her mother's face when she told her she had lost the gem-encrusted heirloom, the only piece of jewelry that her mother had ever entrusted to her. Her sins were mounting. She had not kept her word to Colin, and now she had lost a valuable bracelet that was significant to her family.

They searched near the well, all around it, and then continued on toward the stable. As she was staring down at the ground, Colin rushed up close to her.

"I thought I saw something. It was only a feather." He sighed and shook his head.

As he went back to searching, she noticed again how he seemed to have regained his strength and was no longer pale. He still had a few bruises visible on his face, but they were fading, and his thick hair completely covered the stitched-up wound on his head. It was as if she was seeing him for the first time. Now he appeared as he must have been before the attack — not pitiable and weak and raving mad, but strong and handsome and determined. He had said he was the son of a wealthy lord back in England, and she had no reason not to believe him. Perhaps she shouldn't treat him so much like a servant.

"Thank you for trying to help me."

He looked up at her with raised eyebrows.

"When you told me to jump and you would catch me."

"Oh. Of course."

"And I am sorry for not coming back to the healer's chambers to visit you. I thought about you a lot and prayed for you."

"You thought I was addled." There was no anger in his tone. "That the blow to the head had brought on madness. It's understandable. Besides, you are the daughter of Duke Wilhelm. Your family would not have thought it prudent for you to befriend someone like me who could have been a beggar, a ruffian, anything."

"Frau Lena thought my presence made you anxious. She said perhaps I shouldn't visit you anymore. But I am ashamed that I did not come back to see if you needed me to translate for you."

"The priest came and helped me, so I was not completely alone." He gave her a crooked smile, making his right eye squint.

"I didn't think about the priest. I am glad he came and helped."

She couldn't be sure, but she thought he rolled his eyes again before going back to searching the ground. He was entitled to a bit of resentment, but she wouldn't let him get away with too much insolence.

They searched all the way to the stable, keeping her left arm close to her side and trying not to move it, and still she did not find the bracelet. "I need some more water."

She walked back toward the well. She dropped the bucket over the side and it splashed into the water below. When she reached with her good arm to pull it back up, Colin drew near and peered into the well.

"Halt!" He grabbed her arm.

She stopped pulling on the rope, leaving the bucket of water dangling, and leaned over to see what he was staring at.

Something sparkled, caught on a stone that jutted out slightly a few feet down into the well. "My bracelet! You found it! It must have slipped off my wrist."

"Yes, but now we have to get it out without sending it into the water below. Careful." He took the rope from her, and the front part of his shoulder inadvertently brushed against the back of her shoulder, as he slowly and carefully pulled the rope. The windlass creaked as the bucket rose. He continued to pull, making sure the bucket didn't sway and hit the bracelet and knock it off its precarious perch.

The slight brush of his shoulder against hers made her feel strangely warm.

"How will we ever get it out?" Her voice was a raspy whisper, as if talking might cause the bucket to bump the bracelet into the deep well below.

"I will go see who I can find to help." Colin hurried toward the stable. Soon he reappeared with the scowling stable master Dieter and stable boy Fritz as he led them up the slight hill to the well.

"What does he want?" the stable master asked Margaretha.

"He wants you to help me get my bracelet out." She pointed down into the well. "It must have come loose and fallen off my wrist when I took a drink."

"Will you translate for me?" Colin asked her in his smooth English accent.

"Of course."

"Tell them to each grab one of my feet and lower me down far enough that I can reach the bracelet."

"Oh, that sounds dangerous—"

Before she could say anything else, he hefted himself up onto the top of the well's wall on his stomach and teetered on the edge.

Quickly, she yelled, "Grab his feet!"

Dieter and Fritz lunged forward, grabbing Colin's legs. They hugged his ankles as they lowered him head first into the well.

Margaretha held her breath as he inched closer to where the bracelet dangled. If he didn't grab it carefully it could easily fall, sinking to a watery grave, and then they'd never find it. But the thought of Colin himself plunging head first into the narrow well was what made her heart pound against her chest and her stomach turn in circles.

She shook her head and blinked hard to get the image out of her mind.

He was almost close enough to reach the bracelet. "Just a little more," he said, his voice echoing back at them.

Fritz and Dieter looked grim as they clutched Colin's ankles.

He reached out with his right hand, and Margaretha closed her eyes, too afraid to watch.

"I got it!"

The two men slowly pulled Colin up until his stomach was resting on the top of the wall. He pushed himself up using his elbows, then held out the bracelet to Margaretha.

"Thank you." Margaretha cupped the bracelet in her hands. It wasn't even broken—all the jewels were still in place, but it had come unclasped.

She stared up into Colin's dark blue eyes. "I truly do want to thank you. You risked your life to help me, and then you risked it again to get my bracelet."

One side of his mouth crooked upward. "My father says I'm reckless and impulsive—like my grandfather."

"Your grandfather?" she prompted.

"My grandfather once threw himself in front of a wolf that was attacking a servant girl."

"Oh! Was he killed?"

"No, but he lost an eye and was never able to use his left hand again."

"I hope nothing like that ever happens to you."

Colin's lip curled as he stared down at her. He chuckled, then laughed, throwing his head back and pressing his hand to his chest. It was a pleasant sound.

"What are you laughing about?"

He shook his head. "No, nothing like that has ever happened to me. I flew off in a fury, following after the man who killed my sister's best friend. I was attacked and left for dead, carted to Hagenheim Castle by a potter and his apprentice, and was saved from death only by the kindness of strangers."

Margaretha couldn't help smiling, and marveled again at how much better he looked with clean hair, a shave, and color in his cheeks. "I can see that you are like your grandfather. But I thought English lords were proud people who would never risk their lives for a maidservant, a woman outside their own class—" With an intake of breath, she covered her mouth. "Forgive me. I don't mean to offend you."

"You are quite right. English lords are a proud bunch, and it was a strange thing my grandfather did. But he was not a lord at the time. He was merely the second son, and he is not your average English lord. His nature was passionate and impulsive ... like mine. My parents were right." He raised his brows and shook his head. "I've always wanted to right wrongs and protect damsels, just like my grandfather."

The look on his face reminded Margaretha of her father. "Righting wrongs and protecting damsels is good."

"But not the kind of activities expected of me. My father says I should be pursuing an advantageous marriage, and planning how to expand my holdings and secure the ones I have."

"Those things do not appeal to you?"

He shrugged. "It is my duty, and when I return, I will not shirk it." He reached above his head to take down the ladle for the water bucket. He handed it to her, and she used it to take a long drink from the bucket.

"I always love the way water tastes right out of the well. Once it's been transferred to earthen pots and pitchers, it seems to lose its fresh taste." She handed the ladle to Colin and he dipped it into the bucket and took a drink as well.

"This water is very good."

The stable master had reached the stable and turned back to yell, "Get to work!"

"He will be there soon," she called pleasantly but firmly to the stable master, who gave her a curt nod and disappeared into the stable.

"How is your shoulder? Better, I hope."

Margaretha tested it, moving her shoulder and arm around. "Only a little sore. I've escaped unscathed, it seems."

He smiled and shook his head. "I should get back to work."

"Wait." She touched his arm, which was warm, his muscle reassuringly solid. A shiver traveled through her fingers.

He was giving her his full attention.

"I ... I want to do something for you, since you helped me so selflessly." When he didn't say anything, she went on. "You said you needed me to spy for you, to listen to Lord Claybrook's conversations with his captain of the guard."

"No, it's too dangerous. You're too much of a ... flibberti-gibbet." He mumbled the last word, which sounded like gibber-ish, not English.

"A flibberty what? Is that an English word?"

He frowned and shook his head. "Never mind."

"No, I want to know what you said. I want to learn it if it's an English word."

"It's not a well-known English word."

"What does it mean?"

75

He looked away, not meeting her eyes. "Oh, it means ... someone who wouldn't make a very good spy."

"You have a word in your language that means 'a person who wouldn't make a good spy'?"

He frowned again, but his look was pensive.

"But if I spied on him, it would help you to know his plans. My spying on Lord Claybrook would return the favor you did for me, wouldn't it?"

"You are a courageous girl, Lady Margaretha, but I cannot have you putting yourself in danger. I've just witnessed you almost get killed by a horse, and I don't want to be responsible for something worse happening to you."

"You helped me and now I will help you."

"No. Thank you for offering, but I don't want you to—"

"Why not? I can do it."

His frown deepened, along with his faraway look. "This could end very badly."

"It won't end badly. Besides, I want to do it, to thank you for what you did for me today, and for keeping my secret about riding the black stallion." She smiled, confident she could do this. For him. "It will turn out well. You'll see."

Chapter
10

Seven days after Colin le Wyse had been brought to Hagenheim Castle on a cart, half starved and half dead, he was cleaning out the castle stables and brushing down the horses.

At least he had his strength back.

As he brushed down another horse, he relived the events of the day before. His heart beat at a frantic pace at just remembering how Margaretha had flown, head first, off that demon-possessed horse's back. He thanked God that she had fallen just short of the well instead of falling against its stone—or into it, where she might have struck her head and drowned.

Even though she sometimes chattered incessantly, treated him like a lack-witted servant, and was naive in not taking his warnings seriously enough, she had a sweet smile and kind nature. The thought of Claybrook being anywhere near her made his heart sink, especially when he imagined her spying on the man. If that criminal were to discover her, he would probably kill her. He could only hope Claybrook would never believe her capable or clever enough to spy on him.

Not that Colin thought she wasn't. She was intelligent. But he could easily imagine Claybrook underestimating her.

Even so, if Claybrook caught her eavesdropping, he would

kill her the way he had killed Philippa—by strangling her and throwing her body in the river.

He never should have asked her to spy.

If only Duke Wilhelm would return to Hagenheim, Colin would find some way to talk to him. If the duke was a good man, as everyone said he was, he would surely investigate his claims and soon discover that Claybrook was a heartless, devious, power-hungry devil.

At least Margaretha was safe for now.

Men's voices drew near from the other side of the stable. As he continued to brush the large war horse, five men rounded the corner of the building. The one talking was Claybrook.

The image of John's mangled body and vacant, staring eyes swept over him. If he had a sword, or any weapon, he could kill Claybrook now. But that would not be the right way to bring him to justice. No. When he confronted Claybrook, he wanted it to be in front of many witnesses, after everyone already knew of his treachery and foul, black heart.

Colin kept brushing, but he slowly moved so that the horse was between him and Claybrook.

Claybrook was leading a brown horse by the reins. He handed him off to one of the four men who were with him.

"... We have two days," Claybrook was saying, in English. "We'll talk more tomorrow morning. Tonight I must continue wooing Lady Margaretha."

Claybrook didn't immediately leave. He looked around the stable yard. Colin kept his head down, squatting to rub the horse's legs and hide his face behind the gelding's flank.

"*Du.*" The guard holding the reins was looking at him. *Du,* Colin had learned, was the German word for *you.*

Colin recognized the man. He was one of the men who had attacked him and his faithful friend, John. "*Du,*" he said again.

Then he said something in German that Colin was fairly certain meant, "Come here and take this horse."

Colin straightened slowly. He had no choice but to walk across the stable yard and take the horse from Claybrook's guard.

He slumped his shoulders and kept his head down slightly as he walked. All the while he was thinking of what he should do if Claybrook or the guard recognized him.

But by the time Colin reached out to take the horse's reins, the guard wasn't even looking at him, and Claybrook had turned and was walking away. Colin watched as the men strode out of sight.

What was Claybrook plotting? He'd said something about two days. Was he planning to do something evil in two days?

Colin had to find out.

Margaretha sat in the Great Hall sharing the evening meal. Lord Claybrook sat beside her, telling her about his travels. She tried to behave normally, but she couldn't stop thinking about what Colin had said about Lord Claybrook killing his sister's friend, a young woman who was pregnant with his child. While Claybrook told her about the weather, things they had seen and people they had met, she turned and looked into his eyes. Was it her imagination, or did he look cold and devious?

Colin had been willing to risk his life for her. He had retrieved her bracelet from the well, and she could do this one small favor for him. She could spy on Lord Claybrook to find out if he truly did have some dastardly plan.

Pretending to be interested in his stories was difficult, except when he mentioned her father, Duke Wilhelm. But her father had not been able to journey back to Hagenheim, as he was investigating reports of bandits attacking merchants along the north road to Hagenheim.

After describing his uncle's castle and holdings west of Hagenheim, Claybrook leaned closer to her. "You would look lovely presiding over the Great Hall at Keiterhafen Castle with me."

Margaretha raised her eyebrows, trying to look innocent and interested. "Has my father consented to our betrothal?"

A smile crept over his face. "No, but I think he will. If you wish it, that is."

She couldn't argue with that. If she wished to marry Lord Claybrook, her father would consent. And now she shivered at how close she had come to marrying this man. She had been thinking that she could stay near her family, and that Lord Claybrook had seemed like a kind person. If Colin had not warned her, would she have become his wife?

After the meal, Lord Claybrook addressed Margaretha's mother. "I am tired from my long journey. If you do not object, I would like to retire to my chamber."

"Of course. I pray you have a good night's rest." Her mother smiled at him.

"*Gute Nacht,*" Margaretha said.

"*Gute Nacht,*" he replied.

A few moments after he left, Margaretha told her mother, "I need to go to the garderobe."

"Yes, *Liebling.*"

Margaretha entered the corridor, lit by torches in the wall sconces, and instead of turning right to go to the garderobe that she and her sisters used, she took off her slippers so her footsteps wouldn't make any noise and turned left, hoping to follow Lord Claybrook.

Hearing someone inside the men's garderobe, she hid herself around the bend in the wall and waited. When the person came out, she moved forward and caught a glimpse of Lord Claybrook's back as he walked down the corridor toward the chamber where he slept.

Someone was coming toward her from behind. She was passing her younger brothers' chamber, and she opened the door and slipped inside, leaving the door open a crack. She held her breath, waiting for the person to pass by. When he did, she saw it was one of Lord Claybrook's guards.

He knocked on Claybrook's door, which quickly opened. Margaretha crept out of her brothers' chamber and tip-toed closer. She pressed her body against the wall in a particularly dark nook and listened.

"Tell Reginald I'll speak with him an hour after sunrise in the apple orchard."

"Yes, my lord."

Margaretha hurried back to her brothers' chamber and hid inside until the guard walked past. When his footsteps had faded, she darted out and hurried back to her own chamber on the other side of the castle.

Her heart was still pounding sickeningly against her ribs as she sank down on her bed. "I can hardly wait to tell Colin," she whispered, "that I spied and eavesdropped on Lord Claybrook." Her heart soared and she giggled.

Tomorrow morning she would be in the apple orchard, out of sight and perched high in the branches of her favorite climbing tree. She would find out what Claybrook could have to say to the captain of his guard in the apple orchard so early in the morning. Thus she would return Colin's favor — and perhaps discover the truth about whether Lord Claybrook was a murderer.

Margaretha was awake and dressed before dawn. The only other people who were up were some of the servants — the cooks and kitchen maids and some of the guards. Margaretha moved quietly out the door, trying not to wake her sisters, who slept in the same chamber.

The dew on the grass wet her hem as she walked, and the air felt heavy in the dim gray light of morning. The birds seemed to sing quietly, as though afraid to wake the babies in their nests.

Margaretha wrapped her arms around herself against the chill air. Once in the orchard at the bottom of the small hill, she picked the tree that she had often climbed as a child. Soon she was sitting in the crook of a branch, halfway up, hidden by new leaves. She leaned back against the trunk, holding on to another branch, and settled in to wait.

She had rearranged herself several times on her uncomfortable perch before she finally heard someone coming. Peeking through the leaves, she saw Lord Claybrook's guard captain entering the grove of apple trees and coming to stand almost directly below her. A few minutes later, Lord Claybrook himself came to stand under her tree. Little of them was visible besides the tops of their heads.

Her heart thumped hard against her chest as she tried not to move, not to even breathe too loudly. She must hear what they would say.

Lord Claybrook's low voice said, "We need to act fast, before Duke Wilhelm and his son get back."

Margaretha's breath caught in her throat. What did he mean?

"My uncle's guards should arrive late tonight."

"I thought they wouldn't be here for two more days."

"I received a missive from him last night. They will come tonight, but we will wait until dawn. Then we attack. We shall cut them off from the town by closing the castle gate. Fifty soldiers should be enough to control the townspeople, while we will use the rest to defeat Duke Wilhelm's guards. We'll confine the family to the solar in the center tower."

A sound like a rushing wind filled Margaretha's ears. She

fought back panic. But she had to keep listening and find out whatever she could.

"How many guards do you think are left at the castle?" Lord Claybrook asked the question calmly, as if it was a matter of little consequence.

"About thirty. Most of his guards and soldiers are with the duke."

"Excellent. We can subdue thirty guards in no time."

"What did you want to do with Lady Margaretha?"

"We will have the priest marry us immediately, in the castle chapel. Once we kill Duke Wilhelm and his oldest son, Valten, there will be no one to object. Lady Margaretha will think the guards were attacking on my uncle's orders, and that I am her savior. Even the king will sanction our marriage." Lord Claybrook laughed.

Margaretha clung to the tree branch she was leaning on, her stomach tumbling like a stone rolling downhill.

The two of them spoke of who would attack where, and of killing the guard at the castle gate first. Margaretha became so dizzy, she had to close her eyes and hang on tight. She heard little of what they said next, unable to defeat the panic that overwhelmed her senses. She focused on breathing in and out; she couldn't faint.

After what seemed like a long time, Lord Claybrook and the captain of his guard started walking back toward the castle. Soon she couldn't hear them at all.

"O God, what shall I do?" Her voice shook. She began to climb down out of the tree, which was difficult, the way her arms and legs were shaking.

I must tell someone. But who should she tell, since neither her father nor Valten were home? She didn't want to terrify her mother. She should tell her father's guards, but she had to be careful. If Lord Claybrook found out she knew his plan . . .

She stumbled over her own feet as she ran through the orchard and up the hill toward the castle. Would her father's guards even believe her story? Perhaps not. But there was one person she knew who would.

Chapter

11

Margaretha ran through the town gate, then the castle gate, and across the stable yard. The sun was already shining over the horizon, but the stable was still dark. She blinked, waiting for her eyes to adjust, and then she saw Colin dumping oats into a bucket. He looked over his shoulder, and when he saw her, gasping for breath after her long run, he dropped the bucket and hurried toward her.

"What happened?" He grabbed her arm.

"Is anyone around?"

"The other stable boys, but they don't speak English."

She whispered, "You were right," and paused to catch her breath. "I spied on Lord—on him. It is just as you said. We're all in danger." She glanced around. Two other stable boys were bringing oats to the horses. They glanced at her curiously but looked away when she made eye contact with them. She leaned even closer to Colin. What did it matter if it looked like she was being much too familiar with a servant?

"He is planning to attack the castle guards and take over the castle and the town."

"When?"

"At dawn tomorrow. He will make it look like he is saving us from his uncle. He will force me to marry him and kill my father and brother when they come home." Her voice caught on the last word and a dry sob escaped her throat.

"Don't worry." Colin clasped her hand. "We will stop him, now that we know his plan. Good work, my lady."

His words and the expression on his face helped her take control of herself. But would Colin know what to do? How could he keep Lord Claybrook from killing her father and brother? Or from forcing her to marry him?

"We have no weapons. We must tell my father's guards, the ones who are left. But how, without looking suspicious?"

"We will find a way. The element of surprise is on our side, as long as they don't know that we know."

Without warning, anger welled up inside her, stoking an internal fire that spread upward to the top of her head. "How dare he think he can take over my town and my family? How dare he talk of killing my father and brother? That hat-wearing, impudent, conceited ... I don't know enough English words to insult him properly." She had never struck anyone in her life, but she could slap his face if he were in front of her now. "If he thinks I will marry him—"

"Listen. We don't have much time. We need to form a plan."

"Oh, Colin, if it wasn't for you warning me, I never would have guessed what a devil Claybrook is. I thank God you came." She squeezed his hand, too overcome for a moment to say anything else.

"You can thank me later. Now we must get word to your family and somehow get you all to safety."

"Yes. Yes, we must."

The stable master entered the stable and yelled, "What is this? Boy, get back to work!"

"I am sorry, Dieter, but I have need of him at the castle. You must give him the day off from his duties in the stable and allow him to ... that is, I need his services. You must excuse him."

Dieter stared hard at her. Finally, still scowling, he said, "I shall speak with your father about this when he comes back."

"Of course. I do not blame you, and you are right to confirm with my father that what I am telling you is true. Farewell." She clung to Colin's hand as she ran out of the stable toward the castle.

"Wait." He pulled on her hand when they were halfway across the stable yard. "We mustn't excite suspicion. Slow down."

This was life and death. Her whole family was in danger, especially her father and Valten. Never had she faced such a dangerous situation. "I must be brave," she muttered to herself, but in German, because she didn't want Colin to know what she was saying. "I must be wise and shrewd and brave. And I've never been wise or shrewd or brave in my life." She took a deep breath and covered her eyes with her hand. "God, help me."

Claybrook was about to attack Hagenheim and kill Duke Wilhelm, and Colin's only ally was Lady Margaretha, a sincere but sheltered girl at best, a heedless flibbertigibbet at worst.

And now she was muttering to herself.

"One thing you must not do," he said, halting her and getting so close to her she was forced to look into his eyes. "You must not call me by my name."

"Colin?"

"You cannot call me that."

"Shall I call you Gawain again?"

"That is fine. Or perhaps what the stable master calls me. He calls me *Froschjunge*."

She stared back at him with wide eyes and her mouth hanging open. "Colin, that—"

"Don't call me that name."

"I don't think you want me to call you *Froschjunge* either. *Froschjunge* means 'frog boy.' "

Frog boy. He might as well be the court jester. He huffed and started walking toward the castle. "Just call me Gawain. And don't walk beside me. It shouldn't look like we are together. You should walk in front of me. I'm just a lowly stable boy, or so everyone is supposed to think."

Lady Margaretha must have been remembering what Claybrook had said, because she looked properly frightened. "Of course."

She hurried to pass in front of him and walked at a reasonable pace all the way to the castle, entering through the door to what turned out to be the Great Hall. He followed at a respectable distance behind her—respectable for a servant, which he was tired of pretending to be. He must have lost his mind, setting off after Claybrook to avenge Philippa's death. After all, it wasn't as if she was his sister or even his love, although he had once hoped to marry her. When she had begun to show interest in Claybrook, he had ceased to think her suitable as a wife. And when he'd found out Philippa was pregnant with Claybrook's child . . .

He'd come after Claybrook in a fit of rage, wanting to avenge Philippa's death, stirred by outrage at the injustice of it, so sure that he could overcome Claybrook himself. Since then he'd suffered deprivations, danger, had been nearly beaten and starved to death, and now had the humiliation of being thought of as a lowly stable boy, eating in the kitchen with the other servants and sleeping on a pile of straw.

His life was in as much danger as ever, and many more lives were at stake than just his own, including Lady Margaretha's entire family. And Lady Margaretha was in danger from a fate worse than death—marriage to Claybrook.

He followed Lady Margaretha up the stairs. No one was

around to question what he was doing in the castle. She led him up to the solar where a woman he assumed was Lady Rose sat stitching something. Also in the round tower room was a beautiful pregnant woman who looked to be near her time, as well as a girl a little younger than Margaretha who was playing with another girl of about six years.

If the two younger girls were Margaretha's sisters, and the pretty pregnant woman was the Earl of Hamlin's wife, along with Lady Rose, they were all about to receive a great shock. And he had to think of a plan to save them. He would rather forfeit his own life than allow them all to die, as he had allowed Philippa and John to die.

⁓

Margaretha approached her mother. "I have something I must tell you, but promise me you will not become too alarmed."

"Of course, darling. But first ..." Mother was the picture of calm as she laid her embroidery across her lap and smiled up at Margaretha. "Lord Claybrook asked if you would go riding with him this morning. He said he would wait for you in the Great Hall. I told him you would be awake soon." Her face clouded. "What is amiss? You look pale."

"Mother." Lady Margaretha took her hand and knelt before her. "I have discovered something about Lord Claybrook."

She was speaking quietly, and Gisela moved closer to listen. How she hated to frighten them all, especially when Gisela was so near her time. Even Kirstyn and Adela turned their attention to Margaretha as she went on. "He is not the man he pretends to be."

"He's not Lord Claybrook?"

"He is Lord Claybrook, but he isn't the harmless person he would want us to believe him to be. He intends to use his men to attack Hagenheim."

Her mother drew back slightly while her sisters gasped. "How do you know this?"

"I overheard him telling the captain of his guard. They were making plans to attack while Father is away. He will pretend his uncle, the Earl of Keiterhafen, is attacking us, but it was his plan all the time. And I never would have known if not for this man." She turned and looked at Colin. "He is from England, from the same region as Lord Claybrook, and he knows of Claybrook's treachery there, where he actually murdered a young lady. He came here to warn us. He warned me, but I didn't believe him at first."

Mother's eyes were round and her face had turned pale. "Are you sure?"

"Mother, I heard Lord Claybrook with my own ears. He is plotting to take over Hagenheim. Believe me when I say that we are not safe. Our family must flee, and we must send word to Father and Valten about the danger. It is Lord Claybrook's plan to kill them both."

Gisela stood. Adela began to cry, and Kirstyn rasped, "That can't be true. What kind of person would do such a thing?"

Colin stepped forward and said in English, "We need a plan, and we must not let Claybrook know we are suspicious of him."

"What is he saying?" Her mother rose from her seat, her embroidery falling to the floor.

"He doesn't speak much German, Mother. He says we need a plan and we must not let Claybrook know we know his plans."

Colin kept speaking and Margaretha translated his words to her mother, Gisela, and her sisters. "We must get the family out of the castle, but quietly, so Lord Claybrook does not become suspicious. We must alert the guards who are still here at the castle and in Hagenheim, and we must send a message to Father and Valten alerting them of the danger."

"We can go to the house beside the river," Gisela said with a grim set to her mouth, "where Valten and I stayed for a few days after our wedding. It's in the forest. I doubt Lord Claybrook or his uncle even know it exists."

"Yes, that is a good idea," Mother agreed.

Margaretha translated their conversation to Colin, who said, "But they must not all leave the castle at once. It will attract too much attention."

Margaretha translated his words to Mother and Gisela.

"I am assuming it is far enough away that they will need horses?" Colin asked.

"Yes."

Looking grim but determined, Colin went on. "They should go in two groups, an hour apart. If they are asked where they are going, one group will say they are going on a picnic by the stream. The other group will say they are going for a ride, or to visit ... someone, and will return in a few hours. Make up a likely story. By nightfall Claybrook will probably realize they have escaped him, but by then it will be too late."

Mother and Gisela agreed, while Kirstyn tried to comfort and reassure Adela.

"In the meantime," Colin went on, "you and I will alert your father's guards to what Claybrook is planning, and find one of them to take a message to your father. But we must be careful." Colin pinned her with his blue eyes. "Some of the duke's guards may not be loyal to your father anymore. Claybrook may have bribed them or otherwise won them over to his side."

Margaretha nodded. She was surprised she felt no fear, only excited energy surging through her. It was good to have a plan of action, and Colin seemed to know what to do.

When they were ready, Margaretha embraced first Gisela, then Kirstyn and Adela, kissing their cheeks. Her mother hugged her, then looked into her eyes. "I will be praying for you. You will not be afraid, but you will do whatever you have to do to stay safe." Her look was fierce, even with tears in her eyes.

"I love you, Mother. God will keep us safe."

She and Colin hurried away down the stairs.

Chapter

12

As they reached the bottom of the stairs, Lord Claybrook entered the Great Hall only a few feet in front of them. She shrank back, instinctively throwing her arm back as though to hide Colin, who flattened himself against the stone wall. Lord Claybrook walked confidently through the doorway, never glancing in their direction.

Margaretha sat down on the steps, placing her hand over her heart. It vibrated against her hand, so hard was it pounding. "He nearly saw us."

"If he sees you," Colin whispered, "do not act as if anything is amiss. But if he sees me, our plan is ruined." He grabbed her upper arms, forcing her to look at him. "You must help me find a few loyal guards, men you are certain would never betray your family. Then you will need to go to Claybrook in the Great Hall. Since he asked your mother to tell you to meet him there, he will become suspicious if you don't show up."

Margaretha's heart fluttered. He seemed so wise and capable, his hands warm and reassuring as they gripped her arms. Thanks be to God that he was here, helping her.

"Will you come with me?" she whispered.

"Yes, but you must lead the way."

He let go and she hurried to leave the castle by a back door. Colin followed just behind her to the gate.

When they arrived at the gate house, a guard was there, but Margaretha did not know him. With him was one of Lord Claybrook's guards, wearing the blue and gold of Lord Claybrook's uncle. Margaretha smiled at them, hoping she didn't look suspicious. A glance behind her showed Colin hanging his head, no doubt trying to hide his face.

Margaretha turned back toward the castle, and when she did, she saw more of Claybrook's guards near the stable. Were they trying to keep track of who was coming and going?

She clasped her hands and bit her lip as she walked, keeping to the back side of the castle so as not to be visible to Claybrook from the windows of the Great Hall. *God, have you truly entrusted me, a girl who has never faced danger of any kind, to help save Hagenheim? To place such a responsibility on me, when I never imagined I would need to do anything like this . . .*

"Do you know where you're going?" Colin whispered behind her.

Margaretha kept walking as she turned her head to answer. "Of course. I know every foot of these — oh." She ran into something . . . or someone.

"Careful, Lady Margaretha. You should look where you're going."

She took hold of his massive arm. "Bezilo." He was as loyal as any of her father's guards. She would wager her life on it. "We must speak with you, Bezilo, but we need to go where no one will hear us. Please come with me." They were near the flower garden, which was behind the castle, sheltered partially by trees. She led the two men through the short iron gate and motioned them to follow her to the shade of a low-hanging mulberry tree.

Once they were under the relative seclusion of the thick leaves and branches, she told Bezilo in a hushed voice, "We are in danger. Lord Claybrook is trying to take over Hagenheim."

Bezilo's eyes went wide. "I knew it. I never trusted that fool-ish looking foreigner."

"Well, my friend—for indeed, I consider you my friend and one of my father's most trusted guards—this man here is also a foreigner, from England, and if not for him, we would not have known of Lord Claybrook's treachery."

Bezilo turned to Colin and nodded.

"We don't have much time," Margaretha went on without translating for Colin. "I need you to get a message to my father as soon as possible. We need to let him know that Claybrook is plotting with his uncle to take over Hagenheim and kill my father and Valten. But I'm not sure where Father is."

"Duke Wilhelm and Lord Hamlin were checking out some reports of brigands to the north. I shall find them, don't worry."

"What did he say?" Colin asked, tapping her arm. "Translate for me."

"Just a minute," Margaretha told Colin, barely glancing away from the guard. "How will you leave without Claybrook's men seeing you? His guards are milling about the stable."

"I can leave the castle gate on foot and get a horse from town."

"They're watching the castle gate as well."

"I'll say I'm going to see my sister who sells vegetables in the *Marktplatz*."

"What are you saying?" Colin demanded.

Margaretha explained briefly to Colin what Bezilo planned to do.

"Good." Colin nodded approvingly at Bezilo, as if with the authority of Duke Wilhelm himself. "But before he goes, he should alert the other guards that there will be a fight in the morning at dawn, or probably sooner. Or perhaps he should alert one guard and let him tell the others, but only the ones they are certain are loyal."

Margaretha relayed his message to the burly guard.

Bezilo grunted. "Very well, I shall. But do you have a plan, Lady Margaretha, for you and your family to escape?"

"Yes. We shall say we are going to visit someone, or that we are going on a picnic. You must tell Father and Valten that we are at the manse in the forest."

"I will. Now I am off to warn the other guards. You two stay here a moment so that we are not seen together."

Margaretha translated to Colin as Bezilo walked away. Colin looked sharply at her, his hands clenched into fists. He had changed so much since the first time she saw him, lying almost lifeless on Frau Lena's narrow bed, covered in dust and grime and dried blood. And then later, wearing those green-speckled clothes.

Now, even with the brown woolen tunic and hose of a stable boy, when she looked into his intense blue eyes, he made her breath catch in her throat. His hair was clean, thick and wavy, a dark-brown-almost-black which set off his bright blue eyes. His expression was less wild but every bit as intense as when he had demanded to speak to Duke Wilhelm that first day. His cheeks were no longer hollow and his shoulders brawnier after eating the hearty fare the cooks fed the servants.

It must have been a powerful spirit that had brought this foreigner, this peculiar stranger, to their town. He had come and everything had changed. She'd always felt so safe, and if not for Colin, she never would have suspected Lord Claybrook of being a murderer and a violent usurper.

"Margaretha, we must hurry. Claybrook will be expecting you."

No one besides her immediate family members called her by her given name with such familiarity, but she was not in any mood to scold him for it.

She followed him out of the low garden gate and back toward the castle.

Colin dropped back to follow behind her as they walked. "I will hide in the library, which I saw across from the Great Hall," he said quietly.

"Very well." Ahead of her was Hagenheim Castle, a place more dear to her than any other. Its soaring towers never failed to fill her chest with contentment. To her left was the town of Hagenheim, where lived the families of the maids and other servants she had grown to love. There was Irmele the cook, who made her favorite cake for her birthdays. Irmele's sister, whom she loved and talked about so often, lived near the Marktplatz with her many children and her husband, a butcher. Margaretha's maid, Britta, had several brothers and sisters who lived in two large family homes on the street behind the Rathous, the older ones married. Margaretha had visited them once with her, and they had treated her like a queen. She had asked to hold Britta's infant niece, and the baby had spit up on her, making Margaretha laugh, but horrifying everyone else. They had scrambled to clean her shoulder with cloths, apologizing profusely until Margaretha had made them laugh at themselves over all the fuss.

Hagenheim was a place where everyone knew which days to come to market and exactly where to find the town's butchers, tanners, bakers, and blacksmiths. No one ever left, very little ever changed. Everyone smiled and spoke to each other, and everyone knew each other and knew what to expect from another day in Hagenheim.

Would that now change? Would the townspeople's safety be shattered because of Lord Claybrook? She simply couldn't imagine her father allowing that to happen. Even if he wasn't here, wouldn't he come and save them before that peacock Claybrook could lift his hand against them?

No, instead of counting on her father to save them, she must trust her own wits, which she'd never placed much value on before, as well as this young foreigner, to save her family, her town, and everything she had ever known. As strange and frightening as it was, it was equally exciting to think that she and Colin were pitting themselves against a dangerous foe and outwitting him until her father could come. Her father would be so proud of her—if she could manage to get her family out before Claybrook captured them.

As she rounded the side of the castle, bringing the gatehouse into full view, her eyes were drawn to the girl on horseback just entering the castle yard.

Her heart sank to her toes. "Not Anne."

"What is it?" Colin hissed behind her.

"Only my cousin, coming for an ill-timed visit."

Anne had already seen her, so Margaretha waved and pasted on a smile, starting forward to meet her. "I shall take Anne with me to see Lord Claybrook, which may provide a helpful distraction."

But when Margaretha glanced behind her, Colin was gone, probably to the library to wait for her.

Margaretha met Anne as a stable boy trotted forward to take Anne's horse.

"You look beautiful." Margaretha clasped her cousin's hand, bracing herself for Anne's reply.

"Oh, Margaretha, you always say that and I never believe you are sincere." Anne half frowned in her sardonic way. "But the blue color of this dress does set off my complexion perfectly. And don't you look like the sweet little girl you are." She smirked, looking down her nose at Margaretha. One might think by her tone and her words that Anne was at least ten years older, instead of only ten months.

"Come into the Great Hall, Anne. I have someone I want you to meet."

"Why? Who is it?"

"An English earl, Lord Claybrook."

"An earl? Is he married?"

"No, as a matter of fact, he's not."

"One of your suitors, Margaretha? Surely you don't want to introduce me to him. Perhaps he will prefer me over you." Anne smirked.

"If he does, I don't mind." Margaretha smiled pleasantly.

"Is something wrong with him? He must be vile and ill-favored."

"Some say he is handsome, but you may see for yourself." Margaretha changed the subject of conversation, asking Anne about her father and mother, Margaretha's uncle and aunt, Lord Rupert and Lady Anne. Some might have thought it strange they gave their daughter the same name as her mother, but she looked so much like her, it seemed appropriate.

"Father and Mother are well, as usual. I decided to come and visit you, Margaretha, since dear Jaspar is away. I am never so discontent as when Jaspar is away. I miss him so much."

Anne sighed dramatically as she spoke of her brother. Margaretha had never understood the way Anne fawned over her younger brother, Jaspar. He was a year younger than Margaretha, and he had ever been as insufferable as most young boys, more so even than her own brothers. He was so accustomed to getting his own way, he expected everyone to give him whatever he wanted.

"I think you shall be … too distracted to be discontent here with us, Anne." Margaretha smiled. But perhaps she was being wicked by not telling Anne to flee for her life. Knowing Anne, she would make such a loud fuss that Lord Claybrook would hear of it and realize Margaretha knew what he was planning.

No, she couldn't risk revealing the truth to Anne.

Anne followed her into the castle, asking Margaretha, "Do you think my hair looks well? Perhaps your maid could pin it up a bit higher."

Margaretha turned her attention to her cousin's silky, light brown locks as they walked. "Anne, your hair is beautiful, as always." Not a hair was out of place, even though she had ridden five miles from her parents' country house.

"He is an earl, after all. If you don't want him, and if he is sufficiently wealthy, I might take him off your hands." Anne smiled when she didn't think Margaretha was looking.

Margaretha had no illusions that her cousin would respect the fact that Lord Claybrook was her suitor. But she hardly cared, and at the moment she didn't have time to dwell on her cousin's lack of loyalty.

As they drew closer and closer to where Lord Claybrook would be waiting, Margaretha had to concentrate on not appearing nervous. She had to remember how she had treated Lord Claybrook before and behave exactly the same way. She could not allow herself to excite his suspicion or their plans would not work.

Taking a steadying breath, hardly listening to Anne's complaints about how dirty the roads were and how her gelding had soiled his legs and her dress, Margaretha entered the Great Hall with her cousin beside her.

Lord Claybrook stood to welcome them.

Margaretha's blood went cold at the sight of him, but she forced herself to smile even as part of her wanted to demand that he explain how he could pretend goodness while his heart was as black as the devil himself. She must focus on the part she was playing.

"Lord Claybrook, may I introduce my cousin, Lady Anne? She is the daughter of Lord Rupert Gerstenberg. Anne, this is Rowland Fortescue, Earl of Claybrook."

"It is my pleasure to meet such a lovely young lady, one who is also Lady Margaretha's relation." Lord Claybrook smiled as he bowed over Anne's hand and kissed it.

Anne's eyes were wide, and there was a definite hint of interest in her upraised, arched brows. She began talking with Lord

Claybrook in her most superficially charming way, asking him about himself and complimenting him with smiles of her own. But Margaretha barely heard what they were saying. Her mind was flitting to Colin, probably hiding in the library, to Bezilo warning the guards of the impending attack by Claybrook's men, and to her father, wherever he was. When would he come to save them?

"Lady Margaretha, you look thoughtful." Claybrook's thin lips curled in a slow smile.

"Oh, I was only thinking about the ride my mother said you wanted to take me on. But since my cousin Anne is here, let us stay and chat, or perhaps play a game of chess."

He gave her a sharp look out of the corner of his eye. Or was she only imagining it?

"I think it will be just as well to stay here and take a ride another time." He was studying her.

She smiled. "Thank you, Lord Claybrook. I don't particularly feel up to an outing today."

He was wearing another elaborate hat today, but the liripipe wound around the hat and then was secured to his shoulder, to make it more suitable for riding, she supposed.

A movement in the corner of the room caught her attention. One of Claybrook's guards was watching them, standing near the door to the corridor. Had Lord Claybrook always had a guard stationed nearby?

"Shall we set up the chessboard?" Margaretha smiled cheerfully.

While Anne spoke with Lord Claybrook, Margaretha tried not to look nervous, but her eyes seemed to dart without her consent to the doorway, and her hands shook slightly as she clumsily set up the chess pieces. At the same time, she found it extremely difficult to look Lord Claybrook in the eye without shuddering. She could only hope he didn't notice.

Anne played the first game with Lord Claybrook. She took a lot of time in selecting her moves, but she still lost to Lord Claybrook fairly quickly. She complimented him in his great wisdom and skill. As they were setting up the game again for Margaretha to play with Lord Claybrook, the guard by the door seemed to be watching someone in the corridor, then slipped out. A few minutes later, a loud scuffle, along with shouts of "Halt!" and "I have you!" and "Cease or you die!" came from the vicinity of the library and corridor.

Margaretha tried not to show understanding. Instead she tried to appear shocked and confused. Meanwhile, Lord Claybrook's face went hard as he stood and strode to the door. He stopped abruptly and turned back to stare at Margaretha.

She tried to imitate Anne's blank but curious expression. "Who is that? What is happening?" Anne asked innocently.

Margaretha shook her head. "I don't know." Her voice sounded breathless.

Another of Lord Claybrook's guards ran past the open doorway. There was scuffling. Claybrook disappeared through the door. A few moments went by and he reappeared, his face red.

Behind him, Colin stumbled forward as a guard shoved him. He met Margaretha's eye for the briefest moment, then looked down at the floor. The guard held his hands behind his back.

Lord Claybrook ground out between clenched teeth, "Do you know this man?"

Margaretha's breath seemed to leave her entirely. She concentrated on breathing and shrugged. "A stable boy?"

"What was he doing in the library, meeting with one of your father's guards?"

"I do not know, and I am astonished at your using that tone of voice with me. What is the meaning of this? You only need to send for the stable master and he will come directly and take this man back to his duties and punish him, if suitable."

"I have a better idea." Lord Claybrook turned to Colin. "Why don't we ask him?"

Claybrook slammed his fist across Colin's face. Margaretha cried out, then pressed her hand over her mouth to silence herself.

Bright red blood oozed from Colin's lip as he glared at Claybrook.

"You'll be sorry," Colin growled in English.

Claybrook laughed, then clicked his tongue against his teeth. "Not before you are sorry." He also spoke in English as he stepped forward menacingly. His guard still held Colin's hands behind his back as Claybrook stood nose to nose with Colin. "What does Lady Margaretha know? If you told her anything you shouldn't have, then I may have to kill her."

Margaretha pretended not to understand their English, even as she trembled at Claybrook's words.

Colin tried to focus his thoughts in spite of his blurred vision and ringing ears. "The lady knows nothing. I'm just a raving lunatic to everyone in Hagenheim. No one here speaks English." He could only hope Lady Margaretha would pretend not to understand them.

"If everyone believes you a lunatic, why did the duke's guard come into the library to speak to you?"

"I don't know what he was doing in the library. He couldn't have been coming to speak to me. I don't speak German." Colin licked his lip and tasted blood.

"I thought I killed you already. Why didn't you die?" Claybrook stared at him. Then he motioned to his two guards. "Take him into the woods and kill him. And make sure he's dead this time. I don't want to have to deal with him again."

The guard began dragging him, wrenching his shoulders.

"Wait!" Lady Margaretha's voice was shrill. "What will you do to him?"

Claybrook turned his attention on Margaretha.

Without divine intervention, Colin would soon die, and if Margaretha wasn't careful, Claybrook would kill her too.

Claybrook smiled like the serpent he was. "Do not worry, Lady Margaretha. My guards will take him back to his stable master."

Lady Margaretha looked panic-stricken. Would she give away the fact that she did know who he was and that she did speak English? That she knew Claybrook was lying and was sending Colin to be killed?

"If he was in the library, then—then he should be punished. No stable boy should be lurking in the library. Obviously he was up to something wicked. You—you must throw him in the dungeon. Yes, right away. Throw him in the dungeon until my father returns home. He will be able to decide a proper punishment for him."

Claybrook narrowed his eyes. "Perhaps you are right."

"Of course I am right." Lady Margaretha stood tall. "Take him to the dungeon. But by all that's holy, stop dragging him. I'm sure he can walk."

The guards obeyed her and allowed him to walk out between them. But he could tell by the suspicion on Claybrook's face that Lady Margaretha, as well as her plan to get her family to safety, was in danger.

God, no, not Margaretha. Please don't let her get killed.

Chapter
13

Margaretha lifted her chin and looked down her nose at Claybrook, mimicking Anne's imperious expression. She followed the guards and Colin out into the corridor. *God, please have them take him to the dungeon and not into the woods to kill him.* She held her breath, watching to see which way they went. Just as they disappeared through the doorway that led down to the bleak, cold dungeon, another of Claybrook's guards came from the other direction. When Claybrook saw him, he excused himself and stood in the corridor, then stared at Margaretha, as if waiting for her to go back inside the Great Hall to join Anne.

Margaretha stopped in the doorway and tried to listen to what his guard was saying, but he spoke in such hushed tones that she didn't catch a word.

Someone grabbed Margaretha's arm. She jerked away.

It was only Anne. Her cousin didn't seem to notice her reaction, but whispered, "Lord Claybrook is quite handsome. I think he fancies me. Did you see the way he smiled at me?"

"Anne..." What could Margaretha say? She couldn't tell her the truth about Claybrook, not here with Claybrook so close. However, as annoyingly self-centered as her cousin was, she was still her cousin and Margaretha wouldn't want to see her come to harm. So she warned, "He isn't everything he seems, Anne. Be careful of this one."

"I should be careful, eh?" Anne's sly half smile set Margaretha's teeth on edge. "I think you only want him for yourself."

She didn't have time for this. "Do as you please. I hardly care." She had to allay Lord Claybrook's suspicions and still save poor Colin from Claybrook's men and the dungeon. One false move, one wrong word, and Claybrook would kill Colin, and maybe even Margaretha and her family.

Lord Claybrook walked over to her, a challenge in his up-raised brow. "You haven't forgotten our chess game, have you, Lady Margaretha?" But his eyes were flinty, and she was certain he had more on his mind than a chess game.

"Of course I haven't forgotten. Shall we play?"

They sat facing each other, the game board between them, with Anne hovering over Margaretha's shoulder first, then Claybrook's. Margaretha had always been a good player, but in her distraction she made a blunder, allowing Claybrook to capture her knight.

"You aren't letting me win, are you?" Claybrook waggled his eyebrows at her.

It rankled that he would accuse her of doing what Anne had done earlier. "Of course not. You simply must be the better player." Better to let him think she was unskilled rather than that she was purposely losing.

The footsteps of several people sounded from the corridor, drawing closer. Margaretha heard her mother say, "This is outrageous. You may tell Lord Claybrook that I am angry and disappointed ..."

Oh no! Mother and the others! They should have been half-way to the manse in the forest by now.

Claybrook's foxlike eyes were trained on her. She had to

choose her words carefully. "What is my mother saying? She sounds vexed."

"Does she?" Claybrook's artificially innocent tone grated on Margaretha like a poke in the ribs.

With as much indifference as she could muster, Margaretha said, "I'm sure there is nothing amiss. She is probably scolding my little brothers about something." She fixed her eyes on her chess pieces, but her mind was racing. Lord Claybrook knew what her mother was vexed about. His guard was probably reporting only moments earlier that they stopped her mother and family members from their outing and brought them back to the castle to hold them hostage.

She moved her king forward to show she was not worried as her mother's voice grew more distant and indistinct. But her face was burning and her stomach sinking. How would any of them escape now?

"Are you sure you want to do that?" Claybrook studied her.

"Of course." How could she possibly care about the chess game?

Claybrook immediately captured her king with his knight.

"Chess is a silly game. I've never been very good." Margaretha tried to smile but failed. Her lips felt frozen, her insides trembling.

"You know who that stable boy is, don't you?" Claybrook's voice was raspy and cold, sending a chill down her back. "He came here and warned you about me, didn't he?"

"I don't know what you are talking of."

Lord Claybrook propped his elbows on the table, bringing his long, slender fingers together in a point in front of his lips. "You speak English fairly well. You told me so the first day I met you. I wonder, did you know where your mother and sisters were going this morning?"

"They were going on a picnic. Why do you care?" She tried her best imperious look again, but her lips trembled.

"That young Englishman my men took to the dungeon shall be your undoing, Lady Margaretha. Now I think you had best tell me the truth."

"The truth about what?" Her heart beat haltingly inside her chest. She couldn't pretend much longer. He already knew she knew. Still, if there was a chance that he might believe her ignorant of his plans ...

"Yield yourself to my will, for I will have my way. The strongest always prevails, and I am the strongest." He leaned toward her.

"What are you talking of? That stable boy? What does he have to do with you preventing my mother from going on a picnic?"

"Spare me the feigned innocence. If you cooperate with me, I shall still marry you, and I might even spare that English boy, who thought he could stop me and has once again failed. But if you do not cooperate with me ..." He looked down at his hand, as though examining his nails. He started clicking his tongue against his teeth and slowly shaking his head. "Who is to say what might happen to the English lad and his noble ideas of justice, not to mention Lady Rose and your sisters?"

"Are you evil enough to threaten my mother and sisters? How dare you."

Anne's eyes were round, her mouth hanging open in a look of disbelief. But Margaretha had to keep her mind focused.

"I wouldn't marry you, not ever. You must be mad if you think you can intimidate me that much. And if you harm my family members, I will see you delivered to the king's royal judges and hanged."

Lord Claybrook's face twisted into an ugly sneer. She couldn't believe she had ever thought him handsome. "You will be begging me to marry you before I'm finished with this family and this town." His voice was like the hiss of an adder.

What should she do? What sort of tactic could she employ? She had to escape, to go get help. She feared Claybrook had stopped Bezilo from going to warn her father—might even have killed him. She had no doubt he was capable of killing Colin or a guard, but would he dare harm her mother—a duchess—and her other family members? He had already promised to kill the Duke of Hagenheim and his heir.

Margaretha's words and actions now might mean life or death to many people. She had to think.

She would intentionally refrain from mentioning Colin in the hopes that she could pretend she didn't care about him and perhaps make Claybrook forget about him, at least temporarily. There was the tunnel that led underneath the town wall. It was her best chance of escape, or going to get help, if she could reach it. And if Claybrook's uncle was bringing his guards, she would need to get help from someone who could send an army to take Hagenheim back from the villainous Claybrook and his evil uncle.

Her mother's father, the Duke of Marienberg, would be able to send soldiers, and along with her father's knights who had accompanied him, when they returned, there would be enough men to defeat Claybrook.

At least, she hoped it was so.

She only had to escape and make her way to Marienberg.

"I would never beg to marry you. And if you hurt the people I love, you shall be forced to kill me, because I will never consent to be your wife."

He stared at her a long time, then caught her chin between his thumb and forefinger, grasping her arm with his other hand. "That would be a pity."

She wrenched her face out of his grasp.

He barked to his guard, "Don't let these two out of your sight," pointing to Margaretha and Anne. And Claybrook stomped out of the Great Hall, his footfalls echoing off the flag-stone floor.

"Margaretha!" Anne gasped. "What is this trouble you've got me into!"

"I'm sorry you came when you did, Anne. Not the best time for a visit, but it's hardly my fault Lord Claybrook is trying to kill my father and take over Hagenheim."

"What?" Anne's incredulous look was not becoming. Her eyes bulged and her cheeks and lips drained of all color. She went so pale, a blue vein was visible above the bridge of her nose. She then made a sound like she was choking. After visibly swallow-ing and blinking, she said, "He wouldn't kill me, would he? After all, I'm only a cousin ... your father's niece." The last word came out as a squeak.

Margaretha didn't answer. She was staring at the guard Claybrook had ordered to watch them. He was staring back at her with cold, heartless eyes. Another guard stood in the open doorway. One guard might have been possible to trick, but two?

"I'm afraid I have to go to the garderobe." Margaretha stepped right up to the nearest guard. "It's not far and I will be back soon—"

Anne scurried across the floor and bumped into Margaretha's side. "You're not going without me." She grasped Margaretha's arm with both hands.

"You're not going anywhere," the guard said in a heavy English accent. Then, abandoning his German, he said in English, "You are fortunate Lord Claybrook doesn't tie you up and gag you."

Margaretha opened her mouth to reply, then decided she wouldn't give him the satisfaction of speaking to him in his na-tive language. She retorted in German, "How disrespectful, dar-ing to speak a foreign tongue in my presence. I will have you know, I am a duke's daughter, and I am not accustomed to this sort of treatment. Your Lord Claybrook will be sorry he didn't stay in England when my father, Duke Wilhelm, is finished with him."

The guard said nothing, only stared back.

Ranting at Claybrook's guards was not likely to bring about any positive effect. She had to think of a clever plan, some way of escape.

"What will you do to get me out of here, Margaretha?" Anne's breath in her ear made her draw away, but not far, as Anne still clutched Margaretha's arm. "Since he's *your* suitor, I'm holding you responsible."

"What happened to you thinking he likes you?"

"I am not amused, Margaretha. I want to go home."

If only Anne *could* go home.

"You can't keep us in this room all day," Margaretha said to the guard, "without allowing us to go to the garderobe. I drank a lot of water this morning and nature waits for no man—or woman."

"When Lord Claybrook returns, you may ask him."

Margaretha crossed her arms, but with Anne hanging on to her, it was a little difficult. "If he doesn't return soon, you'll have to take us with you to look for him."

He raised his eyebrows just enough to let her know that he was not agreeing to anything.

"I am not accustomed to being treated in such a manner." She was afraid she didn't sound very intimidating, but she had to try. "And where are my brothers and Gisela?"

He did not answer her.

"If you or any of Claybrook's other henchmen dare to hurt them, Duke Wilhelm will make you all regret you were born, and regret you left your little island across the sea."

She walked over to the windows facing the courtyard with Anne still hanging on to her arm. The blacksmith in his courtyard smithy was pounding something with his hammer. A kitchen maid was fetching water from the courtyard well. People were going about their daily tasks, unaware that everything was about to change—that a mad Lord Claybrook, with the help of his uncle, was about to take over the castle and the town and subject everyone to his will.

God, please let there be no fighting and no one killed. But it was a strange request. After all, when her father came back, of course there would be fighting. The thought of any of the Hagenheim people being killed, whether they be guards, knights, or innocent townspeople, made her knees weak.

And the first person to die in this conflict would be Colin, if Margaretha couldn't help him escape.

Chapter
14

The guard shoved Colin roughly toward some steps that he could only assume led down to the dungeon. The guard held his hands behind his back. He stumbled and slipped and nearly fell more than once, only to be yanked up by the guard.

A voice called in German from below, down the dark stairs in front of them.

A man came into view, obviously the gaoler, as a ring of keys hung from the leather strap around his wrist. He stood in a pool of light below a torch that was affixed to the wall at the bottom of the stairs. He stared back at them from beneath wiry white eyebrows, his stooped shoulders causing him to crane his neck.

The guard who was crushing Colin's wrists said something in a gruff voice.

The gaoler's keys rattled. He mentioned Duke Wilhelm amid all the German words. His eyes narrowed suspiciously, as though he didn't trust what the guards were saying to him. No doubt he wasn't used to taking orders from foreign guards.

While Claybrook's guard and the gaoler were talking, Colin looked around, hoping for a chance to escape. He didn't see any other prisoners, and a few steps farther down, arm and leg irons were attached to the wall. The floor was bare and a little damp, but there were no loose keys lying around or doorways of escape that he could see.

The gaoler and the guard appeared to be arguing, but the only thing he could make out was "Duke Wilhelm."

How could he take advantage of this situation? He couldn't speak their language and the gaoler couldn't speak his.

The priest! Hadn't he translated for him with Frau Lena? Perhaps he could beg for his assistance again and then gain his help in escaping. He suddenly remembered the German word for "priest."

"Priester!"

The gaoler barely glanced in Colin's direction. He would have to get his attention some other way.

"Help me!" he cried in English. "I do not belong in this dungeon. Lord Claybrook is trying to—"

Claybrook's guard cuffed his ear, making his head ring and stars dance before his eyes. But at least his use of English, a foreign language to the gaoler, had caught his attention and, Colin hoped, awakened his suspicions even more.

The gaoler shook his head, then mumbled grumpily and grabbed Colin's arm. To Colin's great disappointment, he helped the guards fasten an iron band around each of Colin's wrists.

"Priester! Please, I need to speak to the priester!"

He found himself chained to the wall in the dark, smoky dungeon. The gaoler looked at him curiously but walked away behind Claybrook's guards, taking the torch and the only source of light with him. Colin was left in darkness.

Colin pulled hard on his chains, but they held fast. *What now?* He sank to the floor, his arm chains just long enough to allow him to sit on the cold stone.

To his surprise, the bob of the flickering torch came into view as the gaoler walked silently back down the steps and came to stand and stare at him.

Colin jumped to his feet amid the clanging of his chains. "*Hilf mir.*" *Help me* was one of the phrases he had learned from the priest. "Priester speaks English. English. You understand?" Would the grizzled old gaoler comprehend and help him?

He looked sharp. "*Sie ein Engländer?*"

"*Ja! Engländer.* Can you go get the priest? Priester? For the sake of Hagenheim and all that's holy!" If only he knew a few more words!

The gaoler unknit his bushy white eyebrows and grunted. "*Ja.*" He turned and walked away.

There was nothing for Colin to do but wait—and pray the gaoler intended to bring the priest back with him.

Margaretha wandered about the room, peeking at the guard every so often out of the corner of her eye. Gradually, she made her way to the silver candlesticks stored on a small shelf near the windows facing the courtyard. With her back to the guard, and Anne still clinging to her arm, she fingered a small but heavy candlestick just before lifting it and stuffing it into her voluminous sleeve, where she had a hidden pocket.

Anne's eyes widened. She let go of Margaretha's arm. In a burst of familial loyalty and generosity, Margaretha whispered, "If you wish to get out of here, you'd better stay close to me."

Her eyes still enormous and round, Anne took hold of Margaretha's arm again—her left arm, thankfully, since she needed her right hand free.

Margaretha wandered back toward the guard, who only occasionally turned his eyes on Margaretha and Anne. He even yawned just before he perceived her coming toward him.

"You look like an understanding person," she began. "As you can see, my cousin and I are not dangerous. If you could only allow us a few minutes in the garderobe, we would be so grateful." She smiled up at him.

"I am not to allow you out of my sight." His eyes and voice were hard. He was obviously unmoved by her smile.

She switched tactics. "If you do not allow us a few minutes in the garderobe, I'm afraid you will have a mess on your hands that you will not enjoy explaining to the other soldiers in your ranks, nor the servants who will be forced to clean it up." Margaretha placed her hand on her hip, raised her brows, and frowned up at him.

Anne's face turned slightly green and she put her hand over her mouth. Was she really about to heave her stomach's contents onto the floor? Whether she was or only looked like she might, it was the perfect complement to Margaretha's insinuations.

"Come, then," the guard ordered, his voice louder than necessary as he glared down at them.

Margaretha scurried through the door, Anne sticking close to her side, with a second guard following behind. Margaretha headed straight for the garderobe and glanced behind her as she and Anne dashed into the dim, small space designed to allow the ladies of the castle to relieve themselves.

Margaretha whispered to Anne, "You aren't sick, are you?"

"Only terrified." Anne looked at Margaretha as if she was a lunatic. "What are you planning to do? These guards mean to kill us. It's just like what happened at Witten Schloss to my mother's cousins. Their castle was taken over by the Earl of Hildesbaden and they were murdered, run through before they even knew they were in danger."

Anne's voice grew shrill. "I don't want to die." Her eyes filled with tears as she clung all the harder to Margaretha's arm.

"Stop it, Anne," Margaretha whispered. "You must listen to me. We shall get through this and nothing bad shall happen to us."

"How do you know?"

"I don't know how I know, I just know." Margaretha grabbed Anne by her elbows. "Now do as I say and everything will come out right. We will use the garderobe. When we leave, I will hit the guards over the head with this candlestick. I know of a secret escape route out of the castle. We can go for help." She didn't tell Anne that they would have to go through the dungeon to fetch Colin. Anne wouldn't like that at all.

Anne let go of Margaretha's arm, and they both took care of their needs rather quickly. Even so, the guard called, "Hurry up in there or I'll come in after you."

"No need," Margaretha called back. Anne had caught hold of her left arm again as Margaretha slipped the heavy candlestick out of her sleeve and held it behind her back while they emerged out into the corridor. The guard looked them over. He seemed satisfied with their appearance and turned toward the Great Hall. The second guard waited a little farther down the corridor. He was distracted by a pretty maid walking by—Britta, who was probably on her way to the kitchen. Margaretha stepped forward, every nerve under her skin leaping, and raised the silver candlestick. With all the force she could muster, she struck the back of the guard's head.

Britta happened to glance in her direction just as the guard fell. The shock on her face would no doubt alert the second guard, so Margaretha ran forward just as the second guard was turning toward her.

He grabbed the hilt of his sword and began drawing it from its scabbard. Margaretha struck him across the side of his head before he could get the tip of his sword free. He fell to the stone floor, his sword clattering down beside him, and didn't move.

No time to check if they're still breathing. She dashed down the corridor, tucking her candlestick in her sleeve again.

Britta's eyes were almost as round as her open mouth.

"Follow me!" Margaretha called to Britta in a loud whisper over her shoulder. Without waiting to see if Britta would follow, Margaretha headed to the dungeon. Her hands shook, but a sense of power surged through her limbs. She felt as if she could save them all.

"If you get me killed," Anne said in a shaky voice, "I shall come back and haunt you, Margaretha. I shall not rest until I've driven you mad."

Margaretha stifled a rather hysterical laugh. No time to argue with her cousin as she flew down the uneven stone steps into the darkness.

The gaoler had left one torch burning somewhere up the steps. The light was barely enough for Colin to make out the rats that scurried by the far wall. The smell of smoke, mold, and human excrement was almost like a tangible thing, closing in on him in the dark.

The light grew brighter and he heard footsteps, quick and soft, not at all like the gaoler's heavy footfalls.

He stood up, making his chains rattle, as three young women appeared, hurrying down the steps.

Lady Margaretha led the two others. She smiled when she saw him. No one had ever looked more beautiful or been a more welcome sight. Her eyes flashed with a wildness that matched the tone of her voice, for of course, she was talking. Most of it was in English, although she occasionally slipped into German.

"Colin, we have come to rescue you before we escape. I've knocked out Lord Claybrook's two guards who were watching Anne and me, and this is Britta, a maid who was in the corridor. Do you think we have time to go get my family? Claybrook might catch us, though, and we must—"

"I don't know half of what you're saying, but if you have the key to my irons, I will be very grateful." He shook his chains to make sure she understood.

Before she could answer, Lady Margaretha and her two companions turned at the sound of voices and more footsteps.

"*Wer ist da?*" the gaoler's voice called as he and the priest came into view.

Margaretha turned and spoke to the gaoler and the priest coming down the dungeon steps. Colin wasn't sure what she told him, but the gaoler looked at her as if she had just told him to go kiss a toad.

Colin suspected Margaretha was demanding that the gaoler let Colin go, and the gaoler was arguing with her. The priest, who turned to Colin with a surprised look on his face, began to relay what they were saying.

As Margaretha spoke, the priest translated, "I am sorry to tell you this, but it is Lord Claybrook and his guards who are dangerous. This man came here to warn us to be on our guard against Claybrook, who intends to kill him—and to kill my father, Duke Wilhelm. You must not listen to what Lord Claybrook's guards tell you."

"*Ach du meine Güte,*" the priest said, whatever that meant. He crossed himself, lifting the large cross around his neck and kissing it.

The gaoler only muttered and shook his head before lifting the keys that were dangling around his wrist and sorting through them. He stepped toward Colin and began unlocking his irons.

"We must escape," Margaretha said to Colin while the gaoler loosed him from his chains, "and find help. I don't know if any of our men got through to warn Father, but we must find him. If he is near enough, he can prevent the Earl of Keiterhafen's men from getting into Hagenheim tonight and defeat Claybrook before morning."

The timeframe didn't seem likely, but he refrained from telling her that. "We must secure some weapons."

"I have the candlestick I used to knock out the two guards, but I don't know where we might get swords or knives."

"We should also try to get some money, in case we have a longer than expected journey ahead of us. We may need to go to your father's allies for help. Who is his strongest ally?"

"My mother's family, the Godehards of Marienberg. My cousin, Duke Theodemar, will help us if we can get word to them. We can get there in a few days, if we have good horses."

Anne asked something, and her voice sounded peevish. The young maid with the yellow-blonde hair and round blue eyes stood near the wall, still clutching her arms around herself and shivering, even though it was not very cold. Anne frowned indignantly.

"Attaining horses could be a problem, since the stable is guarded by Claybrook's men."

"If we have to walk, it will take a week at least."

He wasn't sure Duke Wilhelm and Lord Valten would survive a week.

"I have money in my chamber, which we will obtain before we leave. I hope it is enough."

The priest had begun to translate their conversation to the gaoler, Anne, and Britta.

"Father Anselm, would you go up to my bedchamber and get a purse out of the small trunk beside my bed?" Margaretha asked. "It's the trunk with the painted vines and flowers on it, and the purse is a simple brown leather pouch."

The priest nodded and turned to go up the steps.

The gaoler said something in his gruff voice and started up the stone steps behind the priest.

"Where is he going?" Colin asked.

"Back to his post. He will tell us if he sees Lord Claybrook's men coming this way." Margaretha's face was a vibrant contrast to the young maid, who looked terrified, and Anne, who looked angry and irritable. Margaretha's eyes were wide and animated, and she spoke in a lively voice. "I can't believe I knocked out two men and escaped. I hope I didn't kill them or permanently injure them. But we have to think about what we will need to bring with us on our trip. Besides money and weapons, we should take some warm clothing and some food, in case we need to avoid entering the villages. I still can hardly believe Lord Claybrook would be foolish enough to try to take over Hagenheim. I hope my little sisters are not too frightened by all this. Adela can cry for hours when she's sad or afraid."

Not only had she spied on Claybrook and discovered his plot, but she had escaped from two of his guards. Margaretha, whom he had accused of being a flibbertigibbet and thought of as the pampered daughter of a duke, who talked on and on when she was excited. He never would have believed it.

His mind went back to what she had said earlier and he interrupted her chatter. "You knocked out Claybrook's guards with a candlestick?"

"Not just one, but two guards." Margaretha smiled as if she had just won a jousting tournament. She pulled a silver candlestick from her sleeve and held it up.

He had to admit, "I am impressed, Lady Margaretha."

She smiled and seemed to be blushing, although it was hard to tell in the dark dungeon. "I rather enjoyed it. I only hope neither of them were seriously injured."

He had no such hope as he rubbed his wrists where the irons had chafed his skin. They waited for the priest to return, and while Margaretha seemed to be trying to comfort her cousin and the maid in their native tongue, he began thinking of a plan to escape from the castle. How many doors led out of the castle?

Wouldn't they all be guarded? It would take a miracle to get out without Claybrook's guards seeing them.

Margaretha turned back to Colin and said in English, "We will save my mother and sisters and brothers and bring them with us, won't we? Claybrook has stopped them from leaving as we had planned earlier. Please. We must take them with us."

Her face was very near his in the dim torchlight of the dungeon. He was struck with the beauty of her delicate features in the mellow light of the torches.

Dwelling on Margaretha's beauty at a time like this? He blinked to clear his thoughts. "I don't want to discourage you, but I think it unlikely that we will be able to get your mother and siblings away from Claybrook's guards."

Would she be logical and accept his reasoning?

"May we not at least try?" Margaretha seemed to be pleading with him with those deep brown eyes of hers.

He found himself saying, "We can try, but if they are guarded, you must accept that, having no weapons — besides your candlestick — we will not be able to overcome the guards and take your family with us."

"But if there is only one, or even two guards, I am sure you and I can defeat that many."

"If there are only one or two, or even three, and if they do not see us ... I will consider the attempt. But remember, Margaretha." He stepped even closer to her, touching her shoulder to make her listen. "We must escape in order to get help for everyone, including your father. We must escape." He emphasized the words.

"I know you are right. Thank you for at least considering the attempt. Perhaps God will make a way."

"But before we go to find your family ..." He looked at the two other people around them. The maid's eyes were wide in her pale face as she huddled against the wall, looking on.

Margaretha's cousin stood with her hands in fists drawn up to her nose, as if to stifle the smell of the dank dungeon. "We have to make a plan of how to escape the castle."

"Oh, that is easy." Her eyes brightened again. "Here in the dungeon there is a secret tunnel."

"In the dungeon?"

"Another entrance to the tunnel is hidden in the castle yard, but it is near the castle gate and we couldn't get there without being seen. Besides, what better place to hide a secret entrance to a tunnel than the dungeon? No one would ever look for it there, and the dungeon prisoners could never find it because they are bound by chains. I think it a most genius idea of my father's, although the actual tunnel idea was my uncle, Lord Rupert's."

"That's my father," Anne chirped.

The existence of a secret tunnel that led out of the castle was the best news he'd heard … ever.

Footsteps sounded above and the gaoler called in a hushed voice, "Father Anselm." The priest returned with Margaretha's purse. She tied it to her belt.

Colin grabbed her hand. "Let us go. Tell the others to stay here. We will try to free your mother and family and return." Colin started up the steps.

Chapter
15

Margaretha hurriedly translated his words for Anne and Britta as she followed Colin up.

Britta's face appeared frozen in terror, while Anne looked as if she was biting through a horseshoe, but Margaretha couldn't worry about them now. As Colin had said, they *must* escape, and she didn't want to leave her family behind.

When they reached the top of the dungeon steps, the gaoler said he hadn't seen any guards. They continued on, with Colin holding her hand behind him. He looked around every corner before moving forward and allowing her to follow.

They started up the castle steps toward the family's solar. Margaretha's heart thudded in her ears, making it harder to listen for any trace of a guard's footfall or voice. She moved her own feet as silently as possible, treading lightly, moving deliberately. Colin's steps were quieter than a baby's sigh as he led her up the narrow, steep stairs. The feel of his hand around hers invigorated her. Together, she was certain they could overcome a couple of guards who had less to lose than they did.

They crept slower as voices became audible above them. They were muted, but blessedly feminine. She thought she recognized her mother's.

Colin strained forward, then jerked back, plastering himself against the wall of the stairwell. His eyes met hers as he placed his finger to his lips.

"Let me — " Margaretha had begun to say, *Let me go up first*, but Colin pressed his fingers against her mouth and shook his head.

He leaned down and pressed his lips to her ear. "Guards, four feet away."

His breath caressed her ear. Margaretha tried to ignore the warm shiver that swept through her. She mouthed, "How many?"

He held up four fingers.

"May I see?"

Colin looked reluctant, but he finally nodded. He traded places with her, stepping down while she stepped up, their shoulders brushing in the tight space. He had nice hair, the way it curled so thickly but smoothly over his head and on the back of his neck. She might tell him if she was able to talk. But perhaps it was better he didn't know she had noticed such a thing.

She carefully stretched forward, peeking around the curve of the staircase. Finally, she saw Claybrook's guards standing outside the door. Their backs were to her, and she could only see two, so she leaned farther forward and saw the legs of two more.

Even Margaretha wasn't optimistic enough to believe that the two of them could defeat four trained, heavily armed guards. Perhaps if they enlisted the aid of the gaoler and the priest ... But she couldn't imagine Father Anselm doing anything violent, and the gaoler was old and might not even be willing. No, she had to trust that she would be able to get help and come back and save them. Besides, she didn't think Claybrook would harm her family. He had no reason to kill them, and the king and the rest of the nobility of the land would look quite unfavorably on such a thing.

She'd felt so much hope when they had started up the steps.

Now her heart was like a huge stone in her chest as she followed Colin back down.

Colin looked carefully before going around any corners, and soon they were back in the dungeon without having encountered anyone along the way.

Anne clasped Margaretha's arm again. "Get me out of this rat-infested hole. I will not stay here another minute."

"With God's help, we will be out of here soon." Maybe then Anne could lose that frustrated, fearful tone in her voice that was dancing on Margaretha's nerves.

"Weapons," Colin said, breaking into her thoughts. "Can you ask the gaoler to give us any weapons he has on him?"

"Of course." Margaretha approached the gaoler, and he readily bent over and removed a dagger and its sheath, which was strapped to his thigh underneath his tunic.

"This is all I carry." He handed them over to Colin. "But if you can wait, I can fetch a mace that I keep in the Great Hall."

Margaretha translated.

"No, too unwieldy. We must be moving fast. But thank you." Colin eyed Anne and Britta. "Who is going with us, and who is staying at Hagenheim Castle?"

Anne and Britta looked to Margaretha to clarify.

Margaretha had assumed they were both going. "Cannot they both go?"

"They can, but we do not know where we are going, exactly. They should know that now. I want to give them the choice."

Margaretha translated for the two young women, but added, "You should come with us to avoid the chaos that is certainly coming."

"Will I be able to go to my family in town?" Britta's lip trembled as she spoke.

Margaretha thought for a moment. "I don't see why not.

126

Once we are out, you can always go back in—that is, until the fighting starts. Then the gates will probably close."

Britta let out a squeak, like a mouse in a trap.

"Don't worry. All will be well. Colin and I will protect you, and probably there won't be any fighting anyway, if we can find—"

"We must go. Tell them to decide now." Colin's manner reminded her of the black stallion just before he bolted.

Margaretha turned to Anne and Britta. "Will you go with us?"

"Do I have a choice?" Anne asked irritably.

"No, unless you want to go up to the solar and turn yourself over to the soldiers who are guarding the rest of my family."

"Which way do we go?" Colin asked impatiently.

"We must get torches first." Margaretha took one down from the wall, and Colin walked halfway up the steps to grab another.

"This way," she said, starting for the tunnel to the right. She hoped Anne and Britta were behind her as she led the way. The tunnel narrowed until it was only wide enough for one person.

"A spider!" Anne's voice reverberated off the stone walls. "Get it off."

A scuffle ensued, followed by, "Ach! I am so angry with you, Margaretha."

"What did I do?"

Anne's voice came from behind, "You led me through a dungeon and through a spider web, which is still in my hair, and a spider crawled up my arm! I even saw a rat run by! If I die in this stinking hole, I will never forgive you."

Margaretha sighed. "I am saving you, Anne, from an evil man. Please try to remember that."

The light of her torch showed that the tunnel ended just ahead in a small chamber complete with chains and iron manacles and two wooden benches. Margaretha stepped into it and walked straight to the back wall. Feeling with her hand, she found a stone that jutted out. She pushed down on it and the wall shifted. She pushed harder and a four-foot by two-foot section of stones opened up like a door on a hinge.

Colin grunted behind her. "I need one of these."

Margaretha smiled. Here was another secret she had never talked about. She couldn't wait to tell her brothers how wrong they were about her.

She had not been allowed to know about the secret tunnel as a child, but a few years before, her father and mother had shown her and her sister Kirstyn where the tunnel was and how to open the secret door, in case there was some terrible event and they needed to leave the castle. Margaretha had dreamed of using it, of how exciting it would be to lead the castle household to safety while evil brigands attacked. All her imaginings were so close to today's reality that it gave this moment a dream-like quality.

She truly was here, and she truly was leading people to safety through the secret tunnel — but more importantly, to get help.

She pushed the wall open as far as it would go and bent low to fit through the small opening, holding her torch before her.

More spider webs greeted her as she stepped into the seldom-used tunnel.

⚮

In awe of the secret passageway, Colin almost whistled when Lady Margaretha pushed on a stone and the wall opened up before her. He had to figure out how they did this before going back home to England.

Anne poked his shoulder, hard. Then she conveyed, through a mixture of crude hand signals and a little broken English, that she wanted his torch, so he passed it back to her. Now he followed close behind Lady Margaretha as they entered the tunnel.

He only hoped Anne didn't set his hair or clothing on fire.

A loamy smell of damp earth met his nose, but it was better than the stink of the dungeon. He put his hand on the wall. Apparently it was made of packed earth, except that, a few feet farther on, a wooden pillar held up some wooden fortifications of the ceiling.

Lady Margaretha was explaining, "The tunnel is not long, but we should hurry so that our torches don't choke us with their smoke, since there's nowhere for the smoke to go."

He glanced behind to make sure both young women were still there. They wore looks of relative horror, but they were staying close. Margaretha glanced back at him, and her expression was the opposite — smiling, with a glint of triumph in her eye.

They continued on. A soft rustling sound seemed to be coming from just ahead. Margaretha stopped abruptly, and Colin nearly bumped into her back. A rat ran across their path, squeaking in apparent alarm, its eyes glowing in the torchlight. It skittered past, along the wall behind them. Anne screamed, then Britta joined her.

"Shh!" Margaretha warned them.

"You shh! I've never been subjected to such filth or ill treatment." Anne huffed. Her voice turned whiney as she said, "Can this day get any worse? Why did I ever think coming to visit you was a good idea?"

They had walked but a few more steps when he heard what he thought was a tiny chirping sound, so faint he might be imagining it. Then he caught a glimpse of something as it darted silently by his head. Colin ducked.

"A bat!" Anne screamed again.

Margaretha suddenly plastered herself against his chest, burying her face in his shoulder and clinging to him with one hand, while she held the torch in her other hand away from them.

He wrapped his arm around her, to protect her.

The bat hovered above them, and Colin felt a tiny breath of air on his face from the creature's wings. Then it flew away.

"Is it gone?" Margaretha asked, and he felt her shudder. "I'm sorry." She pulled away from him, but he let his hand linger on her back. "Rats don't bother me, but I'm frightened to death of bats." She turned away from him and started forward again. "I think he's gone. Let us go."

He almost wished the bat would come back. He liked the way she had felt against his chest. Had it only been his protective instinct that had caused his arm to tighten around her?

Anne made a sound that was a cross between a groan and a sob, but she continued walking behind them. She probably had not witnessed Margaretha's momentary panic at seeing the bat, it was so dark and narrow in the tunnel, and Colin had been blocking her view.

They went around a bend in the tunnel, and Margaretha seemed to slow and pick her way carefully. He soon saw why. A snake skeleton lay in the middle of the path. "Watch your step," she said.

He stepped over it, then heard behind him, "Ach! I hate this place. What next?"

It seemed as if they had walked quite a long way when he saw a tiny glimmer of light ahead and some wooden steps leading up to . . . the ceiling?

"We are here." Cheerfulness pulsed through Margaretha's voice. "There is a door at the top of these steps. We will have to push hard to get it open."

Colin took her torch from her and handed it back to Britta. He and Margaretha climbed the steps. Standing with their shoulders braced against the door, they stood so close that he could feel her breath against his cheek. But he tried not to dwell on it and joined Margaretha in pushing with their shoulders. The wooden door above them began to move, causing dirt and debris to rain down around them. They continued pushing, and soon the midday sun flooded the dark tunnel. When there was a half-foot crack, Colin said, "Wait a moment," and looked out.

They were surrounded by grass, and straight ahead was a beech tree forest. To the left and right it appeared that they were at the edge of the meadow that bordered the wall around the south side of the castle, and just beyond the meadow was the forest. But most importantly, he didn't see any of Claybrook's soldiers.

He nodded at Margaretha and the two of them continued to push the heavy door the rest of the way open. In doing so, they displaced what seemed to be hundreds of leaves, dead grass, and a few insects.

They were out! Now to get out of the open before someone saw them.

Then he saw something—or someone—moving in the shade of the trees. It might already be too late.

Chapter
16

Margaretha brushed the dead leaves and dirt from her hair. Dust clogged her throat, making her cough. Colin held the door for Anne and Britta as they climbed out of the tunnel, then let it down slowly so it wouldn't slam. As she kicked the leaves and grasses back over the wooden door to disguise it, she noticed Colin staring tensely into the trees.

Anne started to speak in her whiniest voice.

"Quiet!" Colin whispered, and motioned with his hand, violently striking the air in a downward motion. Then he squatted.

They all followed his example and sank down where they stood.

Rustlings, like someone brushing against tree limbs, came from the forest. Several feet away, three men emerged, stepping into the meadow. They were walking away from them and didn't seem to notice Margaretha and her companions.

Two of the men wore the red and gold livery of Claybrook's guards, while the third one, in the middle, walked between them with his head down. Even just seeing him from behind, Margaretha recognized Bezilo, her father's guard.

Was that blood running down Bezilo's jaw and neck? It seemed to be coming from his ear. Margaretha's stomach churned. He was holding his arm with his other hand, bloody and obviously injured.

Should they cower there in the meadow, hoping not to be seen? Shouldn't they rather try to save Bezilo?

Colin was pulling out the dagger that the gaoler had given him as he looked her way. He gave a small nod and she knew he was thinking the same thing she was.

He motioned to Anne and Britta to stay, then to Margaretha to come. Her heart leapt; Colin trusted her to help him in a fight.

Colin slowly stood, and Margaretha did the same. He stepped toward the three men, who were walking away, and Margaretha followed close behind Colin, who angled toward the trees, making himself less conspicuous. They followed the men for a short way before Colin began to close in.

One of the men turned. "Who's there?"

Colin froze. Margaretha held her breath. "*Guten Tag*," she said, forcing a smile and dropping a quick curtsy. Hopefully, in her disheveled state, they wouldn't know who she was. "We were on our way to Hagenheim, to market. Can you point us to the nearest town gate?"

"Who are you?" The guard on the left looked suspicious. "Are you Lady Margaretha, Duke Wilhelm's daughter?"

"Who, me?" Margaretha laughed, a rather hysterical sound, even to her ears. "This *is* my best dress, but not fine enough for Lady Margaretha, surely. I'm only the chandler's assistant, and I work in the Marktplatz."

Both guards, though still holding on to their prisoner between them, were now fully attentive to Margaretha and Colin. Poor Bezilo hadn't even lifted his head. His face was bloody, his lips and eyes swollen. What had they done to him? Her stomach twisted but she had to focus, had to play her part and behave naturally.

"Does that man need some help?"

She pointed to Bezilo, but the two guards were looking back and forth between her and Colin. Leering grins broke out on both their faces. Margaretha's cheeks began to burn as she realized what they were thinking—what she and Colin must look like, with leaves and grass clinging to their hair and clothing.

Colin's eyes narrowed, and she noticed he was holding the dagger against his thigh to conceal it. No doubt he had seen their suggestive looks as well.

"Who did you say you were?" The guard looked suspicious again. This time he was staring at Colin. But of course, Colin probably understood very little.

Margaretha had been inching closer to the men, and now she passed Colin and walked toward them. "May I help tend this man's wounds? He seems badly injured. Did he fall off his horse? I've never seen so much blood coming from someone's ear." She continued talking to try to distract the men. She even smiled flirtatiously at the leering guard on the right. "I don't believe I've ever seen you men around here." As she talked, she slipped her hand into her sleeve, her fingers closing around the candlestick. Her heart sped up as she calculated exactly how close she needed to be.

Hearing Colin behind her, she snatched out the candlestick, stepped forward, and slammed it against the nearest guard's temple.

The guard sank to his knees, his eyes closed, and he fell to the ground face first.

The guard on the left was just able to draw his sword from his scabbard when Colin leapt forward and kicked the weapon from his hand. He thrust the dagger point to the guard's throat.

Without taking even a moment to consider her action, and while the guard was staring at Colin, Margaretha swung her candlestick with both hands and hit the side of the man's head. He reeled, then fell like a tree to an ax's blade.

Bezilo had looked up when Margaretha struck the first guard. He stared as though dumbfounded from beneath eyelids swollen almost shut. But when he saw that Margaretha had knocked out the two guards, he seemed to revive. He walked to where the guard's sword had fallen to the ground, and, still holding his arm close to his body, picked up the sword. Then he stood over the first of the two guards.

Colin was staring at Margaretha, his mouth open.

"Lady Margaretha," Bezilo said, "please turn aside. I don't want you to see this." Bezilo was holding the sword above the guard's throat.

With a start, Margaretha realized Bezilo was about to kill the man. "*Liebe Gott.*" Margaretha immediately turned around.

Colin turned his head as well as his expression sobered.

Behind her, Bezilo grunted, and his grunt was followed by a gurgling sound. Margaretha covered her ears and began walking away, as she thought she heard Bezilo walking to the other guard, no doubt to kill him as well. What had seemed like an exhilarating adventure had turned into a stomach-turning moment of the harshest reality life had to offer: death.

God, forgive us.

"It was necessary." It was as if Colin had read her mind, as he appeared beside her, looking at her with those intense blue eyes of his. "He had to kill those men so they wouldn't go back and tell Claybrook."

Margaretha nodded. For once, she had no words. But she had seen what they had done to dear Bezilo, one of her father's most loyal guards and a kind-hearted bear of a man. He was a trained soldier, but his killing the two guards turned her stomach just the same.

A wave of dizziness came over her. "I need to sit." She barely made it into the shade of the trees before she sat down hard, hung her head forward, and concentrated on breathing. She kept her hands over her ears so she wouldn't hear anything Sir Bezilo was doing.

She felt something and looked up. It was Colin's hand resting gently on her shoulder as he bent to look at her face. "You did well, Lady Margaretha. You were incredibly brave, and you saved Bezilo's life."

Margaretha swallowed hard. Yes. She would think about that. They had saved Bezilo from Claybrook's men. "And you too," she said, forcing her lips into a wobbly smile. "Thank you."

After a moment she reached her hand toward him and let him pull her to her feet. The dizziness was mostly gone, which was good, since she had no time for it. Her people, everyone she loved, were in danger.

Men had died, and more would die, possibly a lot more.

Bezilo strode toward them.

"You need a healer," Margaretha said to him.

"I cannot go to Hagenheim Castle looking like this. Those men back there found the note I had written for Duke Wilhelm. I wanted to pass it off to a messenger, someone who could get to him faster than I could, so I could stay here and help you. That plan went amiss, as you can see."

There were cuts above both his eyes. His cheekbones were bloody and bruised, and he seemed to have trouble catching his breath.

"Is your arm broken?"

"It doesn't matter. Lady Margaretha, you must go for help. You must go" — he paused as if to catch his breath — "to your mother's family in Marienberg, to ask the Duke of Marienberg to come with all his fighting men and help your father. I will do my best to get word to your father of the danger."

Anne and Britta came toward them, Anne with a look of disgust on her face as she stared at Bezilo. How dare Anne look at the brave and honorable Bezilo that way!

Lord God, give me patience.

"We will go to Marienberg. Do not worry. But we must get help for you. I am worried about you."

"If you could think of a place ... where I could rest, I would not ... refuse it." His breath was coming in wheezing gasps now.

"The woman who gathers herbs for Frau Lena! I believe her cottage is near here." But would Bezilo be able to walk there?

"Let us go, then. Or simply point me in the right way."

"I will show you. But first ..." Margaretha turned to look at the others.

"I shall go back into Hagenheim and buy horses for us." Colin was obviously impatient to be doing something.

"No. We shall have to buy horses outside the town wall. It is too dangerous for you to be seen inside Hagenheim. Britta." She turned to the pale-faced maid. "We need you to go back to the castle. Or better yet, send a messenger to the healer, Frau Lena, and ask her to come to the cottage of the herb gatherer who lives near the river. She will know who I'm talking about. Tell her I need her to tend to an injured person there. Let her know it is urgent, but do not mention anything that has happened. Lord Claybrook and his men must not find out that we escaped or what we are doing, and we can only hope they will not stop Frau Lena from leaving the castle grounds. Will you do this for us?"

"Yes, Lady Margaretha." The whites of her eyes were visible all the way around her irises.

"Now, you must stop looking so afraid."

"I don't know how!" she said in a plaintive whisper.

Margaretha took her hand. "Listen to me. Take a deep breath. Now close your eyes. And when you open them, don't open them so wide, *ja?*" Margaretha smiled at her as she opened her eyes a slit. "That's good. You can do this. You are very brave. We are all brave now. We must be."

Britta took another deep breath and did indeed look much calmer.

"I am sorry, but I do not think you will be able to rejoin us outside the gate once you go back in."

"Oh, I do not mind that, my lady. I prefer to die — that is, I prefer to be where my family is, and where Gustaf is." She burst into tears at the name of her soldier sweetheart.

And she had been making such progress.

"There, there," Margaretha soothed. "You must not cry. We need you. Bezilo needs you if he hopes to recover. Now run to fetch Frau Lena. Quickly."

Britta wiped her nose on her apron and nodded. "Yes, Lady Margaretha. I shall not fail."

"Wait," Colin said. "Margaretha." He stepped quite close to her. "I think you and Anne should go with Britta."

"With Britta? Why? I must go to Marienberg to get help."

"Let me go to Marienberg to get help. You will be much safer here with Britta and her family in the town. They can hide you and Claybrook need never know you're there. Just disguise yourself before you go in —"

"No! You don't know me at all if you think I will hide here when I could be going for help to save my family." The very idea made her breathe hard and her face grow warm.

Colin's jawline was firm and his eyes bored into hers. "Traveling to Marienberg is dangerous. We have no guards. We won't even have horses at first. Thieves roam these roads, attacking and stealing — and worse. It's not safe for you."

"I will not discuss this." When she saw the woebegone flash of anguish in his eyes, she softened her tone. "I'm sorry, but you cannot persuade me. I would never cower in hiding while my family was in danger." She glanced at Britta, who was still staring, apparently waiting for her to give her the final order. "Britta, you may go. Remember all that I said."

Britta turned and hurried away toward the town gate,

glancing at the dead guards on the ground and making a great semi-circle to avoid them.

"What? Are those men over there ... dead?" Anne scrunched her face to such distortion that her upper lip was touching her nose and her eyebrows met in the middle—just above the translucent blue vein between her eyes. It was perhaps her only physical flaw, that blue vein that had fascinated Margaretha since she was a child. She'd often stared at it without meaning to.

"We're at war, or shortly will be," Margaretha said, feigning indifference toward the dead guards, "and we cannot be squeamish about such things. Come, we must go before any more of Claybrook's men find us."

Anne looked alarmed at that and hastened to keep up, as Margaretha started through the trees toward the cottage where Bezilo could rest and wait for Frau Lena.

To think, a week ago her little brothers' teasing had been her biggest trial in life, along with having to decide whether to reject another suitor or marry him. How quickly life could change and turn her world upside down.

Chapter 17

Colin would never have thought the prattling but sweet Lady Margaretha could be such an asset in a war. First, she had saved herself and two friends from Claybrook's guards. Then, she had rescued him from the dungeon and led them all through a secret tunnel out of the castle. And when confronted with two more of Claybrook's guards, she had done exactly what he needed her to do, knocking them out with the candlestick she had hidden inside her sleeve.

He'd never been more shocked — or more impressed — in his life.

But once again, Colin found himself responsible for someone else's well-being — two someones, if he included Anne, although he felt certain she would take the first opportunity to stay behind if they found a safe place for her.

They left Bezilo in the care of Frau Lena's friend, at her cottage in the glen. The noble and chivalrous guard offered Colin his sword, the one he had used to kill Claybrook's guards, but Colin refused it, feeling he could travel faster without it.

Then they continued on, traveling along the edge of the forest next to the road to avoid being seen by Claybrook's guards, who would be searching for them, to a place Margaretha knew where they could purchase horses.

Margaretha chattered cheerfully most of the way, while

Anne muttered frequent complaints. Colin only knew this, of course, because Margaretha, in her pleasant tone, translated for him. "It would be rude not to," she had said.

Often, after Anne whined about something, Margaretha would try to placate her. "Anne, if you walk behind Colin and me, you won't catch your dress on so many thorns."

Or, "Anne, don't worry about your hair. I will re-pin it for you before we arrive at the horse breeder's."

Or, "Do you need a bandage for that scratch? I can make one for you from my chemise."

After less than an hour of walking, Anne spoke, then Margaretha translated, "Are we almost there? My feet are hurting and my shoes are getting ruined."

Margaretha replied in the German language, then translated for him into English, "We are almost there. Only five more minutes, I think."

As they walked, Colin asked, "Did you say this house we are going to was once owned by your sister's family?"

"Gisela, who is married to my brother, Lord Hamlin, lived here before she and Valten were married. And perhaps while we're here, Anne and I should try to get some sturdier clothing for traveling. It's a long way to Marienberg. Gisela probably left some clothes here after she and Valten married."

Anne interrupted Margaretha in her unintelligible foreign tongue. Then Margaretha told him that Anne had said, "I will be traveling straight home as soon as I get a horse. I do not intend to spend any more time trying to fight some war. I am a lady, the granddaughter of a duke! I am not accustomed to such treatment."

Colin glanced back at Anne. He was not the least threatened by her being the granddaughter of a duke. "One of the first places Claybrook's guards will look for Lady Margaretha is your home. It is nearby, is it not?"

After Margaretha translated, Anne made a choking sound, then coughed. "He won't be looking for me, and surely he wouldn't hurt my family."

"How many guards does your father keep? He is the second son, is he not?" Before Margaretha could translate his words to Anne, he said, "Claybrook has more. A lot more. But I do not believe they will harm you or Margaretha. Claybrook still probably intends to marry her, and he has no reason to harm you, Lady Anne. I believe you will both be safe at your father's home."

After she translated for Anne, Margaretha stopped him with a hand on his arm. "I will not stay with Anne at her father's home. I am going to Marienberg to get help. I will not be left behind. Besides, I would rather die than marry Lord Claybrook."

"You won't have to marry him if I bring the Duke of Marienberg here to help your father save Hagenheim and capture Claybrook." Why couldn't she simply do as he asked? "You don't have to be brave and courageous, Margaretha. You should be like your cousin, Anne. She's thinking about keeping herself safe, and you should be too."

He instantly saw that he'd said the wrong thing. Never tell someone they should be like their sister, cousin, brother, or anyone else. Margaretha's face turned red, and she opened her mouth, but Anne hurried to get in front of Colin.

Anne faced him and stomped her foot. She looked a lot like his little sister did when she was three and couldn't have her way. Her nostrils flared and her eyes flashed.

He liked his sister much more now that she didn't throw these little fits.

He started to walk around Anne but she moved in front of him again. She spoke, her eyes still flashing, then Margaretha translated, "How dare you insinuate that I am a coward!"

Margaretha had not translated his words. "You understood what I said?"

"I know a little English," Anne said in English, then, still speaking in English, she asked, "Who do you think you are, insulting me?"

"I know quite well who I am." Colin crossed his arms, looking back at her calmly. "I am the oldest son and heir of one of the wealthiest landowners in all of England. My father was given an earldom by the king of England, which shall pass to me. Therefore, you may call me Lord le Wyse of Glynval." He executed his most elegant bow to Anne.

She glared at him for a few more moments before unclenching her fists and smoothing the skirt of her gown with her hands. "Very well," she said. "Lord le Wyse, I shall do as you say — for now." She spoke the entire response in English.

So she had studied the language. Obviously she had understood much more than she had pretended. Did she speak English as well as Margaretha and only feigned ignorance for pure annoyance?

Margaretha stopped Anne and forced her to look at her. She asked in English, "Anne, do you speak English?"

"Of course." Anne grinned smugly. "I studied under the same tutor you did. Don't you remember? He spent half his year with you and the other half with me."

Not the most forthright girl. He'd have to remember that.

The two of them spoke quietly behind him. They started out in English, with Margaretha saying, "Anne, you should have told us you understood. Why would you make me translate for you and keep such a thing a secret?"

"I was only trying to listen for a while in order to refresh my memory of the language."

But then Anne began speaking in German again and he didn't understand a word. They talked in hushed voices, and this time Margaretha did not translate for him. Anne probably told her not to.

They came to a break in the trees, with a meadow on either side of the road.

"There's the horse breeder's house." Margaretha hurried forward. A large stone and half-timber house came into view across the road in the clearing. Beyond it was a meadow and stables.

Colin listened and looked carefully up and down the road before they ventured out. But no sooner did he get two feet onto the road when he heard horses' hoofs, and he stepped back into the cover of the trees.

Margaretha, Colin, and Anne squatted behind trees as the horses drew closer.

"Who is it?" Anne asked.

Margaretha shook her head and Colin motioned for them to stay quiet. Her question was answered as a group of about five of Claybrook's guards came into view. They slowed when they saw Gisela's old house, then rode straight up to it. Two men stationed themselves outside while the others pounded on the door, then forced their way inside.

Colin whispered, "Claybrook must have known about this place."

Yes, Margaretha had told him all about it. He had asked her all kinds of questions that had led her to go on and on about her family and all their friends and allies, their extended family members, and their family houses. How readily she had revealed the things he could now use against them.

If only she didn't talk so much. But how could she have known he would use the information to try to take over Hagenheim?

Colin went on. "He assumed this is where we would go to get horses, which means he knows we have escaped."

Margaretha looked at Colin. His lip was still swollen. The

image of Claybrook mercilessly striking him rose before her. She didn't want to be the cause of any more abuse inflicted upon him by Claybrook or his men.

"This is my fight, and only mine," Margaretha said quietly. "It is my family that Claybrook is after, my town he wants to rule over. You two should find a place of safety and leave me to travel on to Marienberg alone."

He turned those intense blue eyes on her. "You are wrong, Lady Margaretha, for this was my fight before it was yours. I followed Claybrook here in order to bring about justice after he murdered my sister's friend, then watched his men murder my friend John, and I will not give up until I see justice done." His expression seemed to soften as he added, "I appreciate your courage, but it is you who should find a place of safety. I would feel responsible if something terrible happened to you."

Was he truly so concerned about her?

"And what about my safety?" Anne asked. "Isn't anyone concerned about me?"

"I am concerned about your safety as well, Lady Anne." Colin cleared his throat. "Margaretha, does Claybrook know of your family in Marienberg?"

"We spoke of them a few times. He asked me about them. I'm afraid I told him many things I shouldn't have."

"Then I think you and Lady Anne must go to her home. If none of Claybrook's guards are there, the two of you should stay."

"What if they torture us to force us to tell them where you have gone?" Anne looked as if she might burst into tears.

"You must tell them that I've gone to Marienberg. Claybrook will naturally have assumed this anyway. He will send men to look for me. It cannot be helped, and I would not have them torture you."

Margaretha set her hands on her hips and clenched her jaw. "No. For the last time, I am going to Marienberg."

Colin sighed and shook his head. She hoped this was a sign of his resignation.

They could do this. Margaretha was sure of it. God was always on the side of the righteous, and He would be with them.

~~~

Colin felt sorry he had called Margaretha a flibbertigibbet. She wasn't a flibbertigibbet, she was the bravest, the most stubborn, and the most frustrating girl he had ever met. Why couldn't she listen to him, stay out of danger, and wait for her deliverance like the gentle-bred daughter of a duke that she was?

Trying to reason with her was getting him nowhere. If she had seen Philippa's bloated body after it was pulled from the river, or John's bloodied and lifeless face as he lay dead on the side of the road, maybe then she would understand what kind of danger she was in—and how inadequate he was to protect her.

He had started off this journey so arrogant. At home in England, he was self-assured, but his sense of power had rarely been tested as the son of a wealthy earl. How exceedingly foolish he had been to come here, where he'd had the self-assurance beaten right out of him. He no longer felt as if he could protect anyone.

But Margaretha was determined to go with him, and she would not let him convince her she was being foolish. She wanted to help her family and her townspeople.

He would simply have to bide his time and wait for an opportunity to leave her somewhere safe. And the likeliest place remained Anne's father's house.

"How far is it to Lord Rupert's house?"

"About an hour's walk from here."

Claybrook's guards were still where they were several minutes before. They could get no horses here, so Colin set out with Margaretha and Anne, once again staying off the road.

When they had walked several minutes, they came to a tiny village. They decided not to show themselves together, and since Margaretha was the only one who had money, Colin and Anne waited in the woods while Margaretha went to the village to try to buy some food.

As he sat pondering the road ahead, Anne's voice broke into his thoughts. In heavily accented English, she asked, "My cousin is very beautiful, *ja*?" Anne's expression was coy. When he didn't answer, she added, "But she is ... how do you say in English? Very ... close to her family. I have heard her say she could never leave her family to marry."

He raised his eyebrows at her, wary of what she might say next. However, his curiosity made him say, "So Margaretha doesn't wish to marry? Or hasn't anyone offered for her?"

"Oh, she has suitors enough, but she has turned them all down." She smiled. "I myself can marry anyone I choose." Anne tilted her head down and looked up at him through her lashes, as if she was trying to look demure.

Margaretha had no desire to leave her family, and therefore she would never marry Colin and go back to England — or so Anne wanted him to believe. He didn't doubt it was true, but it didn't matter. He hadn't come to the Holy Roman Empire to find a wife, and Margaretha had shown no signs of wanting him. So why did Anne's words make his heart sink?

"I don't know if you realize this," Anne said, "but you have the most beautiful blue eyes." She leaned back against a tree and smiled at him, fluttering her eyelids.

What a fool he was to tell Anne that he was the son of a wealthy earl. He liked it better when she pretended she only spoke German. In another minute, she would probably tell him *she* didn't mind leaving *her* family to go to England.

"I think I had better see if Lady Margaretha needs any help."
He moved toward the road that led into the village.

"I will wait here." Anne looked at him from beneath half-
closed eyelids.

He had to force himself to walk, not run, in the direction
of the village.

Chapter

18

❧

Margaretha had never bought food before. She had never bought anything before. If she wanted something, she gave the money to a servant and let them go to the market or to a shop for her, or a family member or servant accompanied her to the market and paid for whatever she wanted. But how hard could it be? Besides, she hadn't eaten anything all day. She'd woken up before dawn to spy on Lord Claybrook and the captain of his guard and had missed breakfast, and now the sun was directly overhead. She had been in too much turmoil to notice how hungry she was earlier, but now that there was hope that she might find food, her stomach was growling loudly enough to frighten the birds in the trees.

A woman was coming toward her. Her hair was covered by a cloth tied at the back of her neck. She carried something in her apron as she clutched the corners to her bosom.

"*Guten Tag,*" Margaretha said with a shy smile.

The woman stared hard at her. Finally, she answered, "*Ja, Fraulein. Guten Tag.*" But she still looked suspicious and almost frightened. Perhaps she was only surprised to see someone, especially a young woman alone, come strolling into her village, someone she had never seen before. The woman undoubtedly had lived in the village her whole life. Villagers of the Holy Roman Empire didn't travel much, and they rarely left their village to go live elsewhere, except perhaps to marry someone from another village.

Besides that, Margaretha's lustrous pale-green silk cotehardie and dark emerald undergown, made of fine linen, would cause her to stand out. As she encountered more people in the village's street, she saw that the women were dressed in woolen kirtles of nondescript brown and gray and dull green. Their underdresses were of gray linen, and they kept their hair covered with opaque cloths instead of the light veils that Margaretha and her sisters wore. Only Margaretha wasn't wearing anything on her head. In the chaos of the day, she hadn't even braided it, and it was tied at the base of her neck with a red ribbon. Several strands had escaped, and Margaretha had tucked them behind her ears.

Her dress was not her best or fanciest, but now she felt almost embarrassed to be wearing such luxurious clothing. She would not go unnoticed, walking across Saxony wearing such a dress. She had to find something less conspicuous. How glad she was that she had not put on her grandmother's bracelet that morning. She hoped it was still safe at home. However, she did wish she had the ring Claybrook had given her. She could have traded it for several dresses, as well as for something to cover her voluminous hair, which was as wavy and unruly as her mother's similar chestnut hair.

But first, she had to feed the growling monster in her stomach.

There were only a few shops in this village. Besides the blacksmith, there was also a butcher shop, a brewery, and a tannery. But somewhere ahead, Margaretha smelled bread.

Finally, she found the baker's shop. She walked in and asked for a loaf of his finest bread.

The baker stared at her much like the woman in the street had. He was slathering melting butter on a slice of bread as he sat on a stool. No doubt he was having his midday meal.

Margaretha's mouth watered so much she was afraid to say anything else. Instead, she waited for him to speak.

"Half a mark," he finally said, getting up and grabbing a loaf from a shelf just behind him.

Oh yes. She'd almost forgotten she had to give him money. Margaretha lifted her purse from where it hung from her belt. She opened it and poured some of the coins into her hand, but she couldn't find anything of less value than a mark.

"Two loaves?" She laid the coin in his open hand. He raised his eyebrows and studied the coin, then he gave her two loaves of bread. Margaretha tucked the bread under her arm and asked, "Do you have any cheese?"

He looked askance at her. "No cheese here."

Margaretha nodded to him and left the tiny shop. As she walked, she encountered a woman with a basket of eggs. "May I buy some eggs from you?"

"What will you give me?" the woman asked. She had the most enormous brown mole on her chin that Margaretha had ever seen, and it had several hairs growing out of it.

"One mark?"

"Let me see it."

Margaretha lifted out her purse again, took out a coin, and showed it to the woman.

She didn't take her eyes off the coin, but said, "How many eggs do you want?" as if she was talking to the money.

How many could she carry without breaking them? "May I have five?"

The woman reached into her basket and drew out five eggs, which Margaretha carefully placed in her purse. She gave the woman the coin, then gently closed her purse and let it dangle from her belt.

"Thank you." As Margaretha walked, hoping she didn't break the eggs, she realized she wasn't hungry enough to eat them raw.

But if she wanted to cook the eggs, she would need something to put them in. She had seen the cook at the castle put eggs into a pot of boiling water.

Margaretha noticed a child's face peeking out an open window at her. As she looked at the houses and shops lining the dirt street, she noticed several more men, women, and children gaping at her.

A little girl was walking toward her carrying an armload of wood. "You're pretty," the little girl said.

"Thank you." Margaretha's stomach growled again and she pinched a piece of bread off one of the loaves and put it in her mouth. It was barley bread, coarse and rather tasteless, but it made Margaretha's stomach feel better, so she ate another piece.

She didn't know where she was going and needed to get back to Colin and Anne, so she approached an older, gray-haired man standing in the doorway of a crude house. "Excuse me. Can you tell me where I might find a pot for cooking? A small one, preferably."

There was a shrewd look in his wrinkly eyes. Abruptly, Margaretha was very aware that she was alone, that she didn't have the safety of her name and her family to hide behind, and that it might have been better to ask a woman.

"Come inside and you can have what you want." He motioned with his hand, a too-eager expression on his saggy face.

"No, I will wait here. I can pay you for the cooking pot."

He grunted, then turned and went inside. He came back holding a black iron pot. A young man stood just behind him in the shadows.

Margaretha lifted her purse without untying it and opened it, offering the man two silver coins.

"More," the man said.

She needed the money to buy horses for the long journey to Marienberg. "No. Two is enough," she said. She still didn't like the look on his face.

A woman ran toward her carrying a small iron pot. "Here! You can have mine for one silver coin!" She smiled.

Margaretha liked her face, so she smiled back and gave her the coin. After the woman looked it over, she handed Margaretha the pot. It was heavier than she had expected and she almost dropped it.

The man in the doorway growled, then mumbled something under his breath that Margaretha did not understand. She did not look back again, but walked through the little village the way she had come, toward the hiding place in the forest where she had left Anne and Colin. She put the loaves of bread into the pot while she walked and held it against her hip, keeping it away from her purse, dangling against her thigh, and the fragile eggs inside.

The hair on the back of her neck prickled, as if someone was watching her. She quickened her pace, wishing she had not insisted she could go into the village alone and buy food. She had assumed this small village was like Hagenheim's Marktplatz, a safe and friendly place to buy and sell.

Perhaps she was only imagining that eyes were still watching her. She was almost out of sight of the little wattle-and-daub buildings. As she rounded a bend in the road, she slowed her pace, hitching the pot a little higher on her hip. Her fears were foolish and imaginary.

Footsteps sounded behind her. She turned her head to look, and someone shoved her in the back. She fell to her knees, dropping the pot in the dust of the road.

Chapter
19

Colin stepped out onto the road and walked in the direction he had seen Margaretha go. Perhaps he should not have let her go by herself. After all, how many times had she gone to market to buy food? Probably none.

He had been walking for less than a minute when he heard a startled cry and a hollow, metallic sound, like something heavy hitting the ground.

He began to run, and rounded a bend in the road. Several feet ahead, a man was standing over Lady Margaretha. With one hand he held her by the throat, and with his other hand he was grabbing at her purse.

A roar left Colin's throat as he charged forward. The man looked up just as Colin leapt through the air. He let go of Margaretha's throat. Colin tackled him, knocking him backward into the ground. Without waiting for the man to recover, Colin drew his fist back and slammed his knuckles into his nose.

"How dare you touch this lady!" Colin ground out between clenched teeth.

The scrawny man cowered beneath Colin, holding his hands up over his face. When Colin lifted himself off him, he saw that Margaretha's attacker was little more than a skinny, raggedly dressed youth, not even as old as Margaretha. He scrabbled backward, dragging himself away surprisingly fast on his hands and feet.

Several villagers were coming their way, no doubt to see what the commotion was. Colin allowed the man to get up and run back toward them.

Margaretha. Colin turned and ran back to her. She was on her knees, staring down into her leather purse. He knelt beside her and gently placed his hand on her arm. "Are you hurt?"

She shook her head and touched her neck.

"Let me see." He pulled her hand away. There were slight red marks on her skin, but no bruises that he could see. An image of Philippa's bruised neck leapt to the fore of his mind.

"I am well," she whispered, and lowered her head so he couldn't look into her eyes. Her hands were shaking as she pulled a cracked egg out from among her coins. Her voice trembled as she said, "He tried to take my purse."

The air rushed from his chest at how forlorn she sounded. What was he thinking, allowing her to go alone? "I'm so sorry I wasn't here to protect you." His words coincided with a stabbing pain, like a knife between his ribs, and once again he saw Philippa as she was dragged from the river, her neck covered in bruises ... then John's unseeing eyes staring up at the sky.

"Are you sure you're not hurt?" He wanted to see her face, but he didn't want to force her to look at him. "Let me do that." Colin took the broken egg from her hand and tossed it away. Four more eggs lay inside, but they all seemed to be intact. He drew the drawstring closed and gave it back to her.

He helped her stand, and she wiped her face with the back of her hand. She bent and picked up a black pot sitting on the ground with two loaves of bread inside. "At least our bread didn't get dirty."

Her voice was quiet, and when she looked up at him, she wasn't crying. "I'm grateful you came when you did, or we would have lost the money we need to buy horses." She seemed to make an attempt at a smile.

Should he put his arm around her? He wanted to comfort her but he didn't want to make her uncomfortable. "Forgive me for not getting here sooner." His stomach clenched at the thought of that man hurting her. "If you want me to, I will go find that little pond scum and make him sorry he ever thought about stealing from you."

"No, no, I don't want …" She shook her head. "Please, let us get back to Anne."

Colin walked beside her. She stayed quite close to him, her arm brushing his once, then a second time, as they made their way back to the little cove in the woods.

Once back, they all ate the bread, even Anne, who complained, "This is barley bread! I don't eat barley bread. It tastes like dirt," as she tore off another piece.

Colin built a fire and carried water in the pot from a nearby stream to cook the eggs that had not been smashed when she'd fallen to her knees and struggled with her attacker.

While the eggs cooked, Colin asked Margaretha about what happened at the village. At first she was quiet and barely answered him, but soon she began to tell exactly what had happened, the way the people in the village had looked at her, and what they had said to her. Seeing she was her talkative self again, he relaxed against a tree trunk and stretched out his legs. As long as she was quiet and unsmiling, he worried she might have some hidden injury. Her chatter reassured him that, just as she had not suffered damage from getting thrown from the dangerous black stallion, she had survived her attack unscathed.

Thank you, God.

Margaretha was pleased to see Anne eating one of the eggs. As much as she'd complained about the bread, she hadn't said anything about the egg—although it would have tasted better with a little salt.

Margaretha felt better now that her stomach was full. It was good to sit in their quiet, secluded spot in the forest and rest her tired feet. Her shoes were not very sturdy and wouldn't last long if they had to walk much farther. They needed to find horses, and soon. Her family's lives depended on it.

Margaretha stood. "We should go."

After Colin covered their fire with dirt and poured the water from the pot over the mound, they set out on the south road toward Marienberg.

Anne, as soon as they started walking, grinned smugly at Colin, "I know you want to protect me from danger, but I am quite certain my father and his servants can keep me safe from Lord Claybrook's guards. So, since I know the way and don't need any help, I am going home."

Colin didn't acknowledge her words, and Anne's smile changed to pouting lips and crossed arms.

"You should go home," he announced. "We will escort you there. And I think Lady Margaretha should stay with you too."

"We already talked about this." Margaretha clenched her fists. Heat crept up her neck and into her cheeks. "I am going with you to Marienberg Castle to get men to fight Claybrook. I will not sit like a frightened little girl at my uncle's house."

Anne huffed and crossed her arms again.

Colin's jaw looked like it was cut from stone. She plainly read his meaning.

"Lady Margaretha, you can trust me to go to Marienberg Castle, get help, and save your family." He glanced sideways at her as they walked. "This journey will be perilous. Look what has already happened, when you were attacked at that village. I don't want you to be hurt, and you will be safe at Lord Rupert's manse."

Heat pricked her face. She knew she had been foolish to show her money and purse to all those people in the village. She had not been on her guard when the man ran up behind her and attacked her, and to Colin she must look like a sheltered, naïve girl who didn't know the least thing about taking care of herself. The thought of him having to rescue her suddenly made her furious, mostly at herself.

Margaretha couldn't seem to stop herself from saying, "I will not let anything like that happen again. I will not need you to save me again, and I will not be dropped off like a pile of dirty laundry."

"It isn't like that at all." But Colin's voice did not sound a bit conciliatory; he was not backing down either. "A young, beautiful lady walking around the countryside, unprotected except by a man like me—untrained in warfare—with only a small dagger as a weapon? It is beyond foolish. What kind of person would I be if I allowed it?"

"You do not have a choice in the matter! I have a will of my own, and I am not married, and I have no master with a right to tell me what to do."

She had almost allowed his mention of her being "beautiful" to soften her. But she couldn't allow him to deter her from her purpose. "My family is in danger. I must help them." She felt the tears well up behind her eyes and was horrified. Now was the absolute worst moment for her to be hit with an urge to cry. She swallowed, forcing the tears back. "You need me to go with you. If we both go, we can help each other, and there is a better chance of getting there. Besides, you simply cannot stop me. I am going, and I will not be deterred."

They were standing in the road, glaring at each other. Anne looked on, frowning in obvious disgust.

Margaretha started walking again, as if the argument was over and she had won.

"I will not allow you to put yourself in danger." Colin's tone was adamant.

"You cannot stop me." At the risk of sounding boastful, she said, "I took care of myself and Anne in the castle. I saved us all by knocking out the guards and taking us through the secret tunnel. And therefore, I am going."

"I want you to stay with Lady Anne. Why can't you understand? This will be a dangerous journey." A muscle twitched in his jaw, as if he was clenching his teeth.

She truly did not understand why he was so determined to leave her behind. Unless ... "If I annoy you, why don't you just be honest and say so." She blurted this new thought before she could bite it back. Her heart constricted painfully in her chest. Was he trying to get rid of her because she talked too much? Did she annoy him so much? Well, of course she did. She annoyed everyone when she talked too much, which was all the time.

"No." Colin frowned.

Of course he wouldn't admit it.

"No, you don't annoy me. I just don't want you to get killed."

They walked on in silence. Margaretha quickened her pace so that she was walking slightly ahead of Anne and Colin, since it seemed she could no longer hold back the tears. She knew she probably sounded ridiculous. Perhaps he did simply want her to be safe. In her anguish and frustration, her family's faces rose before her—her mother; her sisters, Kirstyn and Adela; her sister-in-law, Gisela, and her unborn baby; her brothers, Wolfgang and Steffan. And what would happen to her father and Valten when they came back to Hagenheim and found it under siege by that evil Claybrook? Would he manage to carry out his plan to kill them?

If she were honest, the tears also sprang from wondering

if Colin found her company so tedious and annoying that he wanted to get rid of her. But she pushed that thought away.

Instead she considered poor Bezilo, so badly beaten and wounded. Pictured Claybrook's guards, whom she herself had bashed in the head with her candlestick, lying dead on the grass after Bezilo finished them off with the sword. *O God, what has happened to my life?* This wasn't supposed to happen. *Will I be able to make it to Marienberg before something worse happens? Will you keep my family safe until I return? Will I ever be able to return to Hagenheim?*

This was not the sort of prayer to give her the courage to defy Colin, and not the sort that would help her stop crying. She wiped the tears as discreetly as possible, hoping Colin and Anne wouldn't know she was crying, since they were behind her and could only see her back.

O Father God, I know nothing is impossible for You. I am not putting my faith in anything but You—not the money in my purse, nor my status as the daughter of a duke, not in Colin's ability to protect me, nor even in myself. My faith is in You. You are mighty to save, and I will not waver in my faith. I know You care for me, and nothing is too hard for You.

Her tears had all dried up by the end of that prayer. A sense of peace washed over her and she walked with a more confident step. *Thank you, God.*

Colin suspected Margaretha was crying by the way she kept lifting her hands to her face. He sighed. *God, help me. I can't allow her to be killed. Help me convince her to stay with Lady Anne. I just want to keep her safe. Why can't she be reasonable?* But Colin felt no peace at all after that prayer. Was God even listening to him? Surely God wouldn't want him to take her with him.

"What does your home look like?" Anne asked, a flirtatious smile on her face. Uh-oh.

He looked askance at her. "It's ... gray."

"Gray stone?"

"Yes."

"I've always wanted to go to England." Anne smiled meaningfully.

Once again, he wondered why he had told her his lineage. Though he knew why. Pride, stupid pride. He was tired of being treated first like a poor mad indigent, then a mute stable boy. His pride had risen up and he'd declared himself both wealthy and powerful by the world's standards. Now he would have to pay for that bit of folly.

"Is it a castle?"

"In a sense."

"With towers?"

"Yes."

"What's it called?"

"Le Wyse House."

"Not very grand."

Colin shrugged. He was still trying to figure out an argument that would convince Margaretha to stay behind.

"What did you say your father's title was?"

"Earl of Glynval."

"That sounds very well. Is Glynval a grand place?"

"No. It is a small village."

"Oh. But he has land holdings in other parts of England?"

"Yes."

"Are you always so talkative?" Her hand was on her hip.

"Are you?"

"*I'm* not the one with a reputation for talking too much." She angled her head in Margaretha's direction and raised her eyebrows.

Was it his imagination, or did Margaretha's shoulders stiffen? She spun around and faced Anne.

"Anne, you have always treated me with contempt and petty mean-spiritedness, and I'm tired of it. If you cannot treat me as a friend and a relative, the way I have treated you, then don't bother to come visit me at Hagenheim anymore when this is all over."

"Ach! I did not know you had such a temper, Margaretha." But Anne said nothing more to Margaretha, and they continued walking.

Anne tried to make conversation with Colin occasionally, but for half an hour, Margaretha never spoke. Anne even invited Colin to come to visit her when all was done saving Hagenheim and capturing Lord Claybrook.

He was afraid he would never be able to convince Margaretha to stay with her cousin now, although he still hoped she was softening. When they were nearly to Lord Rupert and Lady Anne's home, Colin caught up with Margaretha and took a peek at her face. Before he could say anything, she unclenched her teeth to say, "I'm coming with you. You can't stop me."

No. Not softening at all.

Chapter
20

Margaretha hardened herself to the disap-
pointed look on Colin's face. Even though his lip was swollen
and he still had traces of the blue and greenish bruises on his
face, she couldn't allow herself to feel any pity for him, not until
she was no longer afraid he would try to leave her with Anne.

Anne quickened her pace as they drew near her home,
causing them all to walk faster. The two-story stone house
looked quiet. There was no sign of Claybrook's guards. Colin
asked Anne to wait, but she ran toward the house, leaving
Margaretha and Colin staring after her from their hiding place
behind some trees.

"Margaretha." Colin turned toward her. His expression was
intense, reminding her of how passionate he had been when
she'd first seen him in Frau Lena's chambers. He fastened his
dark blue eyes so powerfully on her that she couldn't look away.

"I will not be responsible for you." There was a note of warning in his voice. "If you are killed, it will be your own fault for
being stubborn." He glared at her. "This is your last chance to
stay here and be safe."

"I will not stay here. My family—every person in the world
that I love—is in danger."

He looked as if he wanted to say more, but he only pursed
his lips, turned away, and started walking.

Margaretha went after him. He stopped when he was parallel to the stable behind the house.

"Do you think it would be wrong," Margaretha asked, as they both stared at the stables, "to take two horses from my uncle's stable? My father will pay him back."

"I was contemplating the same thing. But we must be careful. Claybrook's guards could be watching the house."

"Perhaps they haven't gotten here yet."

Colin squinted as he continued to stare at the stable.

A young man walked out of the door and across the stable yard. He wore the plain brown work clothes of a stable boy, and he walked slowly, not like someone who was anxious or under any sort of watch. "Indeed, I think we can go without fear. I don't believe Claybrook's men are here yet."

"Let me go. You stay here."

"No. You will run off and leave me."

He gave her a shrewd look, and she knew she had guessed the truth.

Without waiting to hear any more arguments from him, Margaretha darted out of the trees and crossed the road just as the stable boy turned and went inside the kitchen behind the house. She ran as quietly as she could. Just as she was almost to the stable door, Colin caught up with her. He darted into the stable ahead of her.

Neither of them spoke as they each worked to saddle a horse. Margaretha's heart pounded in the dark, musty stable, the pungent odor of horse manure stinging her nostrils. Every glance at Colin showed his concentration, that old intensity and determination that so often tensed his features.

They worked quickly, Margaretha whispering a prayer that the two horses they had chosen would prove to be strong yet cooperative.

Finally, both horses were saddled and ready. Colin grabbed

her lower leg through her skirt and boosted her up. Her heart thumped extra hard when she realized he wasn't trying to get away from her.

He vaulted into the saddle of his own horse, and they ducked their heads as they guided their mounts out of the stable door. Margaretha took just enough time to glance around. Not seeing anyone, she spurred her sprightly brown mare forward, following just behind Colin and his tall black gelding.

Margaretha wanted to urge her horse into a gallop, but she held back and kept her at a fast walk. Once they were more than a hundred yards from the house, Colin nudged his gelding into a canter, then an all-out gallop, and Margaretha followed suit. Soon her hair was whipping across her face. She found herself smiling, the wind drying her teeth.

They slowed their pace, not wanting to exhaust the horses. By then she'd decided: it was a long journey to Marienberg, and Colin had not wanted to bring her at all. She would only speak to him if she was forced to. He would see that she was not annoying. Somehow, she would prove that she could stay quiet, and he would be sorry he tried to get rid of her.

It was getting dark. They'd been riding for hours, and Colin still needed to find food.

He had planned to travel off the road, but as the sides of the road were so thickly forested, they had stayed on it to make better time. If they had been walking or riding in a slow-moving, donkey-drawn cart, it might have been different. But they were riding fast horses, and should be relatively safe, or at least able to outrun anyone who came after them. He hoped so, anyway.

After not seeing anyone for several miles, they began to see a few people on the road, so they must be close to a village. He certainly would not send Margaretha to get food again, but if he went alone, he'd have to leave her alone. No, it was probably best to go together.

They rode slowly through the village. He found the bakery, and they bought enough bread for two days. They found pork at the butcher's shop, some cheese and eggs, and bought some blankets and an iron pan, since they'd had to leave their pot behind. They carried their provisions until they were out of sight of the village. Then Colin tied everything to the back of their horses behind their saddles. They mounted and set off again.

When it got so dark they could barely see the road, Colin found a place for them to stop and sleep for the night. It was in the edge of a barley field, at the border of some trees, far enough away from the road that no one could see or hear them. They tied their horses to a tree and fed them some oats they had bought from the villagers. The stream that meandered near the road provided water.

Margaretha rubbed the horses and talked softly to them while he built a fire and fixed a meal of fried pork and eggs and bread. They ate in silence. Was Margaretha too tired to talk? She'd talked to the horses. But now that he thought about it, she'd spoken hardly a word since they left Anne's house.

He put away their provisions after dousing their fire with water and dirt, then wrapped everything in a rough woolen tarp and tied it with a bit of twine. He then handed her one of the blankets. She took it and turned away from him without a word.

He sighed. "Margaretha." He touched her shoulder and she stilled. "Why are you not talking to me? Are you angry?"

She turned partially around. "What was the true reason you wanted me to stay at Anne's and not come with you? Was it because I talk too much and you knew I would annoy you?"

He stood only a foot away from her. The moon was surprisingly bright. He moved in front of her so they were standing face to face.

"I told you why, and it was not because you talk too much." He said the words softly and shook his head. "I told you, I wanted to keep you safe. I let my friend John be killed by Claybrook's men. I let Philippa be murdered by Claybrook. And when you were attacked . . . You could have been killed by that ruffian who tried to steal your purse. If something bad happened to you, I don't think I could bear it."

She looked him in the eye. "Those deaths were not your fault."

This time he looked away. "John's death was." He sighed. He should not tell her what happened, but he found himself saying, "I had put my cloak on John only a few minutes before Claybrook's men found us. They had been told to kill the man with the red cloak." He clenched his fist around the pommel of his saddle and closed his eyes as shame crowded his chest.

"I am so sorry, Colin." She placed her gentle hand over his, and he loosened his grip. "You are not to blame. That was not your fault, and I thank God you were not also killed."

She squeezed his hand, and he felt the shame melt away a bit.

"Thank you for being concerned for me," she said. "No one could accuse you of not caring about your friends, of not being willing to help others. It wasn't your fault John was killed. The blame lies with Claybrook and his men, not you."

A lump formed in his throat. Her skin looked as soft as velvet in the moonlight. He thought of reaching out and brushing his fingers across her cheek. "And you are not annoying." He leaned closer as he realized the truth of what he was about to say. "Life is more cheerful when you talk to me."

"Oh." Her mouth hung open. "Truly?"

"Truly." A warning, like a voice of caution, whispered to his spirit. It warred with the other voice that said how sweet she looked, her face upturned toward his.

He cleared his throat. "We'd better try to sleep."

"Yes." She turned away from him and they spread their blankets, she on one side of the fire and he on the other. It was a cool
night, and so he showed Margaretha how to roll herself up in the
blanket for extra warmth.

When he closed his eyes to sleep, he could still see
Margaretha, the way she had looked in the moonlight. Her voice
was soft and sweet, and her smile was completely devoid of ill
will. But he also remembered Anne saying Margaretha would
never leave her family. England was a very long way from the
Holy Roman Empire.

He should guard his heart, for he could see it was in danger,
and they were still a long way from Marienberg.

Margaretha slept as soundly as she did in her own soft bed in
Hagenheim. She awoke and wondered why she couldn't move her
arms, then remembered she had wrapped herself in her blanket.

Colin was not lying where he had been the night before.
Hearing a noise, she saw him saddling one of the horses. The sun
had not made an appearance yet, but the sky was streaked with
pale pink and orange.

They broke their fast with some bread and cheese and were
soon on the road again.

When the sun was high overhead, they stopped to rest and
water the horses at the small stream that meandered near the
roadside.

"I know I shouldn't complain, but it is hard to sit so long in a
saddle." Margaretha resisted the urge to rub her sore backside as
she watched Colin check the saddles and the packs and tighten
them. Her hands were blistered from holding the reins. They
both stretched and arched their backs while the horses grazed.
"I will be overjoyed to see Marienberg Castle." She didn't want
to tell Colin, but she'd also been thinking of her family back at

Hagenheim Castle, wondering if they were being mistreated, if they were scared or hungry or cold, and if her father and Valten had found out about Lord Claybrook's treachery. Were they attacking Claybrook's guards at this very moment, outnumbered and getting beaten back?

She must be learning self-control, because she stopped herself from mentioning these fears to Colin. What good would it do? She'd probably start crying and that would not help anyone. Tears only made men feel uncomfortable, and they gave her a headache.

"I am grateful to you for wanting to help me and my family and the people of Hagenheim." Margaretha occupied herself with checking the horses' hooves to make sure they hadn't picked up rocks or thrown a shoe. "I know you want to capture Claybrook for your own reasons, but you had no reason to want to help me and my family. If there is anything my father or my cousin, the Duke of Marienberg, can do for you, I am sure they will be pleased to reward you."

Colin had been filling their water flasks while she checked the horses' hooves. He now sat down and stretched his legs out on the ground and fixed her with a serious stare. "Lady Margaretha, I'm afraid you think more of me than I deserve. The truth is, I came here for the sole purpose of capturing Claybrook and taking him back to England to face punishment for his murders."

"So you would not help us if it were not for wanting revenge on Lord Claybrook?"

"Not revenge. Justice." He seemed to think for a moment, then lay down on the grass, reminding her of when he had lain on Frau Lena's sick bed, ranting about Claybrook so passionately that she had thought he was mad. He said quietly, "But I would have helped you and your family, Margaretha, even if I had not known of Claybrook's previous evil deeds." He smiled at her, then closed his eyes.

Something about the way he looked at her made him seem even more handsome. But she refused to think about that. She stepped to the edge of the stream and started washing her hands in the cold water. "I believe you *would* have helped us anyway, and that is to your credit. I am thankful to have your assistance, for whatever reason. However, I must say, I am not sure your desire for justice is not simply a thirst for vengeance. You should be careful to leave room for God's justice."

Margaretha took a drink of the cold stream water. It wasn't quite as good as the well water at Hagenheim, but almost.

"Vengeance?"

Margaretha glanced over her shoulder. The word seemed to have riled him into a sitting position as he squinted at her.

"You think me guilty of seeking revenge, then?"

"I am sorry if I sounded accusatory." She wasn't sure why, but she had to fight the smile that was creeping into her face. He was so intense. "A desire for justice is a good desire, and I believe you have that. I also think you ought to be careful not to let it lead you into vengefulness."

He stared at her but didn't say anything.

"I sometimes say things before I think, things I shouldn't, but I'm not sorry I warned you not to be vengeful." She almost said, *because I care about you*, but her breath hitched in her throat and stopped her. He was almost like an older brother to her, after all they had been through together in such a short time, and she did care ... a lot. Although the way she felt about him was not the same as the way she cared for her brothers, she didn't want to dwell on that too much. When this was all over, he would go back to his family in England, and she would go back to her pleasant life in Hagenheim.

"Perhaps I do want revenge." He picked up a chestnut off the ground beside him, seemed to be testing its weight, then threw it into the stream. With a hollow *plop* it sank out of sight.

"But I think I am justified, after he murdered an innocent girl simply because she was pregnant with his child and he didn't want to marry her."

Understandable, but was it justified? Margaretha wasn't sure what to say, but for the moment, with his lips pursed in that tense way, she didn't think him quite as handsome as she had a few moments before.

Chapter
21

For the rest of the day, Colin thought about what Margaretha said. Their horses made good progress on the reasonably smooth roads. He might not admit it to Margaretha, but he did want revenge. He wanted revenge for his sister's sake, whose innocence and sense of security had been shattered by the indefensible murder of her friend. He wanted revenge for his friend John's sake, who had died because of his loyalty to Colin. He wanted revenge for his own suffering at the hands of Claybrook's guards. And what difference did it make whether you called it revenge or justice? Wasn't it the same thing? Surely God understood that Colin needed to bring Claybrook to justice.

But Colin also knew that it mattered to God what was in his heart. Motives mattered. And he hadn't felt much peace — any peace, if he were honest with himself — since he left England.

He was too tired to think any more about this. It was already dark and they needed to find a place to sleep for the night.

He signaled to Margaretha and she turned her horse to follow him off the road and into the trees. Once again they were able to find the stream that wound close to the road. As he and Margaretha unsaddled their horses and tied them to a tree, Margaretha began saying, "We should only have about two more days of hard riding before we reach Marienberg. The horses are holding up well. I am thankful to see that. I'm not sure my mare at home would have fared as well."

Colin thought he heard horses' hooves. The sound was getting closer, and Margaretha must have heard them too, because she stopped talking and listened.

The horses — there must have been at least three of them — slowed on the road, which was only about twenty feet from where they were standing in the trees. Male voices were talking but he couldn't make out the words. Then he heard, "... stop at this stream for the night."

Margaretha moved nearer to Colin and the horses until she was standing close enough he could hear her breathing. It was too dark for him to see more than the outline of her, but she was facing the direction of the voices.

Four or five horses and riders left the road at almost the same spot where Colin and Margaretha had. The riders dismounted and led their horses to the stream. In the light of the moon, Colin could see that the men were wearing red tunics with gold stitching.

Margaretha grabbed his arm. She leaned close and whispered in his ear, "Those are Claybrook's men."

"Don't move," Colin whispered back to her.

Her hand still gripped his arm. Claybrook's men milled around, talking and preparing to sleep there. If none of them came toward where he and Margaretha and their horses were standing, perhaps they could leave quietly and not be seen.

One by one, the men headed into the woods, no doubt to relieve themselves, then came back. Colin held his breath as the last man headed into the woods, walking within ten feet of them. Margaretha stood still next to him, but the horses were busy munching on what grass they could find at their feet. Would the sound of their powerful teeth biting through the grass reach the man's ears as he walked past?

The man disappeared into the trees.

The others were talking as they set up camp, made a small fire, and seemed to be cooking something. As he added some sticks to the fire, one man said, "That Lady Anne is a fine one. When she marries Sir Reginald, think he'll make her do the cooking?" His voice rumbled with laughter.

Another one snorted and said, "She's too fine a lady for cooking. Reginald will lose all his money trying to keep her in silks."

The first one said, "She must not have any love for her kinsmen. She hardly batted an eye when Reginald told her he was promised a castle and holdings when Duke Wilhelm was dead."

Margaretha gasped and covered her mouth with her hand.

He went on. "She even told us the color of the horses the duke's daughter and Lord le Wyse had left there on." They chuckled.

One of the other men standing nearby laughed so loudly, he drowned out their conversation about Lady Anne.

Margaretha clenched her fist over her mouth as she stared out at the men.

Colin was still watching and trying to listen for the man who was in the forest and had passed so close to them. He suddenly emerged from the trees at the same spot he had entered, about ten feet from Colin and Margaretha, and joined the other soldiers. The loud talking and laughing must have covered up the soft sounds of the horses' chewing, because it didn't look as though he had heard or seen them hiding there.

"What should we do?" Margaretha whispered.

"I think we should go now before things get too quiet." In the darkness, Colin took her hand in his, his heart pounding hard against the wall of his chest. He placed his lips against her hair and whispered, "Take your horse's reins and we'll lead them back, farther into the trees. Follow me."

Margaretha nodded and did as he said. They led the horses away from Claybrook's men. He tried to let go of Margaretha's hand, but she clung to him.

Once they were far enough away that they could barely hear the men's voices, Colin changed course, crossed the road, and walked into the cover of the trees.

"What should we do?" Margaretha asked.

"Are you too tired to ride?"

"No. I can ride."

"I think we should put some distance between us and Claybrook's men. We can stay in the trees until we're past them, then ride for an hour or two. Then we'll try to get a few hours' sleep, get up, and be off again at dawn so they won't catch up to us."

"It is a good plan."

She was standing very close and looking up at him. Her eyes were big and round, but it was so dark he could barely see anything. So why was he so aware of how near her lips were to his? Why did the thought of kissing her seem burned into his brain like a mandate from both the king of England and the Holy Roman Emperor?

What would happen if he leaned down, just a bit closer? Would she close her eyes? Would she stand on tip-toe to reach him? Would she put her arms around his neck?

He was an addlepated lack-wit. She would never want him to kiss her, because even if she cared for him, she would never want to leave her family. She loved them, and rightfully so. As far as he could tell, they were wonderful, loving people. And now they were dependent on them, Margaretha and Colin, to help save them.

Remember why you're here.

Colin stepped back, then turned away from her and continued walking. He had told her the plan. There was no other reason for them to speak to each other.

"Colin, were you frightened?" Margaretha whispered as she grabbed onto his arm and walked close beside him. "I was so scared they would see us, I was afraid to breathe!"

She had no idea he had just been thinking about kissing her. She prattled on, obviously not feeling what he was feeling. That was as it should be. She was blameless and naïve, a sweet girl who was incapable of scheming about making the most advantageous marriage for herself, unlike her cousin Anne, who would sell her own cousin and marry a heartless lout to gain wealth and position for herself.

And he was nearly as wicked, thinking about stealing a kiss from an innocent girl who was alone with him in the dark, far away from her family, when he knew he could never marry her.

He was worse than an addlepated lack-wit.

"Did you hear what they said about Anne?" she whispered. "I can't believe she would agree to marry Claybrook's captain! What a fiend he must be! She must know he is not a good man. Perhaps he threatened her and she had no choice. I know she has always desired to make a good match for herself, but even she couldn't want to marry a brute like that Sir Reginald. And she told them the color of our horses, but you told her to tell them where we were going. But to tell them the color of our horses . . . She may have been afraid of them, but if she had wanted to help us escape, she could have lied about the horses. You may have already guessed this, but Anne has never been a very kind or loving cousin."

They were getting closer to the place where Claybrook's men were preparing to sleep. "I had better stop talking now," she whispered.

The close proximity of danger certainly helped when one was trying to not think about the beautiful girl who was clinging to one's arm.

They walked carefully, and Colin prayed neither of the horses would neigh and alert Claybrook's men.

When they had walked far enough beyond the men that he didn't think they could hear or see them, he turned toward Margaretha and she let go of his arm. "Now we can ride. I'll boost you into the saddle." But his palms started to sweat at the thought of grabbing her leg and tossing her up. Ridiculous. He had thought nothing of taking hold of her and tossing her into the saddle numerous times before. What was wrong with him?

She held on to the pommel of her saddle and stood waiting for the help he always gave her.

He bent and grasped her foot with one hand and her lower leg, through the fabric of her skirts, with the other and boosted her up. But he boosted her harder than he meant to—much harder than he needed to. She soared right over the saddle and cried out—a sharp little cry of alarm—and disappeared on the other side of the horse.

Margaretha landed on her arm and right shoulder in the leaves and sticks on the other side.

Oh no. She had cried out when she felt herself falling. Had Claybrook and his men heard her? Would they come and find them?

She scrambled to get up, pulling at her skirts, which were tangled around her legs. The next thing she knew, Colin grabbed her around the waist and lifted her off the ground.

"Are you hurt?" he whispered.

"No."

His hands still on her waist, he lifted her onto the saddle. Then he mounted his own horse and they started through the trees at a slow trot. They guided the horses onto the road, and after a short canter, they broke into a gallop, the pale moon lighting their way on the deserted road.

They rode without talking, and when Margaretha began to fear the horses would be harmed by how fast they were going, Colin slowed his horse and she did the same.

"I'm sorry I fell, and that I cried out," Margaretha said, "but you threw me over the saddle!"

"Forgive me. I did not intend to. You weren't hurt, were you?"

"No." Margaretha couldn't help smiling at the chagrined look on his face. How had he made such a mistake? "What were you thinking?"

He didn't answer. Was he angry because she was laughing at him?

Finally, he said, "It was an unpardonable mistake, especially at such a time. I am sorry."

"I wouldn't say it was unpardonable. I don't think they even heard us. We were too far away, and they were still talking loudly."

"I hope you are right."

They rode on for what seemed like a long time. Margaretha was hungry and could barely keep her eyes open. Finally, Colin said, "We can stop here."

They guided their horses off the road and into a thickly wooded area. While they tied their horses and prepared for sleep, Colin said, "Please forgive me for throwing you so hard. I suppose I was ... nervous."

"Of course I forgive you. I was not hurt. When I'm nervous, I talk too much and too fast. I also talk too much when I'm joyful, and when I'm angry—all the time, except when I'm sad. Besides, you were only trying to help me get on my horse. You mistook your own strength. But just now I am too tired to talk. And also a little sad, because I've started to think how much I miss my mother and my sisters, and that makes me want to sleep so I can't think about it." Margaretha had just lain down on her blanket, near where Colin had spread his own blanket. She closed her eyes and immediately felt herself drifting to sleep. "I didn't let you say much, did I? It is a terrible fault of mine ..." Her words were getting softer and becoming slurred, so she gave up on her apology and immediately fell asleep.

"You must get up, Lady Margaretha."

She opened her eyes and saw ... nothing. It was still dark. Then she made out a form standing near her.

"I'm sorry, but we need to go." It was Colin. "We don't want to risk Claybrook's guards catching up to us today."

Margaretha sat up, but her eyes didn't want to open all the way. She shook out her blanket and folded it up. Colin took it from her and pressed something into her hand.

"Here is your breakfast. Some bread and cheese. I dare not start a fire, even though the bread is stale and would taste better toasted."

"Oh, that is all right. Did you have some? Good. I am ravenous so I don't mind the staleness." Margaretha chewed the dry food while Colin finished packing away her blanket, then he handed her the water flask.

"It should be daylight in less than an hour," Colin said.

In a few minutes, after Margaretha had finished her bread, they were on their horses and heading south again.

They rode at a fast pace only long enough for Margaretha to remember what she had been saying when she fell asleep the night before. And then they rounded a bend in the road and were confronted with five men and their horses blocking the road.

"Don't stop!" Colin yelled. He seemed intent on riding straight through them.

Margaretha calculated where to steer her mare so she wouldn't trample anyone or hurt her horse. Colin burst through the middle, between two men, who grabbed at his reins but missed. Margaretha tried to do the same, but one of the men seized her by the arm and yanked her off the horse, wrenching her shoulder.

Margaretha screamed and so did her horse, which reared and pawed the air.

She slid out of the saddle and fell on her hip in the dirt. Someone hauled her up roughly by her arm.

At least Colin had gotten away. But then she saw him coming back, driving his horse toward them, a look of intense fury in his face. When he drew near, one of the men threw a stick of wood aimed at his head.

Colin partially blocked the blow with his arm. Margaretha screamed again. Two more men joined in the attack on Colin. One grabbed the horse's bridle and the other grabbed him and dragged him off his horse.

Chapter
22

The men swarmed around Colin. They struck and kicked him.

Margaretha yelled, "Stop it! In the name of Duke Wilhelm of Hagenheim, stop it! Or I will have you all beheaded!" She was so desperate to stop them, she said the first thing that came to her mind.

They did stop beating him and lifted him off the ground. It took three of them to hold him, as he kept fighting to get loose. His lip was bleeding again, and it looked as if they had reopened the half-healed cut above his hairline, because a trickle of blood ran down his forehead.

They hurt him. A dry sob escaped her and tears stung her eyes.

A fourth man seemed to be searching his clothes and soon found the dagger the Hagenheim gaoler had given him. The man, who had dirty blond hair and several days of stubble on his face, grinned as he held up the weapon. He walked toward Margaretha. "And who might you be, invoking the name and authority of Duke Wilhelm of Hagenheim?"

"Don't tell him anything!" Colin shouted, but of course, he said the words in English and the dirty brigand didn't understand him.

Margaretha glared defiantly at the ugly, gap-toothed man. She would not give him the satisfaction of seeing fear in her face.

He looked her up and down, no doubt taking in her dress, which, though stained and wrinkled and even a bit torn, was of fine materials and obviously not the clothing of a poor peasant. "I said ... who might you be?"

He leaned closer, his face only inches from hers as he pointed the dagger at her throat.

"I am from the town of Hagenheim. And Duke Wilhelm does not allow brigands to mistreat his people. He punishes them."

"Is that so?" He didn't look—or smell—as if he had ever taken a bath or washed his clothes. "I don't think Duke Wilhelm can punish someone he can't catch. Can he?"

The other men laughed, a spiteful, malicious sound. Colin finally stopped struggling. Blood ran down his temple, almost into the corner of his eye, and down his cheek. He was breathing hard and there was a tense look of pain in his eyes.

The sight of his injury sent heat rising to her head.

Margaretha's captor held her by one arm, his fingers biting into her muscle. But her other arm was free. While their apparent leader, the one holding Colin's dagger, glanced back over his shoulder at his comrades, Margaretha stomped the arch of her captor's foot as hard as she could. He loosened his hold on her arm and howled. Almost simultaneously, she struck the leader's hand with her fist and knocked the dagger to the ground. She snatched it up, as her captor had released her and yelped in pain.

She held the dagger out in front of her, pointed at the leader's chest. "Now let go of my friend and get out of here, you despicable excuse for a human."

The five men stared at her, open-mouthed and silent.

The leader whistled, then grinned. "A feisty one. We underestimated you."

Margaretha's fury drained away her energy, and her hands began to shake. "That's right. Now let go of my friend and we will allow you to leave."

He laughed, the hateful sound growing louder and louder. The other men joined in. "You underestimate me as well." He drew a dagger of his own from his belt, a dagger that was longer, and noticeably sharper, than hers. "Now throw your knife down or I will cut your friend into little bits." He stepped toward Colin.

"No, stop!" Her chest clenched painfully at the thought of him cutting Colin.

"Then put down your knife."

"How do I know you won't hurt him, or me?"

"You don't know, but if you don't throw down the knife, you can be sure that I will."

"You're evil." Margaretha threw down the dagger.

He stepped forward and picked it up. "Not as evil as some. All I want is your money, your horses, and all your possessions. I will let you keep your lives." His grin once more revealed the gap between his teeth.

He motioned to the man who had originally been holding Margaretha, and that man came toward her.

She stared him in the eye and said as menacingly as possible, "If you touch me again, I shall make you rue it." Her blood still boiled, especially at the prospect of them finding and taking her money. At least she had left her bracelet at home. And the horses! If they dared to take their horses ... how would she and Colin ever make it to Marienberg?

The man halted, uncertainty in his eyes. His leader snarled at him. "Get her. Now."

What good would it do to struggle? Colin was still being held by the three men, and the leader held their only weapon. The man grasped her wrists and held them behind her back.

The leader walked back to Colin and felt all over him. "Your friend doesn't have any money on him. Where is yours?" He turned to Margaretha.

183

The man holding her pushed her forward and forced her to walk toward him.

"We don't have any money." *Father God, please forgive me for lying.*

He curled his lip at her, then snapped his fingers. "Dog Face, go check their horses and bags."

One of the men, a particularly ugly one, moved toward their horses, which had shied several feet away. He only had a little trouble catching them, then he started untying the bundles behind their saddles.

Colin was still being held by two men. If Margaretha could read the look in his eyes, he was calculating how to get away from them.

The leader crossed his arms, still holding the long dagger, and stroked his scraggly beard with his other hand. "If I had to guess, I'd daresay the girl has the money on her person."

The men holding Colin called out places where they thought she might hide it, so crude and lewd in their speech that Margaretha's face went hot.

"You are all disgusting, vile, and demon possessed to speak that way about me."

They chuckled at her protest. No doubt they saw her as weak and helpless. She should again break free from the man holding her, just to show them she could.

The leader moved quite close to her, until he was only inches away. He wasn't much taller than she was, and he leaned almost nose to nose with her.

"Tell me where your money is and I won't hurt your friend."

"You will get nothing from me."

"Oh no?" He grabbed her by the shoulders and shook her violently, causing her head to snap back and forth. The money in her sleeve rattled.

He stopped shaking her. "I do believe I heard something." His thin lips curled into a smile.

He grabbed her left arm. Her captor let go and the leader stuck his hand up her sleeve. His fingers touched her bare skin and made her shudder in disgust. He found her purse and drew it out. He held it up with a shout.

"What do you think, boys? Shall we go to the inn tonight and feast?"

They all let out a whoop.

Margaretha's chest turned inside out as she stared at her purse, all of their money, in the hands of these dirty thieves.

They searched the bundles on the backs of their horses and found their food and blankets. Once they had examined everything, their leader told them to pack it all back up.

"Shouldn't we take the girl's dress too?" one of the men asked. "It would fetch a good price at the market."

"Why not?" the leader replied with his usual grin. "She won't be attending any balls at Hagenheim Castle any time soon."

They all turned lecherous eyes on her, every one of the men staring at her. Margaretha instinctively raised her fists as she felt all the blood drain from her face.

The dirty robbers let go of both Margaretha and Colin, but there was nothing he could do. He had no weapon, and the world had been spinning around and around ever since they'd kicked him in the head. Still, he was prepared to die protecting Margaretha.

His worst nightmare was happening all over again. Someone he cared about was under his protection, but he couldn't keep her safe.

The men were all looking at her. They started to step toward her, and Margaretha's face went white.

No! He could not let them hurt her. *God, no, please.* Colin didn't know much German, but he knew enough to shout, "*Nein! Hier ist* Lady Margaretha! *Herzog* Wilhelm's *tochter!*"

The men froze. They muttered and glanced at each other, wondering aloud if she was truly Duke Wilhelm's daughter. They seemed to be discussing something among themselves. Would they have enough respect for the duke and the fact that this was his daughter, or at least enough fear of what he would do to them, to not harm her? This strategy would backfire if they decided to hold her for ransom. He had sensed the leader at least had a small amount of decency and respect—a very small amount. Besides, they couldn't hope to escape from Duke Wilhelm's wrath if they hurt his daughter.

They couldn't know that, at the moment, Duke Wilhelm's own life was in danger from Lord Claybrook.

The leader shouted something, and the other men seemed to be arguing with him. The leader shouted again. The others mumbled discontentedly and looked downcast. Then he shouted, "*Laßt uns gehen!*" at them, and they turned to go. They had already tied his gelding and Margaretha's mare to their horses, and soon they were galloping off down the road with all Margaretha's money, their horses—Lord Rupert's horses he and Margaretha had stolen from him—and their food and few possessions they had purchased.

Margaretha stood there, looking bereft but unharmed.

Thank you, God. Colin felt himself leaning precariously to the right. The sun was finally coming up—but unfortunately, the world for him was quickly going dark.

Chapter
23

Margaretha ran to where Colin had slumped to the ground and fell to her knees beside him. "Colin! Can you hear me? Please wake up!" She pushed him onto his back. His head was still bleeding, the blood matting up in his thick hair, and his skin was pale.

A sob burst from her. Tears dripped onto Colin's chest as she clutched his arms. "Don't leave me, please!" She sobbed even harder.

She had to stop this. She couldn't cry, not now when Colin needed her to think and to be strong and help him.

Wiping her face on her sleeve, she blinked the useless tears away. She leaned down and placed her ear against his chest. After a moment, "I hear it! His heart is beating." She touched his face. "You will not die, Colin. God will not let you die." She wasn't sure what prompted her to say that, but it felt good.

She needed to get some water to revive him and to wash the blood from his face. But she had no cloth and no water flask, as the thieves had taken everything.

The stream was not too far off, just beyond the road. She scrambled to her feet and headed toward it. As she ran across the packed dirt of the rutted road, the sun, which was just coming up, glinted off something lying on the road. She stopped to look at it. Colin's dagger. The pale light from the east was glinting off the blade. The men must have dropped it when they'd left.

She bent and snatched it up, then ran to the stream.

The dagger had given her an idea. She washed it off, then used it to cut a large piece of fabric from her white chemise. She dunked it in the cold water, then ran back to Colin carrying the dripping cloth.

She sank to her knees beside him and dabbed the wet cloth on the inside of Colin's wrists, as she had once seen Frau Lena do to someone who had fainted. Next, she held the cloth over the cut on Colin's head and squeezed out the water into his hair. Then she wiped his forehead and his face, where the blood was already starting to dry. She dabbed at the blood on his poor swollen lip as well.

He turned his head slightly and moaned.

He was alive. She continued touching the cold wet cloth to his face, which seemed to be reviving him. "Colin? Can you hear me?"

He opened his eyes only a crack. "Lady Margaretha. You aren't hurt."

"No, of course not. But you are. Where is your pain?"

"Everywhere. Mostly my head." She touched the cold cloth to his forehead, and he put his hand over hers, holding the cloth there. "That feels good." His eyes were closed again. "What happened? I can't remember."

Oh no. After thinking he was mad before, would he have gone mad this time, from all the blows to the head? He had said her name, so he at least remembered her. Perhaps if she explained it to him, he would remember.

"We were on our way to Marienberg to get help. Some evil men were blocking the road. They beat and kicked you and reopened the wound on your head. And I am so angry at them."

Margaretha couldn't talk anymore, as tears choked off her voice. How dare those men hurt Colin?

She had to block those thoughts or she would succumb to the angry tears that were damming up her eyes.

"Thank God they didn't kill you." But that was no good, either. Tears flooded her eyes again at how grateful she was that he was still alive.

"Don't cry," he said, and lifted his hand to her cheek. He brushed his fingers over her face.

His touch seemed to startle the tears away. "I'm sorry. I won't." She stared down into his eyes. What was this strange feeling that squeezed her heart and made it hard to breathe, frightening and exhilarating at the same time? But she must think logically. This was no time for foolishness. She went back to work wiping the blood from his face.

Colin was looking at her with a slight frown, a troubled crease between his eyes. Then he turned his head to look at his surroundings. "I don't remember anything after we got away from the castle. It was night and there were some men in red livery ... Claybrook's men."

"That's right. That was last night. Then this morning we got up about an hour ago and started riding. We came upon those horrible men who stole our horses." And our food, and our money, and our blankets. But she didn't want to overwhelm him.

"Where did you say we were going?" He squinted up at her, as though the light was painful.

"To Marienberg, to get help from the duke, who is my cousin."

"Why were we getting help?" He closed his eyes and rubbed his brow.

"Oh dear. Colin, don't you remember?"

"I ... I remember I came here to fetch Claybrook back to England."

"Yes, but that was weeks ago."

"And I remember I was trying to get to Hagenheim with my friend John, and Claybrook's men murdered him and nearly killed me. When I woke up in Hagenheim Castle, you were there, and I found out Claybrook was at the castle."

"Yes. Lord Claybrook was courting me—"

"But you didn't want to marry him. I remember that." He looked at her with wide, excited eyes.

"Yes. I mean, no, I didn't."

He squeezed his eyes tightly shut, as if trying to remember something. "You were on a black horse. I thought you were about to be killed. The horse stopped and you flew off. Were you hurt? I can't remember."

"No, I was not badly hurt. How does your head feel? Are you feeling pain anywhere else?"

"I think someone kicked me in the side, but nothing feels broken. Except my head." He lifted his hand to his forehead and touched the old wound. He winced. "My head feels broken."

"You just lie still." Margaretha didn't know what else to do. "I don't think you should get up. You might faint. Do you remember yet that we were on our way to Marienberg?"

He kept his eyes closed while he talked. "Marienberg does not sound familiar. But I do remember you didn't want to marry me because you don't want to leave your family."

"Well, I ... I ..." Margaretha felt her face grow hot. "I don't believe anything was ever said about ... that, but ... it is true that I had hoped to marry someone near my family."

His lips parted, then his face gradually became tense. He opened his eyes and squinted up at her. "I am talking like a madman again, aren't I? I remember now. You thought I was mad. You and everyone else at Hagenheim Castle, because I was raving about Claybrook, and no one could understand my English, except you. But even you thought I was mad. I remember now."

Her face seemed to be afflicted with a perpetual blush. "I am sorry about that. I should not have doubted you. You were completely justified in warning me, as it turned out. And I don't believe you are mad now, either. You simply need to rest and your memory will come back to you." But she wasn't nearly as sure as she wished she was.

He opened his eyes. "I'm afraid I don't remember much about the last few days ... or weeks. I'm not sure how long."

"Don't worry. It will come back to you."

"But you and I ... we are ...?" He lifted questioning brows at her.

Margaretha wasn't sure what he was about to say, but she was too afraid to wait for it. "We are friends who are on our way to Marienberg. We escaped from Claybrook and his guards and Hagenheim Castle with Lady Anne, my cousin, and a maid named Britta. Do you remember that?"

"Was I in the dungeon?"

"Yes! You are remembering. We escaped the castle through a tunnel that went from the dungeon to a meadow outside the town wall. Then we found Bezilo, one of my father's trusted guards, and we rescued him from two of Claybrook's men."

"Did Bezilo kill them? With a sword?"

"Yes. Britta went back to Hagenheim and we took Anne to her home, where we stole two horses."

"I remember this. It was good that Anne did not come with us. We stole the horses ... What happened next?"

Why did he think it was good Anne did not come with them? "Well, we rode the rest of that day and all the next day. Then that night we saw five of Claybrook's men, who had decided to stop for the night in almost the same spot we had chosen."

"Yes, I remember that. We were in the woods and it was dark. You were holding on to my arm, and I kissed you."

"What?" Margaretha sat back on her heels. "No. No, that

did not happen." She felt herself blushing more furiously than ever, her breath coming fast at the thought. "I can't imagine why you would think ... no, you did not kiss me." *I would have remembered that.*

"Oh. No, of course not. Forgive me. Of course I didn't ... I wouldn't ..." Now *he* was blushing.

He was very handsome when he blushed.

A tragic expression of horror came over his face. "I almost let you get killed—again. Why didn't you listen to me? I told you this trip was dangerous. Why didn't you stay with Anne?" He closed his eyes and his face was pale. "I failed you. I cannot protect you, Margaretha. You shouldn't have come with me."

"No, you did not fail me." Margaretha touched his face, turning it toward her, and his eyes met hers. "You came back when you could have gone on and left me. You saved me." She felt the tears welling up in her eyes again and blinked them back. "And if you hadn't said that I was Duke Wilhelm's daughter, they would have taken my dress. But after you said that, their leader forced them to leave me alone. You saved me, Colin, from being humiliated, losing my dress, and possibly much worse."

The woebegone look in his eyes faded. She must have convinced him that he had indeed saved her. He placed his hand over hers, and her heart tripped at the warmth and gentleness of his touch.

O God, what would I have done if those robbers had killed him?

"You must be so worried about your family," he said. "We should start walking. We have to get to Marienberg." He started trying to sit up.

"Are you sure you are able to get up?" She helped him by taking hold of his shoulder and arm and pulling him. Once he was sitting, he closed his eyes again.

"Should you lie back down? Are you in pain? You look so

pale. Are you sure you won't faint?" He swayed a bit and she steadied him. "I'm sorry. When I get nervous I talk too much and ask too many questions and don't give the other person enough time to answer. You surely remember that. It's my worst fault. I always say that, but the truth is, I hope that is my worst fault, but people often don't realize what their worst fault is, so maybe it isn't—And I'm doing it again. Forgive me."

"I like hearing you talk." He opened his eyes and smiled. "It's soothing."

Who was this man? No one liked her talking. It was annoying, not soothing.

Colin's head injury had loosened his tongue. First he seemed to know that she wouldn't marry him and why, which she had never discussed with him, then he was saying he had kissed her, which he hadn't, and now he was saying he liked hearing her talk. He had also said last night that her talking sounded cheerful, now that she thought about it. Could he truly think that?

This strange conversation was making her heart leap madly. She had to stop thinking these wonderful but confusing things about Colin. She must focus on the task at hand—making sure he was well enough to travel.

"How are you feeling? Are you dizzy?"

"My head is spinning like a drunken man with a wooden leg."

Yes, re-injuring his head had done something to his inhibitions.

"But it is better." He blinked. "I think I can walk now. There's a stream nearby, yes?"

"Yes." He was trying to get up, so she grabbed his arm and helped him to his feet. He closed his eyes and swayed. She wrapped her arm about his waist, pulling his arm around her shoulders to allow him to lean on her.

"Thank you. I'm not sure why I seem to be having trouble standing."

"Could it be the kicks to the head?"

"Possibly."

Margaretha helped him slowly cross the road. He seemed to get stronger as they drew near the stream. She sat him down on the bank, where he lay on his stomach at the edge and drank from his hand. Then he rolled over onto his back and lay still, his eyes closed.

His chest moved up and down and he seemed to be breathing hard.

"Can I do anything for you? Are you all right?"

"I am well. I'm sorry for slowing you down and for letting the horses get stolen. I know you want to get to Marienberg and send help to your family as fast as you can. I will be able to walk after I rest a moment."

"Don't worry. I am tired too. We rose very early this morning. After we rest for a little while, we can be on our way again." Without horses, without food, without money. Margaretha felt the panic rising inside her.

No, she would not think about that. Besides, she was extremely tired, and things always seemed worse when she was tired. She would lie down near Colin, who was already asleep, she could tell by his steady breathing, and take a nap. Then they would both be better able to travel.

Margaretha stretched out on the thick grass and pillowed her head on her arm, tears pricking her eyes at the thought of the blankets that were now gone, tears of exhaustion and the remaining emotions after the attack by the robbers. At least they were alive. She could be grateful for that.

The soft grass actually felt good, and she felt herself drifting to sleep.

Margaretha awoke and sat up. Where was she?

When she saw Colin nearby, the morning's events came back to her. She and Colin were taking a short sleep before continuing their journey—on foot, unfortunately.

"Colin?"

He didn't move.

"Colin? Can you hear me?" She kept her voice low, remembering that Claybrook's men were not too far behind them.

He still didn't move. She stared at his chest. It looked still. "Oh no, please, no." She scrambled over to him on her hands and knees and laid her ear on his chest, pressing as close as possible. She held her breath and waited. There it was. A *swoosh-thump* sound against her ear.

She kept her ear there. His chest was quite warm. Hadn't she heard that people went cold if they were dead? No, he was definitely alive, and this was quite pleasant and comfortable—her head lying on his warm chest, listening to his heartbeat. She sighed deeply.

"Margaretha?"

She righted herself and stared into his bright blue eyes. "I woke up and couldn't see your chest moving and I got scared and put my ear there to try to see if I could hear your heart beating. And it was. Beating, I mean."

He simply stared at her, a sweet, soft look on his face. He seemed to be staring at her lips.

"Of course it was beating. You are alive." She laughed—a nervous sound. "But I'm talking too much again. How do you feel?" She realized she was leaning over him and moved away.

He sat up. "Only a little dizzy. I am well."

"Do you remember what happened to you?"

"Some of it seems a bit foggy. I don't remember why my head hurts, but I remember ... we were going to Marienberg ... to get help to defeat Claybrook."

When he said the name Claybrook, his face came alive. "Let

195

us be off." He stood a little shakily and looked around. "But where are the horses?"

"Oh dear. I do believe sleep is bad for your memory."

"Why? No matter. We must be off. You can tell me what happened on the way."

"Let us go, then."

"Where are the horses?"

"We don't have them anymore. Some men lay in wait for us in the road this morning, attacked us, and stole our horses." Must she explain this to him every time he fainted or fell asleep?

"We will have to walk, then. I know you are anxious to get help for your family."

At least he remembered that much. "Are you sure you are able to walk?" He didn't look very sturdy, and he was still pale.

"I am able." He looked down at her feet. "Since we're walking, you will need better shoes. Those won't last long on these roads."

"I thought of that. Perhaps at the next village I can exchange my dress for something less fine and a sturdier pair of shoes."

"Good idea."

They set out, and Margaretha prayed silently, *Father God, please help us bring help before it is too late for Father, Valten, and the rest of our family.* Losing the horses had set them back several days. It was a harsh blow, a painful setback, but she had to believe that they would still make it to Marienberg and back to Hagenheim in time to save everyone. In her heart, strangely, she felt peace.

They had only been walking for a few minutes when the sound of horses' hooves came from behind them. They leapt off the road and watched from the cover of the trees as Claybrook's men thundered by.

Now that they had lost their horses, Claybrook's men would reach Marienberg before they did.

Chapter
24

Colin did not complain about the pain in his head or how dizzy he felt. And Margaretha did not complain either. Even when the soles of her shoes wore out, she simply wrapped strips of her underdress around her feet.

After a few hours, they came to a village and she was able to do what she had proposed to Colin; she exchanged her green silk cotehardie for a brown woolen kirtle and a pair of thicker soled shoes. She also managed to talk the woman into giving them some bread and two bowls of pea and oat pottage, which tasted terrible but filled them up.

They walked a few more hours before it became too dark for them to see, then found a place to sleep. The stream never wandered far from the road, which was more important than ever, now that they had no water flasks.

Margaretha had been unusually quiet. As they lay down near the fire, she on one side and he on the other, she asked, "How does your head feel? Is it still hurting?"

"A little." It was throbbing, and he was still dizzy, but that was to be expected after being kicked in the head. "I remember everything about this morning, the robbers and their attack. And I think I said some very addlepated things just after it happened. I hope I did not offend you, Lady Margaretha."

"No, of course not." She didn't say anything else. The light from the fire was creating shadows on her face, and she looked sad. And why wouldn't she be? They had been only two days away from Marienberg, but now it would take them at least four more days to walk there. And that was only if they weren't attacked again by bandits.

She turned to her other side. "Ouch!"

"What is it?" He sat up.

She sat up too and held her hand toward the light of the fire. "I got a thorn in my finger." She just stared at her hand, and a tear slid down her cheek.

After all she had suffered today, she was crying about a thorn in her finger?

He went and sat down beside her. It was an impulsive thing to do, since he'd promised himself he'd stay away from her, especially after dark.

"Let me see it." Colin took her hand and plucked the thorn out of her finger. "It isn't so bad. No bleeding."

She slowly collapsed into him, pressing her forehead against his chest, and started to sob. "I miss my mother."

He wrapped his arms around her shoulders. He had to listen carefully to understand her words through the crying.

"What if they are all afraid? What if they are wondering about me, whether I am safe, or whether I was able to get help for them? I know my mother must be worried. What if my father and Valten walked into Claybrook's trap and he ... he ... he killed them?" She was sobbing too hard to speak anymore.

He pulled her closer, cradling her in his arms and rubbing her shoulder.

"I'm dirty and tired and hungry, but we have to keep walking. And I'm so sorry those men hurt you. Twice in one day I thought you might be dead." She clung to his shoulder with one hand, her face still buried in his tunic. "It was horrible."

"Don't worry about me." He brushed her hair back away from her face. "I have had much worse beatings." Well, only one.

"I'm so foolish to be crying. You must think me a lack-wit."

"No, of course not. I think you are brave and sweet and ..." His heart contracted painfully in his chest. "If you want to cry, it's all right. I don't mind." He leaned his cheek against her hair.

"I just miss my mother and my family. I love them, and it hurts so much to know they're in danger."

"I know," he said, wanting to soothe her. "I understand." He didn't like hearing and seeing her cry, but she was so warm in his arms. She was pouring her heart out to him, and it felt good to know she trusted him enough to tell him exactly what she was thinking. Although her words confirmed she could never marry him. She obviously would miss her mother and father, sisters and brothers too much.

His heart sank, but he tightened his arms around her, raising her head up to his shoulder. He couldn't marry her, but if he could keep her safe until they reached Marienberg, and if he could save her family from Claybrook, he could go home knowing he had done something good, that he had made a difference in the life of the most beautiful, worthy, gentle creature in the world.

"What if we don't make it to Marienberg in time? What if we can't get back to Hagenheim in time to save everyone?"

"We will make it. With God's strength, we will get there in time."

"But you are not well. You should be resting, not walking for miles and miles in the hot sun."

"God can do anything." The words were like a revelation, and he drew strength from them. "God likes using the weak to defeat the strong."

"Yes, that is true."

"And God will use us to defeat Claybrook. Besides, my memory has returned, and I am well enough to walk. I think you need to sleep now. You will feel better about everything in the morning."

She sniffed, then took a deep breath and let it out, but she did not make any effort to pull away from him. "No doubt that is also true." She relaxed against him, her head tucked against his neck. He closed his eyes to better memorize the way she felt in his arms, since he must never hold her like this again.

"Will you say a prayer for us before we go to sleep?" She sat up straight and looked at him, her eyes wet and luminous in the starlight.

"Of course." He closed his eyes again and felt her slip her hand inside his.

"Father God, You have graciously kept us alive, and we believe that You have a purpose for us." He had to make this sound confident and positive, for Margaretha's sake. "You will *not* let us die, and You *will* be with us on this journey to Marienberg. You will send Your mighty angels with their flaming swords to protect not only us, but also Margaretha's family in Hagenheim, and all the Hagenheim people. We beseech You to not let the wicked prosper, but to uphold the cause of the righteous, as You have promised. Bless us with safety and peace tonight, in the name of Jesus the Savior." And he did feel peace, after that prayer.

She squeezed his hand. "That was beautiful. I feel better already, like we cannot possibly fail." She flashed a bright smile at him.

"Good. Now go to sleep. And stay away from thorns."

"I will."

He put a few more sticks on the fire while she lay back down. He went back to his place but immediately felt cold and far away from her.

As he lay listening to the fire crackle and hiss, she said, "Colin?"

"Yes?"

"Do you wish I had stayed behind with Anne?"

"No. No, I don't." Even though his heart would be broken when he finally had to part from her, and he regretted he couldn't marry her, he wasn't sorry he had spent these days with her.

He thought perhaps she had fallen asleep, but then she said softly, "Thank you."

Margaretha woke with a start. Dawn was breaking, spreading a gray light over their spot in the woods. Their fire had died, but Colin was still lying on the ground. She sat up. She'd been dreaming that she and Colin were embracing, and she could still feel the wonderful warmth of his chest. And then, in her dream, he kissed her on the lips with great fervency. It had felt wonderfully real, and as she kissed him back, she had thought, *He loves me and doesn't mind that I talk too much!* Then Lord Claybrook's men pulled them apart. Claybrook turned her around and laughed in her face. Then she awoke.

She could still feel the overpowering emotion of kissing Colin. She blinked, hard, although she wasn't too sure she wanted to dispel the feeling. "It was only a dream," she whispered. "Only a dream." She hugged herself, reliving the security of Colin's arms last night, as well as in her dream. She only allowed herself a moment of that, then stood up.

"Colin?" She ran over to him. Would he awaken only to have lost part of his memory again? Her heart beat strangely as she looked down at him. She had not hesitated to press her ear to his chest just yesterday. In fact, she had cried in his arms last night. The dream, the sensation of kissing him, was nearly overwhelming, making her reluctant to touch him now. If he knew what was going through her mind ... Her cheeks heated at the thought.

As she stared down at him, she realized Colin was her friend, but was he more than that? Again remembering their dream kiss, she continued to stare at him.

But he was so still. "Colin?"

He didn't move. Twice the day before she had thought he was dead. Still, she had an almost uncontrollable urge to again fall to her knees and press her ear to his chest.

Then she noticed he was smiling, his eyes still closed. "Colin?"

He opened his eyes. "Is it morning?" He yawned. "I must have been dreaming."

"Do you remember everything—where we are and what we're doing?"

"I think so. We are going to Marienberg to get help from the duke to defeat Claybrook in Hagenheim."

"Thank the saints above," she breathed. "You remember."

"Give me a few minutes and I will be ready to go." He stood up and turned to go into the woods.

"Colin?"

"Yes?" He turned to look back at her.

Unable to think of anything else to say, she said, "I'm sorry I cried ... on you ... last night."

He seemed to be studying her with those clear blue eyes. With a solemn look, he said, "I didn't mind."

What would he do if she ran to him and embraced him? She was so close to doing just that, she shivered and wrapped her arms around herself.

"I'll be back in a few minutes." He walked away.

They had no things to gather, so after taking a drink of water, they were on their way again. As they walked, they discussed how long it would take Claybrook's men to get to Marienberg

Castle and find out Colin and Margaretha had not made it there yet. Wouldn't Duke Theodemar get suspicious? How long would it take Claybrook's men to come back down the road looking for them?

"Perhaps they won't recognize us, since I'm wearing a different dress. They won't expect to see me dressed like a peasant."

"I hardly think anyone who has ever seen you could mistake you." A little half smile lifted one corner of Colin's mouth. "There's no disguising how beautiful you are, and your hair is striking."

"You think I'm beautiful?" Her heart seemed to have expanded and crowded out all the breath in her lungs.

"Of course. You are beautiful." He said it matter-of-factly, then looked at her out of the corner of his eye as they walked side by side.

"My hair is rather unruly, like my mother's. I should probably try to cover it, or at least braid it." Her stomach growled, twisting into a knot, it was so empty. She'd heard Colin's stomach growling earlier. She had no idea how they would acquire food, so she said nothing about the dilemma. A few minutes later, there was a rumble of thunder.

"I do believe it is getting colder," Margaretha said. "And it's about to rain."

The sky had grown quite dark. The wind started blowing, chilling her through her clothes.

Margaretha had heard of desert places near the Holy Land where the sun was always hot and it rarely rained, and of places on the Continent where summers were consistently hot and winters were consistently cold. But in their part of the Holy Roman Empire, the weather was unpredictable, and even in summer they sometimes had cold spells and sleet or hail.

"What is the weather like in England?" she asked as they trudged on. "Is it hot in the summer?"

"Sometimes. It's like your weather here, I think, only with a bit more rain and fog."

An extra cold gust of wind swept down the road and into their faces, making Margaretha shiver again. "You haven't told me much about your family. It will distract me if you tell me about them."

Colin said, "I have two sisters and two brothers. I am the oldest. We live with my mother and father in the castle my grandfather built, in the village of Glynval. My sisters are eighteen and ten, and my brothers are sixteen and thirteen. Or, they were when I left. My littlest sister and brother will have had a birthday since then."

"And you are twenty."

"Yes. My parents are very good people and loved my brothers and sisters and me. My father warned me not to go after Claybrook, that it would be a difficult journey and that I didn't need to let my impulsive nature get the best of me." He frowned, only slightly, but Margaretha saw it, just before he bent down to pick up a stick and proceeded to peel the leaf buds off of it. "He was right, of course, although I didn't think so at the time."

"Why did you go after Claybrook?"

"I was angry." He tapped the stick in his palm to the rhythm of their steps. "I wanted to make him sorry for what he had done to Philippa. She was eighteen when he murdered her. But the only thing I've accomplished is to get my friend John killed as well."

"You've spoken of him before. What was he like?"

He sighed. "John was my father's steward's son. We grew up together, and he came with me to England to try to capture Claybrook." He shook his head. "Stupid, foolish mistake. How arrogant to think the two of us could bring Claybrook to justice. But John was not to blame. He was only following me. I suppose I thought his size and strength and my intelligence would keep anything bad from happening to us."

He seemed careful not to look her in the eye, but she could see the pain in the downturn of his face and hear it in his voice.

"It is a terrible pity what happened to John. I'm so sorry."

As she spoke, fat drops of rain began to fall around them. One landed on Margaretha's head, sending a chill down her spine.

"We should walk in the trees," Colin said. "Come."

He grabbed her hand and they ran off the road into the relative cover of the forest. They kept walking, dodging the tree trunks as the rain grew steadier. They stayed mostly dry for several more minutes, but the cold rain eventually leaked through the leaves and began to drip on their heads and shoulders. The wind, which had died down just before it started raining, began to blow harder, sending drops into their faces.

"It looks like there's a village up ahead," Colin said, and he cupped her elbow and pulled her forward.

The rain soaked through the layers of her clothing. Her linen undergown and her woolen kirtle clung heavily against her legs, making it harder to move. Her teeth began to chatter, and Colin put his arm around her shoulders as they trudged on through the wet undergrowth.

They emerged from the trees and into the edge of a small village. In front of them were plots of land, sectioned off, with small green plants growing in rows. They did their best to walk around the edges of the plots, as the rain was coming down hard now. Colin led her toward the small, thatch-roofed houses at the other end of the fields, and headed toward the door of the first house.

Colin knocked on the door of the small wattle-and-daub structure as the rain pelted the back of her head. A little girl with bedraggled blonde hair opened the door and stared at them.

"We are looking for shelter from the storm," Margaretha said.

"No room!" A man's voice shouted from somewhere inside the dark, dirt-floor house. "Close the door, Joan! You're letting in the rain!"

The little girl lowered her gaze to the floor and shut the door.

Chapter
25

Margaretha and Colin hurried down the street of the village as the cold rain continued pelting them. A young woman stood in the open doorway of another low, thatched-roof hut. She motioned to them to come inside.

They ran to the doorway. A wooden sign hung above the door with a crude painting of a loaf of bread.

As they ducked inside, the smell of freshly baked bread made Margaretha's mouth water. The room was pleasantly warm.

The young woman motioned toward two stools. "You're strangers here. Where are you from?"

Margaretha and Colin sat down. "We're from—" Margaretha stopped. Claybrook's men might come and ask the villagers if they had seen them. "North of here. We're on our way to visit relatives." Her relatives, not his. The less she revealed, the better.

"Is he your husband?" the woman asked.

"No. Um, he's my . . . brother." *God, forgive me.*

But instead of smiling at him the way Anne had when she discovered he was the son of a wealthy earl from England, the woman simply nodded.

Margaretha was well aware that she and Colin were dripping water everywhere. "I'm so sorry. We are making a terrible mess."

"It's only water. Are you hungry? Because I have some fresh

bread my husband took out of the oven a few minutes ago. He's angry because he knows no one will come buy it now that it's raining."

"I'm afraid we don't have any money," Margaretha said, the words coming out slowly and regretfully.

"Here." The woman turned and took a loaf off the rough wooden shelf behind her. "Take it."

It was fresh oat bread. Margaretha immediately tore it and gave half to Colin. They both broke off a piece and ate it.

It was still warm. Tears came to Margaretha's eyes in gratitude for the woman's kindness.

"Maud!" a man's voice boomed from beyond the open doorway at the back of the tiny room.

"You'd better go." The woman's eyes flew wide. "That's my husband and he will be angry if he knows I gave away the bread."

"Thank you," Margaretha said, squeezing the woman's hand and turning to go. She stuffed the bread inside her kirtle, between the woolen dress and her undergown, and she and Colin ran back out into the cold rain.

They ran down the street and soon saw another house almost hidden by trees, as it was set off the road and away from the village and the fields. It was much larger and was made of stone instead of the wattle-and-daub construction of the rest of the houses and chicken coops. They tromped through the mud and undergrowth toward it, but instead of heading toward the front door, Colin led her around the side of the house toward what looked like a barn.

At the back of the barn there was a smaller door. He opened it and they went inside.

The smell of hay and dung assaulted her nostrils, but the barn was relatively warm and dry. The only light came from the door. He left it open a crack, and they sat down on the hay.

They each took out their half of the loaf of bread and resumed eating.

The horses snuffled restlessly in their stalls. But another sound came from the other side of the barn, away from the horses' stalls, and it seemed to be coming closer. Colin hid his bread behind his back and moved in front of Margaretha, as though to protect her.

A small boy emerged from the shadows, staring at them with wide eyes. But it wasn't them he was staring at. It was the bread in Margaretha's hand.

His cheeks were thin and he wore a long ragged tunic with no sleeves. His bare arms were bent, and he squatted in the straw. Bare toes peeked out at her.

Margaretha's heart clenched. "Are you hungry?" She broke off a large portion of her bread and held it out to him.

Like a little bird, he crept forward two steps at a time, then reached and took the bread from her hand, looking into her eyes for the first time.

"You need that food, Margaretha."

The sound of Colin's voice sent the little boy running back the way he had come. The foreign language probably startled him as well.

"We have a long way to walk, and you need your strength."

"He's only a little child and obviously hungry. How could I not share my bread with him?"

Colin tore off an equally large piece of his bread and handed it to Margaretha.

"No, I can't take your bread. You need it as much as I do."

The little boy shuffled back toward them, now looking at Colin's bread. Judging by the huge lump in his cheek, he had already stuffed all the bread Margaretha had given him into his mouth. He held out his hand to Colin.

Colin sighed, but held out the bread. The boy snatched it and backed away.

Margaretha caught Colin smiling. "What are you thinking?"

"I was remembering something John taught me a long time ago. There is more than one way to get food." He put another bite of his bread in his mouth, then got up.

His movement caused the little boy to dart away into the darkest part of the stable.

"I need to find a long piece of twine and some sticks."

"Whatever for?"

He looked around until he found a ball of twine. "To make a snare."

"Oh."

He started to go back out the door.

"Wait!" Margaretha stood and touched his arm. "Are you sure you should go into the rain? It is so cold. And if you snare some game, couldn't the landowner do something bad to you?"

"Only if he catches me." He smiled at her and went out the door.

The cold wind swept in, chilling her wet clothes and hair. Margaretha shivered and sank back down on the floor. "O God," she whispered, "I'm so miserably cold and wet. Please keep Colin safe and don't let him get caught snaring game. But let him catch something, because we're very hungry, and so is this little boy." She could barely see him, as he still hung back in the shadows. She buried her face in her hands so the little boy couldn't hear her whisper, "And please let me stop thinking about that dream when Colin kissed me. Help me remember it was only a dream." Her stomach immediately twisted—whether more from guilt or hunger, she wasn't sure. She shouldn't even think about Colin kissing her, since they weren't likely to ever marry.

Was it possible that he might want to marry her? Could he

ever love her in the way she wanted to be loved? He had never said anything about love or marriage, the way her suitors had.

She would do well to remember that Colin lived in England. He had a life there, a family and responsibilities and duties— an inheritance. He was the oldest son of an earl and should marry someone else of noble English birth, someone with ties to England's king.

Colin surely never imagined marrying her—although he had mentioned it in his addled state after getting kicked in the head. But a suitor kissed a girl on the hand or cheek, and married people kissed on the lips, but Colin had never kissed her, even on the forehead, like a brother or friend might.

It was foolish to be thinking about such things when there were much more serious things to be decided, particularly, how they would reach Marienberg before they starved or froze to death.

Margaretha could not control the chattering of her teeth. If only she could take off these wet clothes. She pulled her knees up and wrapped her arms around her legs, put her head down, and went back to praying.

The little boy was moving around. His little feet came pattering toward her. She lifted her head and he was standing before her with a blanket. The gray blanket engulfed his outstretched arms, and he peered over it, his eyes barely visible.

Margaretha took it. "Thank you." She wrapped herself in it, surrounded now by the smell of horses. She was still wet and cold, but his thoughtfulness made her smile.

"Do you know where I could get some dry clothes?" She hesitated to ask. After all, if he knew where to get clothes, he wouldn't be wearing the ragged, insufficient clothing he was wearing.

He stared at her with large brown eyes. Then he motioned with his hand. He turned and hurried away.

Margaretha stood up and followed, still clutching the blanket around her wet shoulders. The little boy scrambled up a ladder and disappeared above her.

She tested the ladder. It looked sturdy enough. She started climbing with one hand, holding the blanket with her other hand, and soon reached the top of the ladder. Her eyes adjusted to the bit of light that was shining through the cracks in the walls, and a loft, piled high with hay, loomed before her. The little boy was at one end, brushing the hay off a trunk.

Margaretha climbed the rest of the way up, stepping onto the wooden boards covered with stray bits of hay and straw. The little boy held out a bundle of blue cloth.

She took it from him and held it up. It was a blue cutaway surcoat with lacing down the front that was made to be worn over an undergown of some type of finer, softer material. The surcoat was of finer wool than the kirtle that she had traded her silk dress for. But since she didn't want to put her wet undergown back on, she went and lifted the lid of the trunk. She found a pale gray cotehardie, of lighter material.

The boy motioned for her to stay there, in the loft, then he scrambled back down the ladder and out of sight.

Margaretha looked around. There were no windows where someone might see her from outside, and no way up to the loft except by the ladder. So she quickly dropped the blanket and stripped off her heavy-with-rain kirtle, then her clinging undergown. Her teeth chattered as the air touched her bare, wet skin, and she pulled the enormous gray cotehardie over her head as fast as she could. The dress was made for a larger woman, but at least it was dry. She then pulled on the sleeveless blue surcoat. The sides were open all the way to her hips on both sides, exposing the gray cotehardie beneath. It smelled slightly musty and was not the warmest garment, but it would do. She then wrapped the horse blanket around her. She would smell like horses and musty hay, but at least she wouldn't freeze to death.

Margaretha wrung as much water as she could from her kirtle and undergown, and spread them out to dry. Then she went to rummage through the trunk again. Colin would be terribly cold and wet when he returned.

God, please let there be some men's garments in here.

She found a fitted, thigh-length tunic of fine linen — a summer garment and not very warm — and a pair of woolen hose. There were no other blankets or clothing, only some rough bags made of hemp for gathering and storing grain.

She tucked the clothes under her arm and went back down the ladder.

The little boy was still staring at her. He was a handsome child. Though he was too thin, his eyes were bright and intelligent. "What is your name?" she asked him.

He simply stared.

"How old are you? Five years old?"

Slowly he opened his mouth, as if his mouth was not used to moving. "My name is Toby."

"That is a fine name, Toby. And how old are you?"

He stared at her with those big eyes. Finally he shook his head.

"You don't know?"

He shook his head.

"Do you have a mother? Or father?"

"My mother and father are dead and buried in the church yard."

The poor thing. How Mother would adore him and take care of him and fatten him up. If only she could take him home. "Who do you belong to?"

His lip seemed to tremble a moment before he said, "Master Steinbek."

"Are these his horses?"

He nodded.

"And where do you sleep? Here?"

"Sometimes." He seemed to relax a little, and they sat down together against the wall. "Sometimes I sleep in the kitchen on a bench. I must keep putting wood in the stove all night. If I let the fire go out, Cook will be angry."

Such a small child for that task! "Do you not have any relatives who would take you in?"

"I have an aunt, but she does not want me. She says she has too many mouths to feed. She has a lot of children." Without pausing to take a breath, he said, "Will you tell me a story?"

"Of course. I know lots of stories." Her mother had often made up stories and wrote them down for her and her brothers and sisters. But Margaretha would tell him one of her own. "Once upon a time, there was a boy who hated injustice."

"What is injustice?"

"Injustice is something unfair or cruel. So when the boy discovered that a wealthy man had unjustly and cruelly killed his sister's friend, a girl the same age as his sister, the boy chased after that man to capture him and bring him back to his homeland to be punished."

Toby stretched out on the floor and lay his head on her leg.

Margaretha laid part of her blanket over Toby, covering his bare arm and bare feet, and went on. "He caught up to the murderer, but his men beat the boy and left him for dead on the road, where he was picked up by a potter and his apprentice. The potter and his apprentice brought the boy to the great and beautiful Hagenheim Castle, where lived a wise healer who tended his wounds and gave him hot drinks made with healing herbs. Soon he was well again, but none of the people of Hagenheim Castle could understand his foreign language, as he was from a country far away."

"What did he do then?" Toby's sleepy voice asked.

"He got a job working in the stables of the castle when he

found out that the murderer was there. There was also a beautiful princess living at the castle, and she was the only person, besides the priest, who could understand the language of the boy, since the princess was well-educated, and studious besides." Margaretha smiled at this bit of vanity. "She and the boy found out that the murderer was plotting to take over Hagenheim and kill the excellent Duke Wilhelm who ruled over the land."

Toby yawned noisily. "What happened then?"

"Then the noble boy and princess defeated the evil murderer."

"Did they chop off his head?"

"Yes, and the boy and all of Hagenheim lived happily ever after."

"Didn't the boy marry the princess?"

Margaretha hesitated. How should she answer? She must pretend his question didn't make her heart flutter. It was only a story, after all. "The boy and the princess were good friends, almost like brother and sister. Besides, the boy was a foreigner and didn't want to live in Hagenheim, and the girl didn't want to leave her family, because they were good and kind to her." Just saying the words, however, made her heart heavy.

"That man who was here, is he your sweetheart?"

"He is only a friend."

A movement made her turn her head. Standing in the doorway, which was open a few inches to let in the light, was Colin.

Her heart stopped in panic. How long had he been standing there?

Rain slid down his face. His hair was as black as night and water dripped off the ends onto his tunic.

But of course, he wouldn't have understood what she was saying even if he had overheard her story, since he didn't speak German. She jumped up to get him the dry clothes she had found.

Chapter 26

Colin approached the door of the stable and heard Margaretha's voice. From the mysterious, slightly playful tone, she seemed to be telling a story. He stopped to listen, but he couldn't understand any of it.

"Colin." She seemed to blush uncomfortably at the sight of him. "I didn't know you were standing there." She let out a strained chuckle, as if she was relieved.

He pushed the door open while she and the little boy stood up.

"You are dripping wet. You will catch a deadly chill." She closed the door behind him, leaving it open a bit to let in some light.

"I set some snares, and now we will have to wait to see if they catch anything."

"That is so clever. I would never know how to do such a thing. But now you must get out of those wet clothes. You're shaking. Toby helped me find some dry clothes and a blanket. And in the same trunk there were some men's clothes." She bent and picked up a bundle and held it out to him. "No, don't touch it." She pulled it back. "You will get them wet. Toby will carry them for you. You can go in the corner and put them on. I won't be able to see you."

She turned and said something to the boy, who motioned to

Colin to follow him, then took the dry clothes and disappeared into the dark corner of the stable.

Colin followed him until it was too dark to see anything, then stood still as his eyes adjusted to the darkness. Toby—that was the child's name, apparently—had led him into an unused horse stall. He shoved the clothes into Colin's hands and left, closing the door behind him.

Colin shucked his cold, wet clothes and managed, after much fumbling, to figure out what manner of clothes he had been given—a long tunic and hose—and put them on. Finally, when he was sure he was covered from neck to foot, he made his way back to Margaretha and Toby.

"You must be so cold. You were out in the rain for a long time. You take the blanket." She took the blanket from around her shoulders.

"I don't need it."

"Nonsense. You're shivering." She wrapped it around him and held the ends together in front of his chest. Her voice was breathy as she said, "And your hair is still wet." She stared into his eyes.

He took the ends of the blanket in his hand.

She let go, breaking contact with him and stepping back. The little boy was gazing languidly at them, his eyes half closed.

"I'll help him get to sleep," she said softly, although the boy would certainly not understand her English. "He's very tired."

She called the boy over to the corner, sat against a huge mound of hay, and took him into her lap.

Seeing the boy's bare arms and feet, Colin said, "There's no sense in you two being cold." He sat close beside her, pulling the horse blanket around Margaretha and the child. He also wrapped his arms around them, on top of the blanket, and leaned his shoulder against the wall and his back against the hay.

"Thank you." She turned to look at him, bringing her face within inches of his.

She immediately turned away. She spoke to the child in German, that strange, guttural language which actually sounded lilting and sweet coming from her. She talked softly for several minutes, until the boy's eyes closed and his breathing became regular and heavy with sleep.

"Why don't you go to sleep too," he whispered against her hair. "I can keep watch. If I hear someone coming, I'll wake you." She felt like heaven against his chest, warm and comfortable.

Turning her head to the other side where he couldn't look into her eyes, she whispered, "Do you think the rain will stop soon? I don't like wasting so much time, but it would be difficult to travel in this cold rain."

"I hope it will stop soon."

She had been sitting rather tensely, her back against his chest, but now she started to relax a little.

"I found a place in the woods, a rock outcropping, where we can cook the game, if my snares yield some."

"What is a 'rock outcropping'?"

"Big rocks creating a natural shelter."

"Oh. That is good." She relaxed some more, leaning farther back, the boy still sleeping peacefully with her arms wrapped around him, the same way Colin's arms were wrapped around her.

She was quiet. He wondered if she was falling asleep. It gave him a warm feeling to think she trusted him enough to fall asleep in his arms. Truly, she was the most gentle, compassionate, sincere girl he had ever met.

But dwelling on her character qualities was dangerous.

"I'm sorry about what happened to your friend, John," she said softly.

That was the last thing they had talked about that morning before it started raining. "John was a good man."

"I have never had anyone close to me die. I had a sister who drowned, but it happened when I was a baby. I know it must be terrible to lose a friend."

"Yes. It was even worse because I ... I was responsible. He would have been home, well and content, if I had not brought him here."

She whispered, "Perhaps you blame yourself to keep from feeling the grief."

He wasn't sure what he thought about that statement. "I was impulsive and overconfident. I thought I could capture a murderer, with only one other person to help me, which also makes me arrogant and careless." Why was he trying so hard to convince her he was a bad person?

"I don't see you as any of those things." Her voice was calm and quiet. "I see you as courageous and caring, noble and generous."

They sat in silence, listening to the rain drip off the thatched roof and the trees outside, the horses snuffling occasionally in their stalls or munching on hay.

He knew he shouldn't say what he was about to say, but ... "And I see you as intelligent, kind, brave, and beautiful."

"I talk too much." Her voice was soft but vibrant. "And I'm a flibbertigibbet."

He also knew he shouldn't do what he was about to do, but ... he raised his hand to her chin and lifted her face until he could gaze into her eyes. Her lips looked soft and inviting, but he did not have the right to kiss her, as he was not betrothed to her and had no hope of being so.

He let go of her chin and closed his eyes.

She leaned her head back against his shoulder, turning so her forehead was nestled against his neck.

"I told you before," he said. "I like hearing you talk. And I was wrong. You are not a flibbertigibbet."

"So you think I am a good spy?"

He smiled as he adjusted his arms around her. "You are a very good spy."

~❦~

Margaretha awoke feeling warm and comfortable. What was so heavy against her legs? She opened her eyes. Toby lay in her lap and Colin's arm was around her, and she remembered. Guilt pricked her at how good it felt to be surrounded by his arms, his warm chest behind her. The sound of his steady breathing next to her ear sent a tingling sensation across her shoulders.

Colin shifted slightly. His breathing changed and became less heavy; he was awake.

"Am I hurting you?" she whispered.

"No. But I should get up. It sounds like the rain stopped." He started sliding away from her.

Margaretha leaned forward and tried not to wake Toby, but he sat up and rubbed his eyes. They all got up and peeked out the door. It had not stopped raining entirely, but it was more of a mist falling from the sky.

"I'll go check the snares."

"We'll come with you." She should probably leave Toby behind, but she had a feeling he would not allow himself to be left.

Margaretha and Toby followed Colin outside, holding the blanket over their heads. Toby seemed to think it was a game and smiled as they darted around the trees and almost lost Colin a few times.

Colin's snares ended up containing three plump hares, one in the noose of each snare. They followed Colin to the rock outcropping, which sheltered them, somewhat, from the heavy mist that clung to their eyelashes.

Colin skinned the hares, which made Margaretha avert her eyes and Toby gasp in delight at his skill. He had found a pile of dry wood that had been covered with an oiled tarp underneath the rock outcropping, and he used it to build a small fire. He also made a crude spit from sticks, and he roasted the hares over the fire. They smelled so good, Margaretha's stomach competed with Toby's to see whose could growl louder, making them both giggle.

When it was done, Colin presented the meat to them on "platters" of wet leaves.

Switching to English, Margaretha asked, "Where did you learn such important skills as catching and skinning hares?"

"I was a boy like most others, roaming over the English countryside looking for adventure. But John taught me about snares and cooking game." A flicker of pain crossed his face as he looked down.

No wonder he displayed so much passion to bring Claybrook to justice. In his grief, he was angry. Her mother had once told her, "When women are sad, they cry, but when men are sad, they get angry."

He handed Toby a piece of cooled meat.

For all she knew, Claybrook may have killed her family members. But somehow, she just couldn't imagine that happening. Her faith in her father—and her brother Valten as well was too great to think they might have allowed a peacock like Claybrook to defeat them. And once they were able to reach Marienberg and her cousin, Duke Theodemar, brought his fighting men, Claybrook would finally receive the punishment he deserved.

The three of them finished the first hare in no time. Never had anything tasted so good, and she enjoyed watching Toby eat so eagerly, even smiling up at her while he chewed.

Surely it would be wrong not to take him with them. He might be in danger on the road with them, but he was also in danger if they left him here to be mistreated by his master.

They ate most of the second one and wrapped the rest in the hemp bag they had taken from the stable.

"The rain has mostly stopped," Margaretha said as they went to the nearby stream for a drink. "There are a few more hours of daylight left."

Colin nodded. "Let us be off, then. Good-bye, Toby. *Auf Wiedersehen!*"

Toby looked like he might cry. He ran and threw his arms around Margaretha's legs. "Take me with you. Please take me with you. I promise I will be good and will obey everything you tell me, if you will only take me with you."

Margaretha translated the words for Colin that were breaking her heart.

"You know we can't take him." There was an edge of panic in Colin's voice. "Tell me you know that."

Margaretha hoped he saw the plea in her eyes. "How can we leave him here? You know he will be treated badly. No one here cares for him at all. He is an orphan, and my mother would dearly love to take care of him, I know she would."

"No, Margaretha, no. Be reasonable. It is not a good idea. He is a human person, not a pet."

"I know that!"

"He won't be safe with us. And we have a responsibility to get to Marienberg and try to save Hagenheim."

"Of course I know that. But he won't slow us down. I'll carry him on my shoulders if he gets tired. I used to do the same thing with my brothers."

"He doesn't belong with us. He belongs here." But Colin's voice was taking on a bit of a pleading tone as well, and she sensed his stance was beginning to weaken.

"His master treats him like a slave. Did you not see the bruise on his cheek and the fingerprint bruises on his arms? Can you bear to leave him here and let him be abused?" Her voice was beginning to vibrate, and she took a deep breath in an effort to remain calm. She didn't want to frighten Toby.

Colin looked almost desperate. "He will be in danger with us!"

Margaretha held out her hands, palm up. "In danger if he goes with us, and in danger if he stays. Please allow him to come with us. He will not be any trouble."

Colin sighed heavily. "What if . . . what if we can't keep him safe? He is a small child. He may be killed if he goes with us."

He was thinking of his friend's death. He was afraid of the child dying, afraid he couldn't keep the child safe. The pain in his eyes made her stomach twist in sympathy.

He said in a defeated tone, "I can't keep you or this child safe. Don't you see? I could not have kept you safe with those bandits who stole our horses. They could have killed you and there was nothing I could have done."

His voice broke on the last word, breaking her heart along with it.

"Colin."

He sighed, making her heart constrict.

His hair was still wet and curled at his temples and below his ears. Several days' growth of beard made him look even more endearing. *Oh, Colin.*

"I cannot tell you to leave him here. I don't want him to be beaten and mistreated any more than you do." Colin hung his head and turned away from her.

Margaretha's heart ached so much, and the only cure for it seemed to be to throw her arms around him. So she did. "Don't worry," she said against his chest. "We won't die. I can't tell you how I know, but I just know that God will keep us safe. I have peace that we will all be well. I know that peace has to be from God."

When she pulled away, still clutching his arms, he was staring down at her. "Peace." He shook his head, a slight movement.

He still looked wrung out and sad. "I haven't had peace since I left England. But I know that isn't God's fault. It's mine."

Margaretha pressed her cheek to his chest again, holding him tightly. "You will get your peace back. God is with you. Don't worry."

When he put his hands on her back and pressed his cheek against the top of her head, she felt even more sure that all would be well.

Chapter
27

❧

Colin awoke the next morning to fog, Margaretha and Toby still asleep. They had gone back to the stable with the idea of trying to steal a couple of horses—and to eventually return them when all was well again in Hagenheim—but when they drew near, they saw two men milling around outside. One looked angry, and the other was calling for Toby, which caused the little boy to cling tightly to Margaretha.

Colin couldn't bear to turn the boy over to them, so they hurried away before they were seen. They had to leave their own clothes behind, wearing the clothing they had taken from the trunk in the barn.

They walked for hours, and the last hour of that time, Colin had carried Toby on his shoulders. They bedded down for the night under a thicket of birch trees, as they could find no better shelter. The air was quite cold, and all three of them rolled up in the blanket they had brought with them, with Toby in the middle. The little boy fell asleep with his face tucked against Margaretha's shoulder and clutching her dress in his hand.

Colin understood why Toby had become so attached to Margaretha in such a short time. And he wasn't the only one.

Margaretha's hair glowed in the morning sun. The rain, mist, and fog had made it thicker and curlier.

He had hurriedly set two snares the night before, which

yielded two more hares. As he built a small fire and Margaretha washed Toby's face with a piece of her undergown she had been carrying around, Colin said, "You look beautiful today."

She turned to him with wide eyes and her mouth open. "My hair is a mess and I've been living like a traveling minstrel for the last week." She laughed merrily, then translated for Toby, who was looking mystified at her.

Toby didn't laugh, he only smiled at Colin and nodded.

"See? The child agrees with me."

Margaretha shook her head. "He only thinks I'm beautiful because he loves me." And she hugged him.

Colin stared at her. Did he, Colin, only think she was beautiful because he loved her? "No, even if we didn't love you, we would still think you were beautiful."

He continued working to build the fire, adding sticks, and eventually noticed that Margaretha was quiet.

"What did you say?" Her cheeks were pink.

"I said you are beautiful."

She was quiet, until Toby grabbed her hand and pulled her away to a patch of pink and blue wildflowers. They picked some and Toby tied the stems to strands of her hair.

Colin kept getting distracted and looking over at them until he burned himself. "Ouch." He blew on his soot-smudged finger.

"Let me see." Margaretha was beside him, reaching for his hand. She held it up to her face. "We have to wash it. Come to the stream."

"Let me finish setting up this spit first," he said. He worked to get two forked sticks pushed in the ground, then laid the stick with the skewered game in the forks over the fire.

He stood and Margaretha and Toby came hurrying up to him with a dripping cloth. She took his hand and gently patted it with the cold, wet cloth. The soot began to wash off.

"Where does it hurt?"

He pointed to the spot on his finger. "It's nothing. Just a little burn."

She continued to dab at it with the cloth. "If you keep it cold, it might not blister."

Her touch was sending tingling sensations up his arm.

"Come over to the stream and hold your hand in the water." She pulled him forward, not asking but telling him. Toby ran ahead of them and started splashing with both hands. Margaretha scolded him, or it sounded like scolding, and he splashed less boisterously.

She pulled Colin's arm, forcing him to squat by the edge of the stream, and dunked his hand in the water. "Doesn't that feel better?" She gazed up at him.

One of the flowers in her hair had come untied and was dangling precariously against her cheek. With his hand still in the water, he reached out his other hand and caught the pink flower. He twisted the tiny stem between his fingers, then he brushed the soft petals against her cheek.

She stared back at him with those warm brown eyes. Her lips were slightly parted. How he longed for her to lean forward and kiss him and tell him that she was beginning to love him, and that she might someday love him enough to go back to England with him.

His heart contracted painfully as he gave her the flower. "It was falling out." He pulled his hand out of the water and let the water drip off. "I think it's fine now. Thank you."

Toby squealed in delight, drawing her attention away.

Colin turned the meat on the spit. While it cooked, he set more snares, hoping to take some fresh game with them when they started their day's journey.

They ate, preparing to leave. During the past day, Margaretha had been even more cheerful than usual, playing and laughing with Toby. But ever since Colin had told her she was beautiful and touched her cheek with the flower, she had been subdued, less talkative. Perhaps she was realizing that he was falling in love with her, since it must be obvious. Did that make her sad? But it couldn't be helped. He couldn't stop, now that he had started. Perhaps it would develop into a brotherly kind of love.

He gathered the bounty from his snares, wrapped them in the hemp sack, and they started walking again.

The road was muddy and slippery after the rain of the previous day. Toby slipped and slid in the ruts. Colin said, "Maybe we can trade our game for some shoes for Toby at the next village."

"That is a good idea," Margaretha said. "But won't it be dangerous to do that? If the wrong person finds out you've been taking these hares, you could get thrown into the stocks, or much worse."

"True. But I'll be careful."

She turned and spoke to Toby, then said, "He doesn't want any shoes. He says he won't wear them even if you buy some for him."

Colin and Margaretha grinned at each other.

"My little brothers would never wear shoes." Margaretha shook her head.

"My little brothers either."

Toby had run ahead of them and was squatting and playing in the mud with his fingers. As they drew near, Toby wiped his fingers on his clothes.

They kept walking and Margaretha grew more cheerful again. She smiled and laughed and talked. The only problem was that she mostly talked to Toby, in German, and Colin couldn't understand her. He would have to learn this language.

But after he and Margaretha were able to get help from the Duke of Marienberg, and after he captured Claybrook, he would be on his way back to England, possibly in less than two weeks. After that, he would have no reason to learn German.

No reason to see Margaretha again.

The thought was physically painful, like a boulder sitting on his chest. But what could he do to change it?

It was another long day of walking. At least they had food, and when they stopped to settle in for the night, he would try to snare more.

They stopped for water late in the day, and Toby fell asleep on the grass.

"Poor thing." Margaretha gazed sweetly at the little boy as she brushed his blond hair off his forehead. "He's not used to walking so much."

"The travelers we met earlier said it is only one more long day of walking before we reach Marienberg."

Abruptly, she looked up at Colin. "What are you thinking?"

The question took him off guard. He could tell her he was thinking how pleased he was that they had brought Toby with them, because he had been thinking that earlier. But the truth was that he had been trying to think how to either convince her to go with him to England, or to convince himself to stay with her here in the Holy Roman Empire. But he had nothing here. He couldn't even speak the language.

She was still staring at him, and again said, "I want to know what you are thinking."

"I am thinking ... that we had better start walking if we want to reach Marienberg by nightfall tomorrow."

"Is that truly what you were thinking?" She raised her eyebrows dubiously.

"It's what I'm thinking now."

She frowned at him. "How is your finger?"

"It is well. No blister, thanks to you."

She smiled back at him. "We have almost made it to Marienberg. Only one more day, and I want to know more about your family. What are your parents like? Your brothers and sisters? I want to hear stories about them and what they look like."

"Why are you so curious about me suddenly?" He couldn't help laughing at the sweet innocence in her face, the way she looked almost guilty at his question.

"I am not suddenly curious. I have been curious about you since the day I met you." She looked pleased that she had been able to turn his question around. "From the first day I saw your bright blue eyes, I wondered what sort of things were tumbling about in your head."

"What sort of madness, you mean?"

"Now don't bring that up again. I have said I was sorry for thinking you were mad when you weren't."

"I am not angry."

"Good. Because I found you interesting, nevertheless."

"Interesting?"

"Yes, of course. And when you went on and on about Lord Claybrook, saying he was a murderer, how your eyes did sparkle and grow dark! It was quite exciting. I have only seen them like that a few times since."

"Even I am intrigued by me."

"It's true. And then when I saw you in the stable, after you were well again, I thought you quite handsome. I even thought about fixing you up with one of the maids, because, I will admit, I am a great matchmaker."

"Fixing me up with one of the maids?" The idea might have made him sad if it were not so ludicrous.

"Oh yes, but don't worry. I would certainly not do that now, not now that I know you are an English earl's son."

"You think me not good enough for one of your maids?"

"You are jesting." She plucked some weeds and threw them at him.

He chuckled. Finally, staring into her eyes, he asked her seriously, "Who would you match me with now?" He held his breath as he waited for her answer.

"Now?" Her expression was sober, almost frightened. "Now ... I would not presume ..." Sounding breathless, she said, "You are too handsome for anyone I know."

"Not too handsome for ... you." He should not say such a thing, but knowing he only had one more day alone with her made him reckless.

"Me? Why do you say that?" Now she looked as if she was holding her breath.

"Because you said you thought me handsome in my stable clothes, and we've already established that you are beautiful."

She seemed to slowly recover her composure. "I did not agree, and therefore that is not established." But a jaunty look came into her eyes.

"It is mutual, then. You think I am handsome, and I think you are beautiful." He stood up and went to her, holding out his hand. She took it and he pulled her to her feet. "I'll carry Toby." She stood only a few inches away, staring back at him. But as long as he believed she couldn't care for him enough to leave her family, he should not be teasing her so flirtatiously. It was not wise, for many reasons.

She stepped back. With temptation out of reach, he bent to pick up Toby and continue their journey.

Margaretha had thought Colin might kiss her. But that was foolish. He was probably thinking of no such thing. He was honorable and good and would not kiss her, knowing they were not betrothed and were extremely unlikely ever to be so.

What was happening to her? Was she so carried away by his broad shoulders and intense blue eyes and thick, wavy black hair?

No. It was more the sweetness in his face, the gentleness in his movements as he picked Toby up off the ground, tenderly holding him in his arms until the child woke up and insisted on walking. It was the uncomplaining courage of continuing on, thinking first of her, of Toby, and of the needs of those back in Hagenheim, and not of himself. It was the knowledge that she could trust him completely, with her life ... maybe even with her heart.

He would never hurt her, not deliberately. It was only her own stubborn heart that seemed set on dooming itself. Their playful conversation had stirred up thoughts and feelings that would have been better left buried.

Soon their journey would be over. Would he try to leave her in Marienberg and go riding off with her cousin and his men to save the world from Claybrook? Probably. But even if she did manage to convince them to allow her to ride with them back to Hagenheim, she likely would not get another chance to speak with Colin alone. And after all they had been through together, that thought weighed her down and warred with the peace she had about reaching Marienberg, and Hagenheim, in time to save her family.

When they finally lay down to sleep, it was another cold night, and again they placed Toby between them and rolled up in the blanket. But instead of falling immediately to sleep as he had before, Toby chattered on about all kinds of things. He said to Margaretha, "The goose girl who herds the geese for Master Steinbek kisses the stable boy on the mouth. Why don't you kiss Colin? I have never seen you kiss him."

Margaretha felt her face turn red, even though she knew Colin, who was lying on the other side of Toby, couldn't understand Toby's German, and Toby had asked the question innocently enough.

"He said something about me," Colin said, eyeing her suspiciously. "Translate, please. It is very dull listening to the two of you chatter on and not understand a word."

Margaretha cleared her throat. "Toby wants to know why you and I don't kiss like Master Steinbek's servant girl and stable boy."

Toby piped up and asked, "Is it because you and Colin are good friends, like brother and sister?"

"I heard my name again," Colin said with a playful smile.

"This conversation is a little ... awkward." Margaretha tried to laugh her embarrassment away, but it wasn't working. "Toby asked if it is because we are good friends and like brother and sister."

"Well?" Colin raised his eyebrows at her. "Is that the reason?" He lost his amused expression, and his eyes turned serious and penetrating. "Are we like brother and sister?"

Margaretha's throat was suddenly dry and she swallowed. She spoke to Toby in German.

"What did you say to him?" Colin demanded.

"I said, yes, we are good friends, but that I would ask you why we don't kiss." Her breath seemed to desert her, making her voice sound raspy.

He was facing the fire, which cast deep shadows over his features. He stared hard at her, but she couldn't seem to look away. "We don't kiss," he finally said, speaking slowly, "because we are not betrothed ... and because we don't want to do something that we would later regret."

"Yes. Exactly." He was perfectly right and reasonable in what he said, so why did his words make tears come to her eyes — tears of longing?

She translated what he said to Toby, who still looked wide awake.

"What is betrothed? What is regret?" he asked.

"Betrothed is when you have agreed to marry someone, and

regret is feeling sorry you did something and wishing you had not done it."

"Why aren't you and Colin betrothed?"

Colin said, "Translate, please."

"He asks why we aren't betrothed." Margaretha's stomach had tied itself into a knot before she even finished her sentence.

Once again, Colin fixed her with that intense gaze of his. Margaretha bit her lip to make sure it didn't tremble.

"We aren't betrothed because—" He stopped.

What was he about to say? If only he would finish his thought! She was afraid of what he would say, but also longed to know what he was thinking.

"Because I am an Englishman and must return to England."

Was it her imagination? Or did he say the words as if they wrenched his heart? He could have said they weren't betrothed because they weren't in love, or because he could hardly wait to leave the Holy Roman Empire and marry an English girl. He could have said many different things.

He swallowed. "And because Margaretha loves her family and would miss them horribly if she left and went with me."

So he thought he knew her feelings on the subject. Margaretha translated for Toby.

Toby yawned. Good. Perhaps he would soon fall asleep and stop asking these questions.

Instead, Toby asked, "Doesn't Colin think you're pretty? Doesn't Colin want to stay here and marry you?"

She knew Colin would insist she translate, so she went ahead and did so. Once again, all the air seemed to get sucked out of her throat and she couldn't say the words without sounding embarrassingly out of breath.

His expression softened, but his eyes were still intense. "I think Margaretha is beautiful. But if I stayed in Hagenheim and worked as a stable boy, I don't think her father would agree to our marriage." He reached out and softly stroked her cheek with his fingers. "But there is a part of me that very much regrets that. Very ... very much." He brushed a lock of hair off her forehead.

Margaretha felt a thrill of pleasure at his touch. Thank goodness Toby was there. But she suspected Colin wouldn't have said what he did if Toby had not been safely tucked between them, forming the perfect little-boy barrier. She glanced down at Toby. His eyes were closed and he was asleep. Uh-oh.

Colin hadn't seemed to notice. He said, "But perhaps Margaretha doesn't feel the same way."

She could discern no hostility in his eyes, only questions. Her heart beat so hard it hurt her chest.

Colin touched her forehead with two knuckles, running them over her temple. He pulled his hand back and tucked it underneath him. "You told me about those suitors that you rejected. If I were your suitor, would you have rejected me?"

"I ... I rejected those suitors because ..." The realization came over her like something that had been right in front of her, but she was only now seeing. "They didn't love me. They didn't like that I talk too much. They looked at me as if they didn't think I could have anything worth saying. Or as if I was a lack-wit. They were annoyed or preoccupied or didn't care. And I want to be loved. I want to love and be loved, and to be respected. I don't want someone to love me simply because I am a duke's daughter. I don't want a disinterested husband. I want someone who loves me passionately. And you, Colin ... I think ..." Once again, her breath betrayed her and she had to pause, her heart pounding in her ears. "I think whenever you marry ... you will love your wife ... with great passion and respect. That's what I want."

There. She hoped she hadn't said too much. But she was more afraid she would say too little. Now if only they could both fall asleep, and if only he would not reject her in his reply.

Chapter
28

Colin's heart leapt into his throat at what she was saying.

He probably sounded like a lovesick boy, but he couldn't stop himself from replying, "You deserve every bit of love and passion and respect that you desire." What did she want him to say? And what did *he* want?

He had one more day with her. Would it be enough? Or would he go back to England and forever wonder what might have been?

Her eyes locked on his, and she whispered, "*Gute Nacht,* Colin."

He wasn't sure he'd sleep at all tonight, but he whispered, "Good night, Margaretha."

The next morning, when the sun was beginning to lighten the sky, Margaretha left Toby asleep in the blanket. Colin was already up and getting a drink from the stream. Margaretha went deeper into the woods to have a few minutes of privacy.

She enjoyed early mornings. What could be better than listening to the first songs of the birds and seeing the squirrels scurrying through the leaves on the ground? It was peaceful.

Today was the last day of her walking journey with Colin, if

God so willed it. Her feet were sore and tired, she had not had a decent bath since she left Hagenheim, but she would miss being with Colin. And she hoped he would miss her.

But she didn't want to think about that.

She turned around to head back to Toby and Colin, but every direction looked the same.

She stared hard at the trees. Nothing looked particularly familiar. She searched for signs of where she had walked, broken branches or trampled leaves, but she could find no evidence of which direction she had come from. Her heart began to pound.

"I only have to wait for the sun to come up to figure out where I am," she told herself.

They had slept next to the stream, as they always did, but she didn't see or hear the water from here. The road was west of where they had camped, but which way was west? With the density of the trees around her, she wasn't sure if she would be able to tell which way the sun was, even when it did come up. The leaves overhead were quite thick.

She had no idea which way to go.

She could call out, hoping Colin would hear her and come for her. But what if someone else heard her, someone not so friendly, like those robbers who had stolen their horses and everything they had of value?

"What would Mother tell me to do?" She bit her lip and closed her eyes to force herself to think.

Pray. Mother would tell her to pray.

Margaretha began to ask God to help her find her way. "If I don't get out of here, I'll be lost away from Colin and Toby. They won't know what happened to me. They might think something terrible happened to me. They might get lost themselves, looking for me."

Margaretha was on the brink of tears. This was no good. Why was she saying such a fearful prayer?

"God, forgive me. You know the way back. Help me find my way."

Opening her eyes, the glow in the sky seemed brighter to her right. That must be the east. Straight ahead was north, and according to what she remembered about last night and where they went to sleep, the road must be straight ahead. If she could find the road, she could find Colin and Toby.

She hurried through the trees. Her heart was still pounding incredibly fast. "God, please help me," she whispered, hearing the desperation in her voice, so she deliberately infused her next words with faith. "God, I know you will help me. You will never leave me or forsake me. Help me find the road and get back to Colin and Toby and get to Marienberg before nightfall. Nothing is too hard for you."

That last thought gave her strength, so she repeated it in her mind as she walked through the thick undergrowth, leaves, and bushes. *Nothing is too hard for God. Nothing is too hard for God.*

The trees began to thin and she could see glimpses of the bare road ahead through the leaves and tree trunks. The closer she got, the more she was convinced that she was near where they had veered off the road the night before. Once she was on the road again, she was certain she could find it.

She broke out of the trees and nearly laughed out loud in relief. To the east, the sun was just peeking over the horizon, as if it lay a few miles down the road. But she didn't see the spot where they had turned off the road the night before.

She looked to her left, and her breath stilled in her throat.

A group of five men—Claybrook's men—and their horses stood in the road looking at her.

<hr>

When Toby awoke, Margaretha was nowhere in sight, so Colin took him by the hand so that he could help Colin collect their game from the snares he had set the night before. Toby was very interested in the snares. Colin could only hope the little boy's excited voice didn't attract the attention of more robbers—or even Claybrook's men, who were doubtless still searching for them.

They made their way back to where they had slept, but Margaretha had not returned. Immediately, he felt a sense of dread. Had something happened?

"Margaretha." He called her name, but not too loudly.

Toby prattled on, but of course, Colin didn't understand him. Where was Margaretha?

Men's voices came from the direction of the road.

Margaretha froze. Her head seemed to float, and her stomach sank to her toes. Was she about to faint?

Claybrook's men sprang toward her, two on their horses, three on foot. She couldn't hope to outrun them, and in a few moments, two of them were holding her by her arms.

"You have led us on a merry chase," one of them growled. He appeared to be in charge, because the other men only stared and let him do the talking. "But we have you now. Tell us where your friend, Colin le Wyse, has wandered off to."

"He isn't here." Margaretha's voice was quiet, solemn, and strangely calm. *Thank you, God, for that.*

"We saw your footprints—two sets of footprints—leading off this road. We know there were two of you, so where is he?"

She saw no way to escape from them. The only thing she could do was to lead them away from Colin. At least he could make it to Marienberg and get help. They would not kill Margaretha, especially if Lord Claybrook still intended to marry her. But they surely had orders to kill Colin on sight.

"Colin is dead." Margaretha burst into tears, covering her face with her hands.

It was not difficult to cry. After all, she had come so close to reaching Marienberg, only to be found by these evil men. And her fear for Colin and Toby was great enough to add to her distress.

"Dead? You're lying."

"He caught a fever and died in the night." She began to sob harder.

"Are you telling me the truth?"

Margaretha could only nod.

Another man said softly, "Let us go. It's the girl Claybrook wants. Let him rot in the forest."

A third added, "We've been chasing this wench for too long. I want to get back to the fighting, if there is to be any."

The leader barked back, "If Claybrook finds out you called his future bride anything but Lady Margaretha, you may not be in any condition for fighting."

He grunted and muttered something under his breath.

Margaretha had stopped crying to listen to them. She hoped they would hurry. At any moment, Colin might emerge from the forest and try to save her. If he did, he would be outnumbered and surely would be killed.

"You will take me back to my mother? Is she still safe?"

The leader looked at her for a moment. "Lord Claybrook had no plans to kill your mother."

"Will you take me to her, then?"

"Of course." The leader dismounted. "You may ride with me, Lady Margaretha. I am Sir Gisborne."

Margaretha nodded.

He helped her onto the back of his horse, where a sort of extra saddle was attached behind his own. Then he and the rest of the men mounted their horses and they set off to the north, back the way Margaretha, Colin, and Toby had come.

O God, please keep them safe. Don't let anything bad happen to Colin and Toby. Bring them to Marienberg, and bring help to Hagenheim.

Colin snatched his dagger out of his belt and glanced down at Toby. The little boy's eyes widened. He took Colin's offered hand and Colin crept toward the sound of the men's voices. Before he reached the end of the forest, he heard horses' hooves, the sound moving away from him to the north.

Colin ran. He made it to the road in time to see five horses and Claybrook's men moving at a fast trot down the road. On the back of one of the horses was Margaretha.

"No. No, no, no." He sank to his knees in the dirt, covering his face with his hands.

"*Was ist das?*" Toby asked, catching up to him.

Colin put his arm around Toby. He had to be calm and in control, for the child's sake. But what could he tell him? They couldn't even speak the same language.

"*Wo ist* Margaretha?" His eyes were wide and trusting as he patted Colin's shoulder.

"Where is Margaretha? She's gone away." By now, he understood a little German, a few basic words and phrases, but it was much harder to speak it. He shook his head at the little boy, wishing he could explain to him. "We must go to Marienberg. Margaretha must go to Hagenheim. But we will go to Hagenheim too. Margaretha *muss nach* Hagenheim *gehen. Wir müssen nach* Hagenheim *auch gehen.*"

Toby tilted his head, understanding Colin's German words, but clearly confused as to why Margaretha was no longer with them.

"Margaretha needs us to go get help. That is what we will do. Come." And they set out again.

Claybrook's men tied Margaretha's hands and ankles together at night to keep her from escaping.

"I shall tell Lord Claybrook that you touched my ankles, that you used undue force, if you so much as *think* about making one wrong move," Margaretha promised the men. She even stipulated which of the men was allowed to tie her up. "Not you! Him."

Why not give them trouble? They didn't deserve her courtesy.

She also made certain to talk without ceasing. She asked them, "Why did you dare to come to this country with Claybrook? Didn't you understand his intentions? Didn't you know he only wanted to take what did not belong to him?"

Finally, after many more such questions, the leader answered her, "Such is the nature of war. A man cannot win a fortune for himself without action, without warring with another."

"I daresay you think these Germans deserve to have their lands and their towns taken from them by force. You have a right to make your fortune at their expense, you think?"

Margaretha gave them no rest. On the third day, Sir Gisborne threatened to tie a cloth around her mouth, gagging her. Margaretha fell silent.

She was overjoyed to finally see the towers of Hagenheim Castle come into view. The men's veneer of manners was wearing thin after she had deliberately plagued them the entire time.

She could hardly wait to see her mother and sisters and brothers again and find out how they were all faring—especially if there was any news of Father and Valten.

As they entered the town gate, it was guarded not by her father's men, but by Claybrook's. Inside, few people were on the streets. The ones who were looked somber, or even afraid. Some looked up and recognized her, sitting on the back of Sir Gisborne's horse, and they covered their mouths in horror, or even burst into tears. When they were passing through the most densely populated street of all, Margaretha called out, "Take courage, Hagenheim! Duke Wilhelm is coming! He will prevail!"

Several cheers rang out as many people raised a fist in the air.

Sir Gisborne hissed at her, "Be quiet! I'll gag you yet."

But Margaretha only smiled and waved at the people who were staring at her from their doors and from their second- and third-story windows. Some of them smiled, and they all waved back at her.

"Claybrook may force his rule over them," Margaretha said to Sir Gisborne's back, "but their hearts belong to Duke Wilhelm."

Sir Gisborne made no reply.

He and his men surrounded her as they walked her through the courtyard. But instead of being taken directly to her family, she was taken to Lord Claybrook, who was sitting like a king on a throne in the Great Hall.

"Lady Margaretha," he said with a smile. "I am pleased my men were able to bring you back safely to me."

Margaretha said nothing. Once again he was wearing one of his elaborate hats, along with a cape of royal blue silk, embroidered with an Oriental design in gold thread. She tried not to feel anything so that her anger toward this man would not overwhelm her. She had to keep a clear head.

"I see you are not inclined to speak today." He smiled that feline smile of his.

"I wish to see my family, if you have not murdered them all yet."

"My dear, you know me to be a ruthless man, but I see no need to dispose of your mother and sisters or the little ones." His lip curled. "Not if you agree to marry me."

So, he would hold her family's lives over her to force her to marry him. She should have guessed.

When she didn't speak, he said, "The wedding shall be . . ."

He looked up at the ceiling, as though contemplating a date. "Tomorrow, at vespers."

Margaretha stared past him at a spot on the wall, refusing to look directly at him. "I want to see my family now."

After several moments of silence, he said, "I shall send your wedding dress to you. You shall be quite lovely in the gown I have picked out for you."

After a few more moments, he waved his hand and ordered some guards to take her to the solar.

Margaretha climbed the stairs extra slowly and began speaking to the three guards who accompanied her in their native English. "A vast army is on its way here. If you wish to save your lives and fight on the side of the righteous, on God's side, you had best change your loyalties when you hear the battle begin."

The soldiers' eyes shifted as they glanced at each other.

"I speak the truth. Duke Wilhelm and his allies will not punish you if you refuse to kill on Claybrook's behalf. Duke Wilhelm rewards good deeds, and you will not be sorry if you offer your loyalty to him, I can promise you."

None of the guards spoke, but she knew they were at least listening. If she could turn a few of his own guards against him, Claybrook would have even less chance against her father and her cousin Theodemar, the Duke of Marienberg. And Colin.

They reached the solar before she could say much else. Inside, her mother and Gisela were sewing, Kirstyn was playing backgammon with Adela, and her brothers, Wolfgang and Steffan, were playing some sort of game on the floor.

"Mama!" Tears sprang to her eyes at seeing her dear mother.

Everyone looked up at her. They all seemed to exclaim at once. Her mother dropped her sewing and ran to Margaretha, embracing her. "Thank heaven you are all safe and well." Margaretha squeezed her eyes shut. "Thank you, God."

Her mother cried softly against Margaretha's shoulder.

"Don't cry, Mama. All will be well."

Kirstyn and Adela added their arms as they also embraced her. Even her brothers came and patted her arm.

"Where have you been?" her mother finally asked, wiping her eyes. "What have you been about? We did not know what had become of you."

Margaretha glanced over her shoulder to make sure the guards were listening. "I cannot tell you exactly, but I believe help is on the way to Hagenheim. Father and Valten shall have all the fighting men they will need to easily defeat the evil Lord Claybrook." She only hoped some of the guards at the door of the solar understood German. But Claybrook would have been clever enough to ensure that.

Her mother looked nervously at the guards and then turned to her daughter and placed her finger over her lips.

"Don't worry, Mother," Margaretha whispered. "I am trying to convert the guards to our side."

Next, she inquired after Gisela and her health.

"I believe she is very near her time," Lady Rose said, smiling at her daughter-in-law.

"I am ready when that time comes," Gisela said. She laid her hand over her stomach and smiled, but her eyes were sad. No doubt she was worried about Valten. Would he return and be able to defeat Claybrook in time to see his first child born? How terrible to be facing the birth of your first child while being held against your will.

Would Margaretha be forced to wed Claybrook before help arrived? She would almost rather die than spend one hour wed to that villain. But she also couldn't allow Claybrook to harm her family members. Tomorrow at vespers, if no one came to rescue her, how could she avoid marrying Claybrook? If Colin was not able to get here with an army in twenty-four hours, she might soon be the bride of a monster.

Chapter
29

Margaretha thanked the maids—Britta was not among them—who brought up the hot water for her bath. They didn't answer, but looked frightened and scurried away. No doubt Claybrook had told them not to speak to her.

When she was safely alone in her room, she sank into the warm water and closed her eyes. Never had a bath felt so good, or been so needed! She scrubbed her skin as well as her hair and scalp with the floral-scented soap. If she hadn't been afraid someone might invade her privacy, she would have stayed longer. But she quickly dried herself off and began to braid her wet hair.

But even the welcome refreshment of the bath could not chase away her worries about her family's safety, the safety of the Hagenheim people, and her questions about Colin.

How long had he searched for her? Did he realize Claybrook's men had taken her back to Hagenheim? Had he and Toby arrived in Marienberg? Did the Duke of Marienberg believe him? Was he able to find someone who spoke English who could help him convince her cousin to raise an army and come to Hagenheim?

For the tenth time that morning, Margaretha's breath caught in her throat. There were hundreds of things that could have gone wrong. And for the tenth time, she told her fears, "Nothing is too hard for God."

She let her braid hang over her shoulder and finished getting dressed.

Yes, there were hundreds of things that could have gone wrong. But Colin was brave. He was the most intensely determined person she had ever met. But more than anything else, she knew God was on their side. God was ever on the side of the righteous.

When she was young, the priest had made her memorize certain psalms. She still remembered Psalm 1.

> *Blessed is the one who does not walk in step with the wicked*
> *or stand in the way that sinners take*
> *or sit in the company of mockers,*
> *but whose delight is in the law of the LORD,*
> *and who meditates on his law day and night.*
> *That person is like a tree planted by streams of water,*
> *which yields its fruit in season*
> *and whose leaf does not wither—*
> *whatever they do prospers.*
> *Not so the wicked!*
> *They are like chaff*
> *that the wind blows away.*
> *Therefore the wicked will not stand in the judgment,*
> *nor sinners in the assembly of the righteous.*
> *For the LORD watches over the way of the righteous,*
> *but the way of the wicked leads to destruction.*

"You watch over us, God. You watch over Colin, and you watch over my family, and the way of Lord Claybrook leads to destruction. I believe, God. Take away my unbelief. I have peace because my trust is in you."

She must not allow Claybrook to take away her peace. She must not allow her fears to overwhelm her trust that God would make a way of escape for them.

The door opened and Claybrook strode in.

For a moment, she was speechless. When she found her voice again, she raged, "How dare you come in here when I have not given you my leave? You will request my permission before coming into my private chamber." She stood and glared into Claybrook's vacant, black eyes.

"I will not ask your permission," he hissed back, his face deadly calm as he leaned so close to her she could count his eyelashes and see his nostrils flare. "You are to be my wife in but a few short hours, and then you shall ask *my* permission ... to breathe."

Margaretha shuddered inwardly. "I do not wish to become your wife—yet. As loyal subjects of the king, we must first send a missive to the king requesting his approval of the union."

"Oh, we shall do that." Claybrook smiled and nodded. "But first, we shall wed in secret, here in the castle chapel, with your family members as witnesses. In the event of any fighting, I want everyone to know that we were married ... especially if you should meet your untimely death in the melee."

Margaretha refused to show any horror. She merely stared at him.

"However, if you cooperate with me"—he smirked and toyed with the liripipe dangling from his hat—"and if you prove to be a good wife, I shall make arrangements so that you do *not* meet your death at the hands of my overzealous guards."

You will never possess me. She did not speak the words aloud. She would let him, for the moment, think he had won.

"But the reason I am paying you this visit is to present you with your wedding dress. It is finer than anything you own, I would wager." He snapped his fingers, and a maid brought in an elaborate gold-and-silver-trimmed dress. She laid it on Margaretha's bed and left the room.

Should she defy him? Or should she pretend to be defeated and go along with him?

"It seems I have no choice in the matter," she said softly, her gaze never wavering from his face.

He smiled. "It is good to hear you speak reasonably. Now examine your dress. I have brought it all the way from London for you, and I want you to see how exquisite it is."

Margaretha looked at the garment. It was not at all to her taste, very gaudy, and the bodice was cut too low. "Truly, I have never been interested in fashions and clothing." She couldn't resist disappointing him.

"Once you put it on, you will see how magnificent it is." He snapped his fingers again and a slim young man entered the room. "My tailor, Gabriel, will make sure it fits properly. Put it on and he will make the appropriate adjustments."

"I have a seamstress who can adequately adjust it for me." Margaretha met his eye, prepared to defy him in this.

He seemed to think about it, then motioned dismissively with his hand. "Very well. I shall call your seamstress—what is her name?"

"Gertie."

"And I will have her come and do the proper alterations." He waved the tailor out of the room, then turned to Margaretha. "I shall see you tomorrow, my dear, on this auspicious occasion of our wedding."

He stepped toward her, as if he intended to kiss her hand. She turned away from him, pretending not to realize his intention. "Very well."

He paused. Would he force the issue? Finally, he turned, but before he left the room, he said, "Tomorrow night, my dear, there will be feasting and dancing after the wedding." Lowering his voice to an icy murmur, he said, "We shall drink and be merry." He walked away, and his laugh floated down the corridor after he was gone.

The next day, Lord Claybrook sent for Margaretha for the midday meal. He even told her which dress he wished her to wear— her dark blue cotehardie with the silver embroidered hem.

She wore her pink silk with the colorful birds embroidered on the bodice.

He frowned when he saw her walking toward the dais where he was sitting in her father's place at the head of the table. He had installed her mother opposite her usual place, at his left hand instead of on the right, and Margaretha he placed to his right.

She said a quick prayer, entreating God to look down and see this boastful peacock in her father's place and to see the injustice of it. "Give me justice against my adversary," she whispered, imitating the persistent widow from the Bible.

The meal was delicious. Margaretha surprised herself by eating heartily. She was aware of the guards stationed all around the Great Hall, and Lord Claybrook smirking and drinking more than he was eating. But in her heart, she felt peace. Colin was on his way to save her, and God would not allow Claybrook to marry her. He would provide a way of escape.

Margaretha had managed to ignore him for most of the meal and talk with Gisela and Kirstyn and her mother, but then he tapped her on the arm and asked, "My dear, what would you like me to give you for a wedding gift?"

A question had been nagging at her all day, so instead of answering his question, she asked, "What have you done with my father's guards?"

At first he didn't answer, only took his time lifting his goblet to his lips and taking a drink, then slowly setting it back down.

"I don't think you should worry about such a thing. But if

you must know, the ones who are still alive are in the dungeon beneath the castle." He narrowed his eyes at her. "And if they refuse to transfer their loyalty from your father to me, then they shall all be hanged."

She tried not to let it show that his words made her feel sick.

"But do not worry, my dear. Once they find out that you, Duke Wilhelm's oldest daughter, are my wife, I think most of them will be more than willing to bow the knee to me."

He had thought of everything. The swine would use her as a pawn in his power game, just as he was using his men to do all his fighting for him. He was nothing without those men, nothing but a cowardly bully and an evil schemer.

No, she would not let him steal her peace. He would still be defeated. After all, her father had many friends all over the Holy Roman Empire. Even now he was probably gathering his forces to attack. Along with Colin and Duke Theodemar of Marienberg, it was only a matter of time before they would come and save Hagenheim from the clutches of this evil man.

Margaretha simply smiled.

The guards escorted her mother, siblings, and Gisela back to the solar, but he ordered two other guards to take Margaretha back to her chamber. She gave Claybrook a cold stare. "Cannot my mother come with me?"

He shrugged. "I suppose." Then he doubled the number of guards he sent with Margaretha and Lady Rose.

"He must think you're dangerous," she said to her mother.

Once they were in Margaretha's chamber and the guards were outside the door—the only way in or out of the room— Lady Rose whispered, "I have an idea. It may only help us gain a little time—"

"Maybe all I need is a little time. I know help is on the way, Mother. Help is coming soon; I can feel it."

"Yes, but unless it comes in the next two hours, it will be too late to save you from marrying him. So we will switch places."

Margaretha gasped at her mother's suggestion.

"We are almost the same height and build, and our hair is similar. If I wear your wedding dress and veil, and you wear a veil as well, then we should be able to fool the guards and Claybrook too. It probably won't buy us much time, especially if he insists on going to the Great Hall and feasting afterward, but it's worth trying."

"But I don't want to escape and leave you here."

Her mother caught her arm and made her look her in the eye. "If you get a chance to escape, you take it. No one here is in as much danger as you are."

Her mother's hand was shaking, even as she held onto Margaretha's arm, and her expression was more serious than Margaretha had ever seen it. "Yes, Mother."

"If the guards still think I am you, and if they take me up to Claybrook's chamber, they won't be paying as much attention to you. Then you can slip away, down to the dungeon, and through the secret tunnel."

"But what will Claybrook do when he discovers you've tricked him?"

"Let me worry about that. I can take care of myself. I wasn't always a sheltered duchess, and I might be able to hide something up my sleeve."

"Like a candlestick?"

"What?"

"I hid a candlestick up my sleeve. That is how Colin and Anne and I escaped. I hit two guards over the head with it."

"That is a good idea." Her mother smiled mischievously, making her look like a young girl.

They looked around the room, but there was not a single candlestick in sight. "He must have heard that story as well."

Margaretha's heart sank a little as they continued to look for anything that might be used as a weapon. They searched and searched, but nothing was small enough to fit in their sleeves — voluminous though they were — that was also hard and heavy enough to serve as a weapon.

Then Margaretha noticed the iron cross hanging above her door. Her mother insisted that all their bedchambers have them. She carried a stool over to the door, quietly set it down so as not to alert the guards outside, and lifted the cross off the nail that held it in place.

The cross was nice and heavy. Good.

"Here, Mother. You can use it on Claybrook."

"You will have more need of it. You're sure to encounter guards when you're trying to escape."

They argued for several minutes, but Lady Rose finally won.

Margaretha put on her mother's dress, which was a dark emerald green. Then she found a black headrail, which she used to cover her hair and tucked into the collar of her mother's gown. She took her black mourning veil, attached it to her mother's gorget, and looked in the mirror.

"I don't even recognize myself." Margaretha giggled at the deception.

In the meantime, her mother had put on the over-decorated wedding dress, with its heavy gold brocade and layers of silk, which were embroidered with silver and gold thread. Then she fastened a fancier gorget to her head, attaching her most heavily embroidered veil.

"No one will ever know you aren't an eighteen-year-old bride." Margaretha shivered a little inside. "But are you sure this is a good idea? I don't want to endanger you, Mother. He is so ruthless, he may kill you if he thinks I have escaped. I don't think we should do it."

"Don't be afraid. I won't allow him to kill me."

"Mother." Margaretha felt ill. "I can't let you do it."

"And I can't let you marry that evil man!" She lowered her voice when she went on. "I lost one daughter, and I won't lose another if there is anything I can do about it."

Her sister, the one who drowned when Margaretha was a baby. Margaretha's chest ached at the pain her mother must still feel over the loss. She must trust God to keep her mother safe.

"All will be well, Mother. I shall believe that God will make a way of escape for you."

"Yes, and I shall believe my plan will work." Her mother held her by the arms and stared into her eyes.

"Very well."

The guards pounded on the door and announced that it was time for them to come down for the wedding. Margaretha ran to the window and gazed out, hoping against her better judgment, knowing that they—her father, Valten, and her cousin and Colin—probably would not be there.

The courtyard was nearly deserted. The only people she saw were two of Claybrook's guards, and they looked as they always did—no one sounded an alarm, and no one moved or looked particularly vigilant.

Her rescuers had not come.

No matter. She would rescue herself.

Chapter
30

Her mother opened the door to the guards and allowed them to lead her and Margaretha down to the chapel, where the priest and Lord Claybrook were waiting.

The priest's eyes were wider than normal, and his lips were pursed. No doubt he had been threatened with some heinous consequence if he did not agree to perform the marriage rites.

Margaretha hung back while her mother walked forward to stand beside Claybrook in front of the priest. Soon, her family members were ushered in to stand as witnesses to the marriage. A glance over her shoulder showed several guards, all with swords drawn, standing by the door of the chapel.

There was another entrance, but it was on the second floor. With an upward glance, she saw a guard standing at the top of the winding stairs, and another at the bottom. Claybrook was leaving no opportunity for escape.

Margaretha felt the weight of the iron cross inside her sleeve. It gave her a measure of comfort, even though she could never hope to use it at the moment, with so many guards around them.

The priest began speaking the rites, unaware that the "bride" before him was Lady Rose and not Margaretha. He spoke slowly, but he soon came to the part where the bride and groom would have to give their consent to the marriage. Just before it was time for the bride to consent, Claybrook suddenly took hold of her veil and ripped it off, revealing the face of Lady Rose.

Claybrook turned and his eyes immediately focused on Margaretha, her face covered with the veil that was supposed to be her mother's. "Ah! I knew you would attempt some trickery." His lip curled in a snarl, showing his teeth like some sort of animal, and he pointed at Margaretha. "Bring her here."

The guards grabbed her elbows and pushed her forward. Claybrook threw back her black veil. "A foolish ruse. You cannot delay the wedding any longer." He grasped her upper arm so tightly, his fingers bit into her flesh. But Margaretha was too relieved that his hand had just missed the cross in her sleeve to complain.

Claybrook turned to the priest. "Get on with it."

The priest repeated the vows. When he asked her if she would vow to honor and obey Claybrook as her husband, Margaretha replied loudly in German, so everyone in the chapel could hear, "I will not."

Claybrook growled and said, "She agrees." Claybrook's voice was emphatic. "Now go on."

Margaretha waited to see what the priest would do. Would he stop the ceremony, defying Claybrook, since Church law stated that no one could be married against their will? Or would he continue with the wedding vows to avoid whatever Claybrook had threatened him with?

The priest only spared Margaretha one quick glance before continuing with the ceremony.

She could have protested further, could have fought Claybrook and run if she was able to break loose from his painful grip, but what good would that do? The guards would only drag her back. They might even hurt her mother just to force her to comply. For now, she would bide her time.

The priest's voice was like the drone of a hive full of bees, dooming her to marry him, whether she consented or not. There was no way out.

O God, save me, save me!

She must keep her wits about her, even though she was trapped and could see no way of escape. How could she ever get past so many guards?

This pattern of thinking was not helping. She must keep looking for an opportunity. She must not allow herself to think that all was lost. God was her peace. Hadn't she learned that on the long journey she had taken with Colin? By focusing on God's power and goodness, she would not panic and her mind would remain clear so she could think of a plan. Instead of sending up prayers full of anxiety, she would trust that God would make a way.

When the priest pronounced them "man and wife," Claybrook took her hand, squeezed her fingers in a vice-like grip, and nodded to the witnesses. "Now we shall eat, drink, and be merry as you honor the marriage between the House of Fortescue and the House of Gerstenberg."

Each of Margaretha's family members alternately looked horrified, disgusted, or angry, but Claybrook didn't seem to notice. He dragged Margaretha forward.

The marriage can still be annulled. She comforted herself with those words, but it was little comfort if she were forced to go back with him to his bedchamber. She simply had to escape.

She numbly followed as he paraded her in front of his men. One of them looked at Margaretha with a lewd sneer. She glared back at him, then faced forward, refusing to look at anyone else.

Throughout the feast, Margaretha calculated various escape routes. When she asked to go to the garderobe, he sent three guards with her and refused her request to allow her mother to accompany her. The guards never turned their back on her, and she wasn't desperate enough to take on three of them—yet.

She forced herself to eat a little bread and meat, to make sure she kept up her strength. But soon, her nervous stomach would not accept any more food.

The only good thing was that Claybrook was drinking heavily, and had been all day. Perhaps he would make himself so drunk he would pass out and she could escape. She wouldn't count on it, though.

Margaretha's sisters kept looking at her with tears in their eyes. She winked at them when Claybrook wasn't looking. All would be well. She didn't want them to think otherwise. Her little brothers also looked frightened for her, desperation and anger flitting over their faces. They wanted to defend her, which proved her little brothers did love her, even though they teased her.

Margaretha refused to look at Lord Claybrook throughout the feast. There was little entertainment — only one troubadour and a juggler. No one seemed in a particularly festive mood. Even the few knights of higher rank who had been allowed to join the feast as guests were subdued.

Finally, when Claybrook was well and truly drunk, he yelled at the guards standing by to take Margaretha's family to their chambers and lock their doors. Then he motioned to three guards to come with him. "Come and escort me and my new bride to our wedding chambers." He chortled drunkenly.

Margaretha walked slowly, and, surprisingly, the guards and Claybrook followed suit and walked slowly as well. *I can surely fight off a man as drunk as Claybrook.* But she preferred to delay the moment of confrontation as long as possible.

They began to climb the stone stairs to Claybrook's bedchamber when Claybrook began to moan. He continued to climb, but he moved even slower. When they reached the top of the steps, Claybrook coughed, then bent over and vomited on the floor.

Two of the guards took hold of Margaretha's arms while the third asked Claybrook if he needed help.

Claybrook ordered, "Take her to her own chamber until I send for her." He leaned over and retched some more.

Margaretha shuddered. She did not envy the poor servant who would be forced to clean that up. But … *Thank you, God, for the reprieve!*

The two guards compelled her to start walking down the corridor to her chamber. When they had rounded the bend, they stopped.

They were looking at each other. Perhaps this was her opportunity!

"Men, if you will help me escape," Margaretha whispered, "I will make it worth your while. My father, Duke Wilhelm, will reward you well—"

One of the guards interrupted her. "We will help you escape, if you have a plan."

"You will? But why?"

"We have our reasons."

"Tell us," the other one said.

"You must take me to the dungeon."

"To the dungeon? My lady—"

"To the dungeon. Pretend you are bringing me there on Lord Claybrook's orders, to clamp me in irons. I will tell you the rest when we get there."

They crept forward and peeked down the corridor. No one was in sight. Then they heard Claybrook retching again farther down the corridor.

The two men compelled her forward. Once at the top of the stairs, they maneuvered around the mess on the floor and hurried down the steps, with Margaretha in the lead.

"We should move more slowly," one guard whispered, "so as not to create suspicion should the other guards see us."

Margaretha nodded and slowed her pace, allowing the guards to take her by each arm again, as though they were holding her captive.

"Why do you want to help me?" Margaretha whispered. Could she really trust them? She was desperate for a way out, so she had little choice.

She stopped and faced them, and they stopped as well, halting in the corner at the top of the stairs that led to the dungeon.

The two men were burly, one with dark reddish hair and the other with light brown. They met her eyes openly. "We thought we could better our status by coming with Claybrook here, but we didn't know what a brutal, unjust man he was."

The one with light brown hair and a crooked nose added, "And we regret being forced to kill innocent men. He promised that if we came with him, he would give us our own estates in exchange for helping him foist a usurper from his family's lands."

"And then we discovered he had lied to us. We don't like the man." The redhead shook his head. "Also, we heard from the kitchen servants that the men of Hagenheim are sneaking out of the town, being lowered down the wall to go and join Duke Wilhelm. They say he is raising an army to fight Claybrook."

"Not only that, but we believe the kitchen servants poisoned Claybrook's wine."

"So that is why he is sick!" Margaretha's heart leapt at the news.

"I heard them say that the last carafe of wine was only for Claybrook and his knights."

"I believe you are trustworthy," Margaretha announced. "But you must tell me your names."

"I am Thomas Stephenson," the red-haired one said.

"Thaddeus Lee," the other said.

"Now I shall tell you a secret that you must not tell another soul." Margaretha cupped her hands around her mouth and whispered in the red-haired man's ear and told him about the tunnel in the dungeon that led outside the wall of the town. Then she told the brown-haired man, as he leaned down and offered her his ear.

"When we get to the bottom of the steps, go to the right."

The men nodded, then escorted her down the dark steps.

"Who goes there?" A guard stood at the bottom of the steps holding up a torch, his other hand reaching for his sword hilt at his belt. The old gaoler was nowhere in sight.

Thomas greeted him and said, "Lord Claybrook ordered Lady Margaretha to spend the night in the dungeon."

Men — her father's own knights and soldiers — lined the walls, chained hand and foot. She even recognized Britta's sweetheart, Gustaf. The sight of them made her clench her teeth and itch to use the heavy cross in her sleeve.

Thomas and Thaddeus had let go of her arms while they talked with the man guarding the dungeon. She heard a thud and turned to look.

The guard sank to the floor. Thomas stood holding his sword at an odd angle. Apparently he had struck the guard with the butt of the hilt. The guard lay unmoving on the stone floor.

"We must set these men free."

Thaddeus was already taking the keys from the large ring hanging from the guard's belt. He systematically unlocked each man's manacles.

The men had obviously been shackled to the wall for quite some time. The ones who could barely walk were supported by the ones who were stronger and not injured.

"Come this way." They grabbed all the torches they could find and Margaretha led them all down the corridor to the chamber at the end, then pressed the trigger stone to open the wall and lead them into the secret tunnel. When they were safely through, they closed the stone wall back into place.

Margaretha led them all as they moved, one in front of the other, in the narrow tunnel. Finally, without encountering any bats or even any rats, they came to the end.

"Here is the door leading out," she said to Thomas and Thaddeus. They put their shoulders up to it and pushed the door open easily. The dark of night greeted them, with stars and moon shining in the clear sky, as they all climbed out of the tunnel and onto the grassy meadow.

"I want to go with you to find my father, but I hate to leave my family. It is possible Claybrook may kill them when he discovers I've escaped."

"I don't think he will," Thomas said. "He will use them for bargaining if things don't go well and the castle is besieged. Besides, he's too sick at the moment to order anyone killed."

That was certainly true.

"But what will happen to these men?" Thaddeus asked her, looking around at the men who had been chained in the dungeon. "Some of them are not able to come with us."

"You are right."

"Lady Margaretha." One of the men approached her, and she realized it was Sir Edgar. "The men who are not able to come with you to find your father will all find succor at my home, which is only a short walk from here. My wife and servants will personally attend the injured ones."

"Thank you, Sir Edgar. That is very good of you."

While Sir Edgar gave instructions to the injured, Margaretha turned to Thaddeus and Thomas. "Do you think we can find Duke Wilhelm without being captured by Claybrook's men?"

"I think so," Thaddeus said. "Most of Claybrook's men are either guarding the city gates or guarding the castle."

Thomas said, "Since you are with us, Lady Margaretha, we should find Duke Wilhelm and his men without much delay, as the people know you and will not be afraid to tell you. But we should hurry, since we don't know how potent the poison was that Lord Claybrook drank. Perhaps he will only be sick for a short time."

As the injured started for Sir Edgar's house, the rest of her father's men that they had rescued from the dungeon joined with Thomas, Thaddeus, and Margaretha, and they started walking east, away from Hagenheim Castle.

Margaretha's feet were still sore from all the journeying she and Colin had done, but she was too grateful to have escaped Claybrook to complain. She walked through the trees, across meadows, crossed a stream, over hills, and still they walked.

One of the men they had rescued from the dungeon knocked on the door to a family friend's house to ask if he had heard where Duke Wilhelm, Lord Hamlin, and their men were. He did not know, but he told them the name of someone who might, and explained where to find him. So they walked on.

Margaretha had not slept well in many days, and she felt she could almost sleep standing up. Finally, they came to the large stone manse that belonged to another of Duke Wilhelm's guards. Margaretha went to the door, along with the others, and knocked. When she had explained to the parents of this guard who she was and that they were looking for Duke Wilhelm and Lord Hamlin, they pulled Margaretha inside and immediately bustled about, finding her a chair to sit on and bringing her a goblet of wine.

The woman of the house told her, "My dear Lady Margaretha, you look worn half to death. Stay here while the men go and join your father."

"Then you know where he is?"

"Bless your soul, yes. My husband has been helping him round up men for the battle for Hagenheim Castle, to take place at dawn tomorrow. These fine men can join him, and you can stay here and rest yourself in a nice warm bed."

It didn't take long for the good woman to convince Margaretha that she should stay and get as much sleep as possible before being reunited with her father. She was almost too exhausted to climb the stairs to the bedchamber the lady had sent her servants to prepare for her. When she did lie down, the bed felt exquisite.

When she was alone and the candle had been extinguished, she pulled the heavy iron cross out of her sleeve and clutched it to her chest, feeling comforted, as it was not only a weapon but the representation of all her hope. "Thank you, Jesus," she whispered, "for Claybrook becoming sick, and for Thomas and Thaddeus helping me escape."

Her thoughts immediately turned to Colin. Where was he? Was he well and safe? Was he trying to come to her? And where was her father and Valten? Had Colin left Toby in Marienberg? Was he safe and happy?

When she had been with Colin, she missed her mother. Now that she had been with her mother, she missed Colin. Remembering how he had held her in his arms when she cried, she felt a strange, almost painful tug at her heart. How she wished to see him again, to talk to him, to tell him everything that had happened to her. She wanted him to hold her again. She wanted him to feel about her the way her brothers felt about their wives. She wanted him to get that look in his eyes that Gabe had for Sophie and Valten had for Gisela.

"Colin, Colin. I escaped. Again. Now I just want you to be safe and come back for me. Please come back." She closed her eyes, her hand touching the cross beside her in the bed.

Chapter
31

It was twilight when Colin and the rest of his party arrived at Duke Wilhelm's encampment. Now they were all gathered—a mighty force, including several men of high rank and all their knights and soldiers who were allied with Duke Wilhelm.

Colin had been surprised to find his father at Marienberg when he and Toby made their way there a few hours after Margaretha had been captured by Claybrook's men. He soon learned Colin's father had felt it his duty to come to Germany and try to bring Claybrook to justice for the heinous murder the man had committed. And he had also come looking for his son, worried that Colin would get himself killed, no doubt. He had stopped in Marienberg because he had heard that Claybrook was on a mission to woo Duke Wilhelm's daughter. He also knew that the Duke of Marienberg was a near relation of Duke Wilhelm, and that Claybrook's uncle lived in Keiterhafen, which was near Hagenheim.

When Colin arrived at Marienberg Castle, speaking only English, the castle servants had not understood him. He had been quite surprised when they went and fetched his father. Colin had been nearly overcome by his father's joy at seeing his son unharmed. He would not admit it to anyone but himself, but there had been a few tears shed, by both men.

Now the plan was to attack Claybrook and his men at Hagenheim Castle an hour before dawn, as Duke Theodemar of Marienberg, Lord Glynval, and all their combined fighting men, had joined Duke Wilhelm and his knights and allies. As they waited for the appropriate time to attack, Colin realized he might finally be able to speak to Duke Wilhelm.

Colin compelled a new friend he had made, Sir Gerek, who was one of Duke Wilhelm's knights, to translate his meeting with Duke Wilhelm. But first, the Duke of Marienberg would make the introductions for Colin and his father.

"Duke Wilhelm," Duke Theodemar said, "allow me to present the Earl of Glynval and his son, Lord le Wyse, both of England. I have only recently made their acquaintance, but I can assure you, they are well worth having as allies. And now I will allow Lord le Wyse to explain why they are here to fight against Claybrook, while I see to my men."

Sir Gerek quietly interpreted for Colin and his father.

The uncle and nephew exchanged a few more words of friendly greeting before Duke Theodemar excused himself.

"Your Grace," Colin began, as he faced Margaretha's father for the first time, trying to appear both humble and confident. "I came to the Holy Roman Empire with the intention of capturing Claybrook and taking him back to England to face the consequences of a murder that he had committed there. I was attacked and left for dead by his men and was brought to your healer at Hagenheim Castle."

Up to that point, Duke Wilhelm had looked at him with piercing but expressionless blue eyes. His brows lifted when Colin mentioned Hagenheim Castle, and as Sir Gerek interpreted Colin's English into German for Duke Wilhelm.

"Before I could recover enough to come to you with my story, you had left Hagenheim. I managed to tell your daughter, Lady Margaretha, of Claybrook's true character, and she bravely eavesdropped on Claybrook and discovered what he was about to do in Hagenheim. We were both captured by him, but we escaped and tried to make our way to Marienberg. We traveled for several days—"

"You traveled with my daughter? Who accompanied you?"

His heart leapt to his throat at the look in Duke Wilhelm's eyes. "Sir, we were alone most of the time." He continued quickly, so as not to give the duke a chance to interrupt. "But I assure you, your daughter is as virtuous as ever, and I wish to ask your blessing and permission to marry her, if she is willing, for I have fallen in love with her."

Duke Wilhelm studied him with slightly narrowed eyes. "And how does my daughter feel? Is she in love with you?"

"I don't know, sir. I would like to discover that myself, as soon as I see her again."

"And where is my daughter now?"

His throat went dry, and he had to swallow, hard, to get the words out. "I do not know for certain. She was taken by Claybrook's men. I believe she should have arrived back at Hagenheim one or two days ago."

Duke Wilhelm said nothing, but stared at Colin from beneath those lordly brows of his. Colin had to force himself not to squirm, but to meet him stare for stare.

"Your father is an earl, from England, and you have no title. Is that true?"

"My father is the first Earl of Glynval, for services rendered to King Richard. I am the oldest son, and my father's family has long held many lands and estates in England, from Lincolnshire to Surrey." He hated laying out his pedigree to prove his worth, as if he was a stallion or a hunting dog, but he would do anything to win Margaretha's father's permission to marry her. "More importantly, sir, you have my word that I would cherish your daughter and treat her well, bringing her back to Hagenheim for visits, whenever feasible, and that I am a God-fearing man whose priorities are God and family."

Duke Wilhelm's tense features relaxed, but he never took his eyes off Colin. "I believe you are an honorable man, Lord le Wyse. If Margaretha wishes it, and if her mother approves of you, you have my blessing to wed."

Margaretha opened her eyes in the strange bed and immediately remembered where she was. She could not have slept long, as it was still quite dark outside. What had awakened her?

A strange noise was coming from outside. It was not loud, but it was pervasive, almost a rumbling sound. She slipped out of bed, still wearing her mother's emerald green dress, and looked out the narrow window.

A hundred men or more and their horses were passing by the house at a fast walk. She immediately recognized her father in his chain mail and sitting on his favorite horse.

Margaretha drew in a startled breath, hurriedly slipped on her shoes, and raced out the door and down the stairs. She ran across the main floor of the house. A young man was guarding the front door, and he jumped up from his stool at the sound of her footsteps pattering across the flagstone floor.

"Open the door," she cried. "It's my father!"

The boy obeyed, unbolting the crossbar and pushing open the massive wooden door.

Margaretha hurried outside. There were so many men. How would she find her father? "Father!" she called out. "Father, it's Margaretha!"

The crowd of men parted, and her father appeared on his horse. He dismounted and came toward her.

Margaretha threw her arms around him. "Father! You're

here! We have been waiting for you to come." His mail hauberk was not comfortable against her cheek, but she hardly cared.

"My *Liebling*, Margaretha." He kissed her forehead. When he pulled away and looked down into her eyes, there was something almost sad about his smile. What was he thinking?

"Father, I'm so glad you've come. Please be careful. Claybrook has guards at all the gates and inside the castle, but he was poisoned last night and I don't know how sick he is, but maybe he will die. I escaped with two of Claybrook's men who were coming to join you."

"Yes, Thomas and Thaddeus told me what transpired."

"Oh, good. They found you."

"And there is someone else here who has found me." Her father stepped back and Colin stepped closer.

"Colin!" Even in his mail hauberk, he took her breath away.

Margaretha's voice set Colin's heart to pounding. When her father stepped away to watch the two of them greet each other, it beat even harder.

She closed the distance and threw her arms around him, as she had done her father. "Oh, Colin, I knew you'd come." She stood on the tips of her toes and pressed her cheek against his—about the only part of his body not covered in chain mail.

"How did you recognize me?" It wasn't what he had planned to say to her upon first seeing her again. But he was very aware that her father was only a few feet away.

"Oh, Colin! You are well! You are here! I thank God." She pulled away to look at him. "You look so handsome in armor." Her smile made his chest tighten. "I must look a fright after walking for hours, then sleeping in my clothes—my mother's dress at that. I probably have spider webs in my hair too, from walking through the tunnel." She rubbed her hand over her hair, which hung loose around her shoulders.

"You look beautiful to me." He longed to say more but a lump formed in his throat. He only hoped that later they would find a few moments to be alone.

Margaretha had yearned to see Colin again, but now she felt shy. It was strange to be surrounded by people, when she so wanted to speak to him alone. And by the look on his face, he was feeling the same thing. Somehow, telling him he was handsome in his armor, and the way he had told her she was beautiful, had seemed incongruous with her father standing only four feet away. She felt herself blushing.

Strange how she was more interested in talking with Colin than with her own father! And it had been longer since she'd seen her father. Should she feel guilty?

The other men continued on their way, and her father was turning to leave too.

Colin leaned closer. He only said, "I have to go," but a world of words were in his eyes.

Margaretha held tight to his arm. "Take me with you."

He got that anxious look, just as he had when she had asked to take Toby with them. "You should stay here. It will be safer." But the edge in his voice proved that he didn't believe she would.

"You must take me with you. Nothing bad will happen to me."

Her father, who had mounted his horse but was still very near them, said to Colin, "The two of you will stay at the rear of the fighting men, and you can be Margaretha's guard. We should be able to defeat Claybrook's men rather quickly, since we greatly outnumber them." He smiled a bit ruefully, as if he knew something she didn't. "I'm sure you'll keep her safe."

Margaretha turned a triumphant smile on Colin. "Yes, you'll keep me safe."

"There's an extra horse in the back," her father said.

Once Margaretha was mounted on a horse, Colin rode beside her, and they cantered until they were near the front of the great company of knights and soldiers. Several carried torches so that they would be able to see their way through the dense forest up ahead.

Colin kept glancing at her, and she at him, but they had little opportunity to talk. The other men crowded around them, laughing and shouting, eager to begin the battle for Hagenheim Castle.

The journey was accomplished much faster on horseback than it had on foot, and soon they were at the edge of the meadow outside the town wall where the entrance to the tunnel was located.

After they tied the horses to the trees next to the meadow, Colin stepped toward her. He was so close, if she had lifted her hand, she would have brushed his arm. He looked into her eyes as if he was about to ask her something important.

Her heart skipped a few beats, and she focused on his perfect lips. How would it feel to kiss them? Did he want to kiss her?

Her father cleared his throat from only a few feet away. "We'll go through the tunnel to attack."

Margaretha and Colin each took a step back. To cover her embarrassment, she did what she always did in uncomfortable moments. "I shall have to tell you both how I escaped from Lord Claybrook last evening, and you must tell me what happened after I was taken by Claybrook's men on the road to Marienberg." She glanced at her father, then grabbed Colin's hand. She gave it a squeeze and tried to let go, but he held on. Her father looked at their joined hands but said nothing, only moved forward, giving orders to various men as he went.

"I got a little lost in the woods that morning," she told Colin, "and couldn't find my way back to where you and Toby were, next to the stream. I was so frightened when I realized I was lost, but I thought if I could find the road, I could find my way back. And as soon as I stepped out onto the road, Claybrook's men were right there, staring at me. I didn't want them to find you and Toby, so I told them you had died. Of course, they didn't know about Toby, but I was afraid they would kill you and leave poor Toby alone in the woods, so I knew I had to go with them."

Colin nodded as they waited behind the men. "I understand." Her father walked forward to the front of the great company of men.

"They did not mistreat me, but they did tie my hands and feet at night so I couldn't escape, which made me very angry."

Colin's brows lowered and he frowned in a dangerous way.

"But first, I should have asked you about Toby. I wondered and wondered what happened to you and to him." She drew close to Colin again. "Is he still in Marienberg?"

"Yes. The housekeeper there is a motherly woman. She says she will take care of him and will send him to us when all is safe here. I do believe she intends to fatten him up. She kept talking about the things she would bake for him—pastries and sweet breads and pies."

"That sounds marvelous." Margaretha couldn't help gazing up into Colin's blue eyes. The dark of night must have been fading, because she could see that they were so blue they were like a stormy evening sky. And the expression on his face ... it reminded her of the way Valten looked at Gisela. She seemed to lose her breath.

"You didn't tell me how you escaped from Claybrook," he prompted.

"Oh yes. After the wedding ceremony last night, I—"

"Wedding?"

"Oh. Yes. Well, Claybrook forced the priest to perform the ceremony, marrying me to Claybrook."

"What?" Colin stopped walking and gripped her hand tighter.

"It is true that the priest pronounced us man and wife, but the only witnesses were Mother, Gisela, Kirstyn, Adela, Steffan, and Wolfgang. And Claybrook's knights. But I refused to give my consent and plainly said so. And afterward, after the feast, when we were going upstairs, Claybrook got violently sick and ordered me to go to my chamber, and the two guards who were with me helped me escape—oh my! There they are! Thomas and Thaddeus!" She waved at the two men, who had obviously joined forces with her father's men. "And Valten! Gisela will be overjoyed to see you."

Valten pushed through the crowd of men and stood before her. She had forgotten how ferocious he could look. He looked ready to bite the heads off of anything that got in his way. "How is Gisela?" But when he said his wife's name, his expression softened. "Is she well?"

"She was well last night. Mother says she is near her time, and the baby could come any day. But she is well, don't worry."

Valten reassumed his usual scowl.

"Did you say you are married to Claybrook?" Colin asked, recapturing her attention, his throat bobbing as he swallowed.

"I suppose, in the eyes of some, I am married to him. But I am sure Father will be able to get the marriage annulled." She bit her lip at the anxiety in his eyes.

Colin took hold of her arm, drawing her close and looking into her eyes. "He did not hurt you, did he? Because if he did, I'll tear his . . ." He stopped and took a deep breath.

"No, he did not hurt me. He barely touched me. I mean, he and his guards forced me to stand in front of the priest, but he did not hurt me. I was too afraid he would hurt my family to fight him. And then there was a feast, he got sick, and I escaped."

273

He put his arms around her, pulling her against him—or against the hauberk, with its hundreds of tiny metal rings. Not nearly as comfortable as she remembered his chest being. Still, it felt good to see how much he cared. It was written on his face and in the way he held her in his arms. "I wanted so much for you to come." She drew in a halting breath, tears pricking her eyelids. "And now you're here."

"Let us go." Valten's strident voice cut into her joyous thoughts. "Let's kill this spawn of the devil, Claybrook, and get back our women and our castle." He drew his sword from his scabbard, making the polished blade ring in the still morning air.

Colin let go of her with a long look, and she stepped back. He and the rest of the men drew their swords. They all filed into the opening of the tunnel, with Valten leading the way.

Her father turned and looked at Colin. "Stay with my daughter. Don't let anything happen to her."

"Yes, Your Grace." Colin took hold of her hand, an intense look in the set of his jaw and the glint in his eye. They stood in the line of men, near the back, who were entering the tunnel.

As they made their way down the steps and into the earthy-smelling tunnel, the only light came from the open door behind them. After they had walked around the first bend, she could no longer see anything. She held on to Colin's hand and clutched his arm, and she felt safe. Though she couldn't see him, she remembered how he had looked a few moments ago, with his sword in his right hand and wearing his mail armor. Colin looked brave and strong. He had come a long way since he lay near death on Frau Lena's sick bed. He was well and whole and . . . beautiful.

And he wasn't afraid of holding her hand in front of her father, which showed his courage even more than the sword and the armor.

When she was near him, she not only trusted him as a good and noble friend. Her heart also leapt and skipped inside her.

Now, feeling the taut strength in his fingers, a tingling warmth spread through her hand and up her arm. Since she could see nothing in the pitch-black tunnel, she thought about how his eyes sometimes seemed to be searching hers, the blue depths speaking to her in a way no one else ever had.

When he left to go back to England, never to return, would her heart break into a hundred pieces? Just thinking about it now made the tears come into her eyes and her chest hurt. How could she let him leave ... without her?

She heard the rustling of the men in front of her and behind, but no one spoke. Finally, the sound of stone scraping stone came from far ahead. Valten, who had gone in first, must have reached the special door that led into the dungeon.

Colin slowed, then came to a stop. Margaretha waited just behind him, since the tunnel was so narrow.

"I need to speak with you later," Colin whispered. She could tell by the sound of his voice that he had turned to face her, and that he was very near. She strained her eyes in the darkness but could make out nothing of his face or even his silhouette.

Margaretha whispered back, "Since we're speaking English, probably no one here can understand us anyway—unless Thaddeus and Thomas are nearby. But I saw them near the front, so I don't think they can hear us."

Colin's breath brushed her cheek as he whispered, "I'm sorry I let you get captured by Claybrook's men."

"That was not your fault. It was mine, for getting lost in the woods. I hope God forgives me for telling them you died."

"I'm sure God forgives you."

He pressed his hand against her cheek. She reached up and touched his face. He had apparently shaved when he was in Marienberg, but not since, so he had a few days' growth of stubble on his jawline where her fingers touched. "I missed you." The darkness surrounded them, and the feeling that they were invisible to the other men before and behind must have been affecting them both, for when she stood on tiptoe to get closer, his hand slid under her chin and lifted her face. His lips touched hers.

Colin, Colin, Colin. It was the only thought she could manage as he tenderly caressed her lips.

His hand sank into her hair behind her neck. She cupped his face in her hands and her fingertips touched his chain mail. She could hardly breathe, but she didn't mind. She kissed him back, because she was in love with Colin le Wyse from England.

"I love you," he whispered, as soon as he pulled away.

"Is that what you wanted to tell me?" She still held his face in her hands. He didn't pull away.

"Yes, but there is more."

"Good. I like more."

She was about to kiss him again when her father's voice boomed, "Men, we are going in. You know what to do."

"Give me your hand." Colin grasped her hand firmly, and they started walking again, a new excitement in the air as the men prepared to fight for Hagenheim.

Margaretha was still trying to get her breathing back to normal after Colin's kiss. She never imagined she would get her first true kiss in the secret tunnel, surrounded by strange men. At least it was memorable.

But she shouldn't be dwelling on Colin's kiss. Even though it was a heavenly kiss. Blissful, even. She needed to remember where she was, and that all these men — possibly including Colin — were about to risk their lives fighting Claybrook to save her family, the castle, and the entire town.

She could think about the kiss later.

They emerged into the dungeon and followed the corridor to the steps that led to the first floor of the castle. Already Margaretha could hear fighting — yells, sword blades striking metal, shouts of rage, a woman's scream.

Chapter
32

Colin gripped her hand tighter. He had the old intense look on his face. She imagined he was thinking how he might best protect her, how he would do anything to keep her safe, would risk his life and defeat any foe—

Her father shouted at the men coming up behind them. "Get to the gate! Make sure it stays open for the ones who are coming from town!" He looked at Colin and motioned with his sword. "Come with me to the solar. Bring Margaretha."

As they hurried down the corridor, her father stepped over the body of one of Claybrook's men lying facedown on the floor. Colin helped Margaretha over the large soldier, and she held her breath, terrified he was only pretending to be dead and would grab her by the leg as she stepped over. But he did not move, and she was soon safely over him.

Her father ran up the steps and she and Colin followed at a slower pace, with Colin keeping his body in front of hers, still holding her hand. Above them she heard Valten's ferocious roar, followed by the great clashing of sword blades, then a cry of, "I surrender! Don't kill me!" It was definitely not Valten's voice.

When they reached the top and Margaretha was able to look over Colin's shoulder, she saw two men on their knees on the floor being guarded by her father and one other man, and two others lying prostrate, obviously either dead or seriously wounded.

Feminine voices, her mother's and her sisters', came from the solar at the top of the stairs, and Colin allowed her to precede him into the room. Valten was striding toward Gisela. He bent and lifted his wife in his arms.

Margaretha moved out of his way. Valten's scowl was truly frightening, and Gisela's face was slightly contorted too, as if she was in pain, as Valten carried her out the door, his steps echoing in the corridor.

"Gisela's water broke." Margaretha's mother hugged her and patted her cheek. "I heard how you escaped from Claybrook when he was sick." She winked and grinned at her daughter. "I am thankful you're well. Now I must go see to Gisela and try to find Frau Lena." She nodded at Colin as she left the room.

Margaretha's sisters embraced her, and even her two brothers joined the hug.

Her father stood in the doorway. "We will take these prisoners to the dungeon. Colin, I leave my family in your charge."

Colin made a slight bow before placing himself in the doorway, his sword at the ready.

Margaretha's brothers and sisters were talking loudly, arguing, and asking questions. Wolfgang was running around, trying to get Steffan to chase him. Margaretha managed to stop Wolfgang, get the others' attention, and order them to sit down on the floor and play a game. She took down the Nine Men's Morris game board and the black and white pieces, and Steffan and Wolfgang began to play. She found the backgammon board for Kirstyn and Adela.

Finally, Margaretha was free to look at Colin and wonder what had happened to him in the past week—and what "more" he wanted to tell her.

Colin stood in the doorway, obviously standing guard over

the room. Truly, with his hauberk and the sword in his hand, he had transformed, from "*Froschjunge*," or "Frog boy," to her very own knight in shining armor.

Colin listened for fighting, but mostly he heard only occasional cheers or laughter, as well as men being brought down to the dungeon from outside. The fighting seemed to have moved into the town, if there was any fighting. He might have been disappointed he'd missed most of it if he hadn't been entrusted with guarding Margaretha and the rest of Duke Wilhelm's family. He felt the significance of the duty, as Claybrook had not yet been found. Duke Wilhelm was searching the castle for him now.

Margaretha approached him. He could hear her soft footfalls and the swish of her skirt. He glanced over his shoulder, the sight of her making his heart twist violently inside his chest.

He should probably turn away—she was far too distracting—but he couldn't quite force himself to do that.

She slipped her hand inside his. "Am I distracting you?"

"Yes."

Her smile grew wider. "Do you think my father's men will defeat Claybrook?"

"I believe they will. He has a lot of men fighting for him, more than Claybrook. Even my father is here with some of his men."

"Your father?" She sounded surprised. "May I meet him?"

"You could hardly avoid it." He couldn't help looking down at her. Her small hand felt sweet and soft in his, and her pretty brown eyes gazed up at him, so trusting.

"Tell me what happened after Claybrook's men took me."

Colin studied her hand as he talked. "I saw you riding away with them, so Toby and I continued on to Marienberg. We must have been closer than we thought, because we arrived at midday.

I was surprised to find my father had arrived in Marienberg only an hour before I did."

"Was he looking for you? How did he know where to find you?" Her teeth were so perfect behind her equally perfect lips. He couldn't help remembering their kiss. Too bad her siblings were in the room.

"He was looking for Claybrook, and he thought if he found Claybrook he would find me. He stopped in Marienberg hoping your cousin might have information—since he'd heard Claybrook was courting you—on his way to see Claybrook's uncle at Keiterhafen Castle. The Duke of Marienberg had just been informed, through a missive he'd received from your father, about the danger to Hagenheim and your family. And then I was able to corroborate the message." He played with her fingers, rubbing the soft knuckles and imagining himself kissing them. He refrained from doing so, just barely.

"So, my father, Lord Glynval, was able to accompany us back here. He was also able to explain to Duke Theodemar the treachery that Claybrook had enacted in England. Armed with this knowledge, along with Duke Wilhelm's message, he had already been preparing to set out the next morning when I arrived with the final details. We decided to set out a few hours later, instead of waiting until morning."

"I am thankful you did." She entwined her fingers in his and pressed the back of his hand to her cheek.

He had to take a deep breath to refill his lungs before going on. "Duke Theodemar supplied me with a horse, and my father had brought my own mail hauberk and sword from home. While traveling here, we received word of where to join forces with Duke Wilhelm and his men."

She had been staring into his eyes with a sleepy, content expression, when her eyes went wide with horror and she screamed. Colin turned as a raised sword came straight at his head.

He ducked and the sword struck his shoulder. Colin raised his own sword and hit Claybrook's wrist, for it was Claybrook who had struck him. The sword fell from Claybrook's hand. He lunged for it, but Colin placed his booted foot on Claybrook's shoulder and pushed with all his might. The kick sent Claybrook sprawling backward.

Claybrook's sword slid across the floor. Colin glanced behind him as Margaretha snatched up the weapon.

"Stay back," he told her.

Claybrook was slow getting up and Colin thrust his sword against his chest. He could easily kill the villain, and he had fantasized many times of doing just that, of running Claybrook through. But somehow, his thirst for Claybrook's blood had melted away, replaced by a much different desire — for Margaretha's respect.

"I will not kill you," Colin said, "even though you don't deserve mercy. But as a wise person lately reminded me, I need to leave room for God's vengeance."

Claybrook was not wearing armor, and the tip of Colin's sword was pricking his skin through his shirt. He yelped like the coward he was, then lay back on the floor. His face was gray and he was breathing hard. "Who poisoned me?" He kept his eyes closed as he spoke. "If not for the poison, I would not have been so easily defeated."

"But you still would have been. Good always conquers evil in the end." God had decreed it to be so since before time.

"What will you do to me?" Claybrook opened his eyes and gazed up at him.

"That is up to Duke Wilhelm. I am done with you. Duke Wilhelm can take you to his king and have you punished. There are certainly more witnesses to the crimes you have committed here. But if you ever again set foot in England, I shall make sure you are given the welcome you deserve."

Colin shouted for Duke Wilhelm. Within moments, he was striding down the corridor with one of his men. "Good work," Duke Wilhelm said. They hauled Claybrook to his feet and dragged him, none too gently, down the stone steps toward the dungeon.

Steffan and Wolfgang were staring, their mouths open, at Colin and his sword. He winked at them as he put the sword back in its sheath.

Shouts resounded from the courtyard and Margaretha ran to the window to look out.

"Father's knights are returning with prisoners. We have won!" She turned to him, her face lit with a big smile.

He came over to the window to join her, stepping around Adela and Kirstyn, who were still sitting on the floor. The men outside were shouting jovially and celebrating.

"It is over, then."

"Which one is your father?" Margaretha asked him.

"That one there," Colin said. "He's wearing a black surcoat with the red and yellow chevron from our coat of arms."

"Oh yes, I see him. And there is my father greeting him. Isn't it wonderful that they are friends? Things seem to have worked out so perfectly in the end, didn't they? Even though they started out so badly."

"Very true." Things had not started out well, but now . . .

Margaretha's gaze shifted to his shoulder. "Did Claybrook's sword hurt you?"

"I barely felt it. The chain mail protected me." He used his fingers to brush back a curl that had worked out of her braid and dangled by her temple. Her hair was as soft as silk. His heart started to speed up.

One of Duke Wilhelm's knights appeared at the top of the steps. Margaretha's little brothers spoke to him in excited tones.

"They're asking," Margaretha explained, "if it is safe for us to come out now."

The knight must have affirmed that it was, because the boys bolted out the door, whooping, and Margaretha's two sisters also left.

Suddenly, he was alone with Margaretha.

⁂

Margaretha was thankful Colin was only wearing the long mail tunic and not the hard metal plates of armor like Valten wore in jousting tournaments. She could snuggle close to him. But did she dare? They were alone, but anyone might come into the solar at any time, as the door was open. She smiled up into his blue eyes. "You said you had more to say to me. How long do you think we have before we are discovered?"

"Not long, no doubt." He stared at her lips. "We should make the most of it."

A delicious shiver went through her stomach at his words, hoping he meant to kiss her, but he frowned.

"Margaretha." His hands gently wrapped around her shoulders as he leaned toward her. "We get along reasonably well, don't you think?"

"Yes, of course." Her heart sank.

"We were vastly good friends on the way to Marienberg, weren't we?" There was a sharpness in his eyes as he seemed to delve into her thoughts.

"After you stopped trying to get rid of me."

He looked sad.

"But I understand why, so it is all well." Margaretha's breath shallowed as she focused on his lips. "You became the best friend I've ever had. You were sweet and kind and courageous and ..."

"Remember when we were in the tunnel and I said I loved you? Well, I didn't mean I love you as a friend, Margaretha."

Their kiss came even more sharply into her memory and she whispered, "I didn't think you did." She placed her palms against his chest, against the hard texture of his chain mail, imagining she could feel his heart beating under her right hand.

"I know you love your family. They are wonderful people, and it's perfectly understandable that you wouldn't want to leave them." His hands tightened on her shoulders. "But I can't leave here without you. I want to marry you and have children with you and take you back with me to England." His expression was almost fierce as he said, "Do you understand what I'm saying?"

"Yes." Oh, why didn't he just kiss her? "I understand."

"Will you marry me? Will you leave your family and come with me? Or must I stay here and work in the stable until your father either sends me away or takes pity on me and makes me one of his knights, so that I'll be worthy enough to marry you?"

"I don't want you to have to work in the stable. You aren't very good at it, and it isn't a worthy goal for a man who will someday be an English earl." She lifted a finger to rub the delightfully prickly whiskers on the side of his face. "You could become one of father's knights, since you do look very good in mail and armor and with a sword in your hand." She smiled teasingly, leaning her forearms against his chest as he wrapped his arms around her back. "But I love you so much, I don't feel any fear at the thought of going with you to your home in England. I want to marry you more than anything else in the world."

"You do?" His brows went up, and his breath seemed to catch in his throat.

"I do. I know I'll miss my family, but I would miss you too much to let you go. I want you to be my family now, for us to be a family together."

He closed the gap between them and kissed her, more intensely this time, stealing her breath and turning her knees to mush.

He ended the kiss and she pressed her cheek against his chest, feeling the tiny circles of the chain mail. "You asked me once why I never married any of my suitors. I knew I didn't want to live without love and passion and goodness. And you have all those things. You are what I wanted all along. The more I understood you, the more I fell in love with you. Only I didn't even realize I was in love with you until ... I'm not sure when, exactly."

She leaned away to look into his eyes.

He touched her hair, and said softly, "I think I fell in love with you when you refused to let me leave you with Anne. Or maybe it was when you came and freed me from the dungeon, then fearlessly led the way through that secret tunnel."

"You say the sweetest things." Margaretha might have laughed if she hadn't felt so warm and comfortable, and if she hadn't been thinking about kissing him again. "Perhaps I fell in love with you when I saw how you took care of Toby and never complained about taking him with us. And when you held me in your arms and let me cry about how much I missed my mother. You didn't try to take advantage of me. You didn't scold me or get annoyed with me. You just ... loved me."

She kissed him. "I love you," she whispered against his lips.

"I am sorry you must leave your family," he whispered back.

"As long as you love me, and I am not alone, I will be happy."

He kissed her, and she was lost in Colin again.

Someone cleared his throat. Loudly.

She looked up. Colin's father, and her own father, were standing at the door.

Margaretha's cheeks went hot. Colin slipped his hand in hers.

"Father," Margaretha began, "I—"

"I already know. Lord le Wyse wishes to marry you."

Lord le Wyse. How noble that sounded. Had he already asked her father if he could marry her?

"We shall speak of this later," her father said, not looking surprised, but Colin's father's eyes were wide and questioning as he stared at his son. "Now, let us go to the Great Hall. Cook has prepared food for us all."

She searched her father's face again, but he did not appear angry. He didn't even scowl at Colin, only frowned a little.

As she passed out of the door, she heard her father say to Colin behind her, "She said yes?"

"Yes, Your Grace," Colin replied.

It seemed her father knew a bit of English. Colin had apparently discussed his marrying her, and her father had not refused. That thought set her heart to soaring. She squeezed Colin's hand, and he squeezed back.

"I just remembered," Margaretha said, as they sat down at the trestle tables in the Great Hall at Hagenheim Castle. "I haven't eaten since my wedding feast last night."

Colin nearly choked on the sip he had just taken from his goblet. He met Duke Wilhelm's eye at the head of the table.

"Father, I'm not truly married to Claybrook, am I?" Margaretha asked. "I heard the priest say we were man and wife, but I did not give my consent, and I escaped him before I was forced to fight him off. Besides, everyone knows that he was heaving his stomach's contents all night."

"Nevertheless," Duke Wilhelm said, "I shall write the archbishop immediately and have him annul your marriage to Claybrook."

"How long will that take?" she asked, echoing his own thoughts.

"Perhaps no more than a month. Perhaps two."

A month seemed like a long time to Colin. Two months was an eternity.

"Margaretha," Duke Wilhelm said, as he pinned her with a serious stare. "I want to know if you have accepted Colin le Wyse's suit to marry you."

"Yes, Father, I have."

She clasped Colin's hand under the table.

"Do you understand that your responsibility will be to your husband? That your home will be England, not Hagenheim?"

"Yes, Father, I understand."

"And that you will not be able to visit Hagenheim whenever you wish?"

"Yes, Father."

Colin's heart sank as he thought he detected a note of sadness in Margaretha's voice. Was he wrong to take her away from her family, a family who loved her? She loved him, but did she love him enough not to resent, after a while, having to live away from her family and the only home she had ever known? She had said she would be happy with him, but would she regret her decision, maybe even regret it already?

She smiled up at him, then attacked her food like a person who was thinking only joyful thoughts. Perhaps she hadn't realized yet the homesickness she would feel, the loneliness for her family, living in a foreign place with only a husband to love her. He must speak to her, to make her understand what her father had been asking her.

With much still to do to restore order after Claybrook's seizure of Hagenheim, the town and the castle, their meal was rather quick. Even so, while they ate, Margaretha managed to charm Colin's father into smiling and laughing. His father even promised to help Colin build her a house bigger than le Wyse House, and to her specifications.

Their fathers stood to be off, Colin's father to assist Duke Wilhelm.

Margaretha also stood. "I shall go up to see if Mother needs any help with Gisela."

"Wait a moment," Colin said, touching her arm. "I think we need to talk."

"We can go into the library, if you wish."

No one seemed to notice them slip into the nearby library. It was rather dark, as the sky outside was cloudy and there was no fire and no candles lit. She turned to him, an eager light in her eyes.

"Margaretha." She was so fair, with her long eyelashes and sweet smile. But he had to give her a chance to change her mind. "I don't know if you realize what you are giving up to marry me. You will live across the ocean from your family. You won't be able to visit Hagenheim very often. Are you sure you understand?"

"Of course I do. I'm not a child."

He stared hard at her.

She sighed. "I know I will miss my family. I have a wonderful family. But I want to be with you." She reached up and pressed her hand to his cheek. "I can't stay at home forever, and I don't want to. I need to have a family of my own."

"Yes, but you will rarely see your parents."

"Don't you think we will be well-suited? That we will be content in our love?"

"I don't know if ... if I will be enough. Perhaps you will miss your mother and will come to resent me for taking you away. Anne said you would never leave your family."

"Anne was wrong." Margaretha's voice was soft as she drew closer to him, never taking her eyes off his. "I will not resent you, Colin. Yes, I will miss my mother, and my father, sisters, and brothers. I will miss Hagenheim. But I am ready to start a new life with you. I am sure we will face problems, but nothing will be too hard for us, because God has brought us together. We must have faith and courage, and I will never regret my decision to love you and marry you and move to England with you."

He didn't think he could possibly love her more than he did at this moment. And at the risk of spoiling it, he had to mention something he was dreading. But if he did not tell her now, she would find out later, when they went to England. "There is one more thing. I want to ask forgiveness for calling you a flibbertigibbet."

"Why? Because I turned out to be such a good spy?" She arched her brows and grinned.

Could she possibly be more beguiling?

"That is not what flibbertigibbet means. It means … but you have to promise not to be angry with me."

"I will promise no such thing." She was still smiling playfully.

"Then you must promise to forgive me and to know that I don't think you are a flibbertigibbet at all anymore."

"Colin, what is a flibbertigibbet?" She narrowed her eyes at him.

"It is a person who … chatters a lot and is not very … intelligent."

Her face instantly lost its playful look. "You thought that about me?" Anger and pain seemed to be warring behind her eyes.

"No, not after I got to know you. Only when you thought I was mad and didn't believe me about Claybrook."

"Oh." She took a step back.

"I regret ever thinking that about you. It isn't true at all." He reached out for her, but she curled her arms into her chest. "Now I know that you are a courageous woman who bashes soldiers twice her size in the head with whatever she finds nearby. You are a woman with a strong will, who never gives up, and is fiercely faithful to those she loves."

The smile came back to her face. "I am powerful, aren't I? I'm the kind of woman you want by your side in a fight, am I not?"

"You are," he readily acknowledged, sighing in relief to see her anger dissipating. "You are the kind of woman any man would want by his side, in times of peace and times of war. And best of all, you are always full of faith in God, and you have taught me a lot about finding peace."

"I'm glad to hear it. And you have taught me that, even though I do sometimes talk too much, I am still a woman of great worth."

"You are indeed a woman of great worth, and I do not think you talk too much." He took her face in his hands and kissed her briefly on the lips. "I am happiest when I can hear your voice." He kissed her again. "And I thank God that you love me." He kissed her for a long time.

Epilogue

Margaretha's wedding day had finally come.
The sky was glorious: Bright blue with big fluffy clouds floating
overhead. Colin, who looked breathtakingly handsome in a dark
blue tunic, his dark brown hair shining in the sun, walked beside
her on the way to the church.

Gisela and Valten's new baby was two months old, and fat
and healthy. She didn't even cry while the priest said the marriage rites over Colin and Margaretha before the bronze doors of
Hagenheim Cathedral. All of the Gerstenberg family was there
for the wedding, along with Colin's father, the Earl of Glynval,
who had stayed to accompany the newly married couple back to
England.

Toby was also there, and he stood beside Steffan and
Wolfgang, learning all their mischievous tricks, no doubt. But he
was smiling and happy. After being with them for a month and a
half, he had grown two inches and his cheeks had filled out. He
stayed close to her mother, who had sent for him immediately
after Margaretha told her about him. She doted on him, and he
was calling her "Mama" after only two days.

Gabe and Sophie had made the trip from Hohendorf with
their two children. Her niece and nephew had grown so much,
Margaretha barely recognized them.

She caught a few glimpses of Anne in the crowd, making nice with her smiles and waves, but Margaretha was not fooled. Her cousin was on the side of whoever could help her gain the most. And since Claybrook and his captain, Sir Reginald, had been defeated and taken to the king to be judged and punished, she would pretend loyalty and love for Duke Wilhelm and his family.

And Colin's new friend, Sir Gerek, was there with a beautiful young woman who looked strangely familiar, although Margaretha couldn't remember ever meeting her.

After the ceremony, they feasted at the castle, and it was quite a contrast to the feast after her wedding to Claybrook. Everyone was smiling and laughing, even her mother and father, whom she knew were a little sad that she was leaving in a few days. They were taking turns holding their grandchildren; they would have sufficient consolation when she was gone.

When the Meistersingers began to play a lively tune, Colin asked her to dance. By the end of it, she was laughing in his arms. Looking down into her eyes, he asked, "Are you happy?"

"Very happy."

He kissed her cheek, and, even though the last two months had been the happiest of her life, the next two months, two years, two decades, promised to be even happier.

Acknowledgments

I want to acknowledge Rachel Hiebert, a courageous sixteen-year-old battling leukemia, and Jess Doerksen, her sweet cousin and a reader of my books, for writing to me and keeping up with the Hagenheim residents. May God bless you both, and I hope you like Margaretha's story!

My biggest cheerleader, Regina Carbulon, who always prays for my writing, with me, and for me.

Friends, beta readers, and critique partners Katie Clark, Carol Moncado, Carrie Pagels, for helping me fine tune the story, and my awesome daughters and helpful first readers, Grace and Faith Dickerson.

My wonderful editor, Jacque Alberta, who seems to have a supernatural sense of what needs to be extracted, tweaked, and added to make the story better.

And last but not least, Brittany Elsen, Sara Bierling, and Adriana Gwyn, who helped me get my German words and phrases correct. I am so grateful to you! And so grateful to everyone who helped with this story. Thank you so much!

Discussion questions for *The Princess Spy*

1. At the beginning of the story, Margaretha is trying to convince herself Lord Claybrook could be a good match for her. Do you think Margaretha would have married Claybrook if Colin hadn't arrived? Why or why not?

2. Colin's original plan was to chase down Lord Claybrook and bring him to task for his crimes. Do you feel this plan would have been successful? Could John have done anything to deter Colin or change his approach?

3. When they first meet, Colin thinks Margaretha is a flibbertigibbet, and Margaretha thinks Colin is addled and impulsive. Do you think there is any truth in these first impressions? What leads you to that conclusion? How did the events of the story impact each characters' behavior?

4. Throughout the story, Margaretha disparages herself because she tends to talk too much. Is this as negative a quality as she and her brothers seem to make it? How might her talkativeness been perceived in the 1300s, when the story is set?

5. In some ways, Margaretha seems independent and assertive—brandishing candlesticks and helping outwit Lord Claybrook—but in other ways she comes across as what could be called traditionally feminine. If she hadn't lived as a medieval noblewoman, and was instead a modern character, what type of person do you think she would be? How might her and Colin's relationship been different?

6. If you had been Margaretha, playing chess with Lord Claybrook after finding out his true intentions, how would you have reacted?

7. From the time Anne arrives at Hagenheim, she is focused on her own welfare, and becomes engaged to Sir Reginald, even spilling key information to Reginald and Claybrook's men while ensuring her safety (and securing what would have

been an advantageous marriage at the cost of her uncle's death). What do you think happens to Anne by the end of the story? Do you think Anne acted the way she did because it was her innate personality, or because it was how she was raised? Why?

8. Throughout, Colin and Margaretha have several misunderstandings that come between them—chiefly Colin's belief Margaretha will never leave her family, and Margaretha's belief Colin doesn't like spending time with her because she annoys him. Do you feel they were holding on to these misunderstandings as a way to avoid their true feelings? Or was there more keeping them apart (at least at first) than they could see?

9. If Margaretha and Colin had never found Duke Wilhelm, what do you think the two of them would have done next in hopes of stopping Claybrook? Why?

10. Toby, the child Margaretha and Colin find in the barn, seems to be a catalyst that finally forces Colin and Margaretha to face their true feelings. How else do you think Toby contributes to the storyline? Do you think Margaretha was right in taking Toby with them to Hagenheim?

11. Margaretha at one point admits she had the perfect man in mind, and it was keeping her from accepting any suitors. Do you think she found the perfect man for herself in Colin? And do you think he hit every box on her "husband-to-be" checklist? Why or why not? Do you think making a list of characteristics is a good or bad idea when it comes to finding a mate? How strictly should such a list be followed?

12. How do you think Margaretha will fare in England?

The Healer's Apprentice

Melanie Dickerson

Two Hearts. One Hope. Rose has been appointed as a healer's apprentice at Hagenheim Castle, a rare opportunity for a woodcutter's daughter like her. While she often feels uneasy at the sight of blood, Rose is determined to prove herself capable. Failure will mean returning home to marry the aging bachelor her mother has chosen for her—a bloated, disgusting merchant who makes Rose feel ill. When Lord Hamlin, the future duke, is injured, it is Rose who must tend to him. As she works to heal his wound, she begins to understand emotions she's never felt before and wonders if he feels the same. But falling in love is forbidden, as Lord Hamlin is betrothed to a mysterious young woman in hiding. As Rose's life spins toward confusion, she must take the first steps on a journey to discover her own destiny.

The Merchant's Daughter

Melanie Dickerson

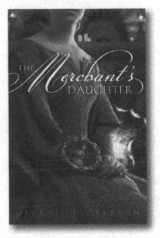

An unthinkable danger. An unexpected choice. Annabel, once the daughter of a wealthy merchant, is trapped in indentured servitude to Lord Ranulf, a recluse who is rumored to be both terrifying and beastly. Her circumstances are made even worse by the proximity of Lord Ranulf's bailiff—a revolting man who has made unwelcome advances on Annabel in the past. Believing that life in a nunnery is the best way to escape the escalation of the bailiff's vile behavior and to preserve the faith that sustains her, Annabel is surprised to discover a sense of security and joy in her encounters with Lord Ranulf. As Annabel struggles to confront her feelings, she is involved in a situation that could place Ranulf in grave danger. Ranulf's future, and possibly his heart, may rest in her hands, and Annabel must decide whether to follow the plans she has cherished or the calling God has placed on her heart.

The Fairest Beauty

Melanie Dickerson

A daring rescue. A difficult choice. Sophie desperately wants to get away from her stepmother's jealousy, and believes escape is her only chance to be happy. Then a young man named Gabe arrives from Hagenheim Castle, claiming she is betrothed to his older brother, and everything twists upside down. This could be Sophie's one chance at freedom—but can she trust another person to keep her safe? Gabe defied his parents Rose and Wilhelm by going to find Sophie, and now he believes they had a right to worry: the girl's inner and outer beauty has enchanted him. Though romance is impossible—she is his brother's future wife, and Gabe himself is betrothed to someone else—he promises himself he will see the mission through, no matter what. When the pair flee to the Cottage of the Seven, they find help—but also find their feelings for each other have grown. Now both must not only protect each other from the dangers around them—they must also protect their hearts.

The Captive Maiden

Melanie Dickerson

Happily Ever After ... Or Happily Nevermore?

Gisela's childhood was filled with laughter and visits from nobles such as the duke and his young son. But since her father's death, each day has been filled with nothing but servitude to her stepmother. So when Gisela learns the duke's son, Valten—the boy she has daydreamed about for years—is throwing a ball in hopes of finding a wife, she vows to find a way to attend, even if it's only for a taste of a life she'll never have. To her surprise, she catches Valten's eye. Though he is rough around the edges, Gisela finds Valten has completely captured her heart. But other forces are bent on keeping the two from falling further in love, putting Gisela in more danger than she ever imagined.